Destiny Rides Shotgun

An Epic True Story Adventure

Duane Eastman

Blackkcoral LLC

Copyright

2024 Blackkcoral LLC

Greenwood MO USA

ctdbooks.com

ISBN (electronic) 979-8-9868635-3-5

ISBN (paperback) 979-8-9868635-2-8

ISBN (hardback) 979-8-9868635-4-2

Library of Congress Control Number: 2024907402

The popular adage, "Based on a true story," applies to this book as does "creative fiction". Inaccuracies are inevitable due to time and distance. As a courtesy and to make the storyline more engaging, the author altered some events, names, and timing. That's the true story part. This book is also a work of creative fiction—some characters, places, names, and situations are the product of the author's imagination or are used fictitiously.

Destiny Rides Shotgun doesn't fit neatly into the existing structure of book genre classifications. It wiggles into Amazon's category of historical adventure fiction but needs some space for its timely splash of potential science based solutions to near future social and climate issues. The publisher suggests a new hybrid book genre: neo scifi.

Duane Eastman was and is an avatar before avatars became a thing. Duane gets blamed for most of the mischief and a lot of the fun. He's just out of sight in Playa del Carmen, Mexico.

Dedication

I am fortunate to have the resources and good health to survive the ordeal of writing a book. I give thanks and am forever grateful to the following:

Mimi and RD, my parents. Hank and Grannyo, my grandparents.

My siblings—Deré, Melissa, Jeb, Leigh, and Maureen. I am blessed by your love and support.

My beautiful, loving wife Arielle, who was there for me along the way.

My loved ones and friends.

Whom and Those who have provided such a wonderful life to me—my eternal gratitude.

Print Versions

You are holding a physical link to the past, a book printed on paper. Books are part of the evolution of humans, and an important vehicle to express intellectual development.

For eons, books have been bound in paper of one sort or another. Paper has unmistakable qualities that trigger human acknowledgement, affection, and respect for its place in history—both culturally and personally. Paper evokes a wonderful, almost magical attachment triggered by the tactile turning of the pages, the aroma of the printing ink, and the intimate and satisfying ability to control the pace of reading and absorption of the content. Many people treasure and revere printed books, including me.

But you can't click on the links!

You will notice links to songs and lyrics at the beginning of each chapter and Interlude. The music of the era was a rallying call to the youth and a worry to the adult establishment. It defined my generation and was a crucial reference point for the story's events and mood.

I urge you to visit the website www.ctdbook.com. There you will find easy access to the music and song lyrics. The "ctd" in the address refers to Connecting the Dots. Dots are an integral part of this book and my life. Even if you don't yet recognize it, I submit they were and are in your life, too.

Besides music, you will also find more relevant, behind-the-scenes information, and a fascinating trove of photographs.

Muchas gracias for your purchase of this book. I trust you will enjoy it.

Duane

Contents

Prologue

Santana: *Soul Sacrifice* > *Lyrics*

During my twenty-second lap around the sun, Scott, Dave, and I were standing on the hot and dusty tarmac of the Kabul International Airport.

We scrutinized the ground crew as they loaded freight aboard a Pan Am flight to Frankfurt, Germany, with an ultimate destination of Cleveland, Ohio, USA. We were also attentive to the ongoing commentary of the Afghan Pan Am Ground Agent named Mohammed.

He had been skillfully paying airport workers according to their status from the wad of Afghani currency (known as *afghanis*) that we gave him. Mohammed guided us through the terminal, past immigration and customs, and out into the bright sun of a warm summer day in Afghanistan of 1973.

Mohammed was a scholarly man and excelled in bribes. Like less fortunate street hustlers, he was fluent in English, Farsi, Pashto, and in multiple European languages. I also heard him converse in Afrikaans. He was sharp and clever—often a person to be wary of. We'd already encountered some textbook examples of that type on the road to Afghanistan.

In the coming months, Mohammed proved himself honest and capable, a valuable resource, and a fine human being.

Noor recommended him to us in Kabul. We spent months at Noor's carpet store enjoying tea, hearing tales, and choosing carpets to ship back to the US.

Oriental carpets are beautiful and timeless objects of art. We knew they were very cool, and all things Afghani were popular in the West, due in part to John Lennon and other rockers wearing "Afghan" coats. However, we knew those coats were from Turkey, not Afghanistan. We came to appreciate the origin and beauty of carpets in those months, sipping chai and learning how to identify fakes as Noor schooled us from abject novices to knowledgeable rookies. He also sold us a lot of his carpets.

It required a keen and experienced eye to identify an antique carpet from a just-woven carpet. And countless "antique" carpets jammed the local market. One day, Noor escorted us on a field trip to the northern part of Kabul on a congested and dusty road that was filled with trucks and buses. Through the choking cloud of street dirt and debris, Oriental carpets littered the road. The traffic wore down the nap of the new carpets, dirt provided authenticity, and the shiny new colors dulled. And that, Noor firmly pointed out, was where so many "antique" carpets originated.

Carpets were fun, and we hoped profitable to import to the US. The trip from Amsterdam to Kabul through Frankfurt was a trial run for us because we had a secondary purpose in mind.

For Scott and me, Afghanistan materialized on our radar screen as the source of the unquestionably best hashish known. We were aware of and had indulged in the other top contenders: Kashmir from northern India, Nepal bordering India and China, and Chitral in northern Pakistan. But in our minds, there was no argument—Afghani was the best. And we intended to go there, find it, smoke it, and facilitate making it available to others.

The sun beat down relentlessly and the temperature rose steadily as we stood with Mohammed on the tarmac. We were a strange sight: three long-haired Westerners gawking as the plane taxied to the runway to prepare for takeoff. The engines roared, and the plane lurched forward and began its journey west.

As the wheels retracted into the fuselage and the plane soared skyward, we turned to walk away. Mohammed gestured at us and said, "*Na!*" (No, stop!) Following his lead, we waited until the plane disappeared from sight. Then he smiled, turned, and led us back into the terminal. We exchanged no words, contemplating what just happened. The lesson presented was unmistakable—never trust without verifying.

And thus we received a brief course in International Business 101. A timely tutorial, and valuable for our stated aspiration.

Noor & Helper in Kabul carpet store

Introduction

Rolling Stones: *2000 Lightyears From Home* > *Lyrics*

Here's the thing. You must truly get your mind wrapped around the era to feel the absolute joy and sense of freedom underlying this book. And music was at the heart of it. Rock 'n' roll was front and center, defining Western culture in its image and values. The era defined individual tastes in clothing and hairstyles, often classifying friends into two musical camps—The Beatles or The Rolling Stones. Without hesitation, I was in the latter camp. Some of my friends were in the former.

To me, the choice was like fishing. The Rolling Stones music was the bait on a hook with a lead weight to sink it into the deep water to catch the older and clever big ones. On the hook was an earthworm—alive, earthy, and active, like the blues and jazz that were the roots of the Stones' music. Their music grabbed you and shook you, made you move and feel the beat. Their music was edgy and naughty. They were the rebels of rock, constantly flirting with danger and often in the midst of it.

The Beatles' music was like fishing with a bobber. It floats on top with a piece of bread as bait to catch whatever might come its way. The bread would disintegrate swiftly, leaving nothing on the hook. I liked some of their songs, but they didn't last long as a group. They may have developed into more of what I liked had they the staying power of the Rolling Stones.

Even if you don't remember, like, or care about rock 'n' roll, it played an important part in the cultural and political evolution of the Western world in the 70s. Wait a minute, think about it. Like life itself, music has evolved. All in existence now has at least traces of previous generations. Rock & roll has prominent jazz and blues DNA. The music of your generation shares the family tree. Give thanks and listen to the music, dear reader.

For the benefit of those who may still scratch their heads in wonder at my assertion of the power and influence that music held over me and my generation, I submit the chart of relevance below.

Rolling Stones vs Beatles	Year	Albums	Shake That Thing	Rebellious	Scare Parents
Stones	1962 - 2022	38	Hell yes	Yep	Oh boy!
Beatles	1963-1970	12	Seldom	Sleepy	Nah

Rolling Stones vs Beatles

The chart lacks scientific evidence, displays bias, and might be slanderous (unintended). It vividly illustrates the musical foundation upon which this book is written. Each chapter and interlude have a hot link to a song and its lyrics from a <u>Spotify</u> playlist. They're some of the most influential sound tracks of my life and events in this narrative. If you listen to the music and give the lyrics a read, you'll drift into the vibe and feel the era. It was a remarkable time, and I appreciate having survived it. If you were there, you might feel the same.

If you passionately seek enlightenment of the relevance of each song played, you can easily do that online by visiting one of the many websites that host song lyrics. I suggest you use the search bar at the top of

Genius.com. Each song rocked me one way or the other, but all resonated with me as I chose them for my book.

While reading, it's important to note that it was during a golden era, the early days of widespread use of "soft" recreational drugs. At least that was true in my experiences, and especially so if you identified as a hippie.

I'm talking about marijuana and hashish and, to some extent, LSD. No hard drugs like opium, heroin, and, in later years, cocaine.

It was also a tumultuous era full of youthful optimism shaded by inexperience with the sledgehammer of history and violent social upheavals. Change was on the horizon, and it was slowly creeping toward us like a fog obscuring the playing field. The "love, peace and happiness" of the 1960s was drifting into the '70s, toward a more traditional American aspirational reality of growing up, having kids, and buying a house.

It was a time before the nasty side of drugs took hold and the underbelly of human behavior—greed, violence, and money—became the norm. A time before soft drug distribution became a ruthless and dangerous behemoth of organizations employing traditional vice activities that are harmful and opportunistic.

But to my good fortune and good luck, this book takes place in a sweet spot of time. That brief era was a flurry of adventure and travel in a world still untraumatized by social media, digital everything, fake news, the internet, and a burgeoning population of humans on an evermore crowded planet.

This story occurred when a good number of pot and hashish merchants had a sense of purpose and took pride in seeking the very best quality and delivering it to an informal distribution network of individuals—not unsavory organizations. That unfortunate aspect was to come later.

Scott, Dave, and I adhered to the credo of *Pride in Workmanship*. We thought in terms of what now are called "Personal Shoppers," seeking the best quality in the best places. A philosophy we took to heart.

In these early days, if one fervently desired the best and had an adventurous streak, one would go to the sources. For blond hash, that was Baalbek in Lebanon. For green hash, Ketama in Morocco. Black hash in Nepal or Kashmir in India. Chitral in Pakistan. But the best hash of all? Afghanistan. And the epicenter was Mazar-i-Sharif.

We wanted the best, and we were up for an adventure. Road trip! Adventure, risk, and profit were the reward for originality, clever thinking, and getting up off one's ass and going out into the world.

People still highly regard the traits mentioned earlier and now call them *entrepreneurial qualities*. I invite you to listen to the music, digest the story, and tune into an era that was instrumental in the upheaval of societal norms and expectations.

Chapter One

One Train Leads to Another

Crosby, Stills, Nash & Young: *Teach Your Children > Lyrics*

Kabul, Afghanistan, is a "far piece," as my grandmother would say, from where I grew up in the middle of the United States. But there I was at the youthful age of twenty-two, standing on the tarmac of Kabul International Airport. Scott, Dave, and I, who were traveling together, drove there from Frankfurt, Germany. That too was a far piece—about 8,000 km (5,000 mi). This story is about my good fortune to get forced off my butt to travel, and my initial fears of what might happen if I did. Then, once off my butt, the story becomes about the adventure, excitement, and enlightenment gained while on the road.

My parents were intelligent and hardworking and made sure to give their children every opportunity to succeed. One of their desires was to impart the beauty of the American national parks to us, while instilling respect and appreciation for the country. With six children, family vacations started with chaos and lurched toward anarchy. Fortunately, our destinations were the national parks in the western region of the US. Must have been strategic parental planning. The majestic beauty and vastness of the parks could absorb the impact of our family tribe and deplete the collective energy of the kids. As the eldest son, I attempted to carve out some private space, but I was rarely successful. In later years, I relished the gift of having five siblings, but back then I needed alone time. I was glad to find seclusion in model car construction, reading books, and the intellectual world of *Mad Magazine*. A childhood much like mine was not uncommon for those who grew up in the 1950s.

From those memories, I am at a loss to identify the provenance of the travel bug in my psyche. I concluded tentatively while writing this book that it was a series of experiences, some fortuitous events, and good fortune that tossed my arse into travel.

However, there must have been hidden travel tendencies deeply rooted somewhere, logically. If so, where did those urges originate? Did I inherit them, or did I catch the travel fever from somewhere else? Was there a triggering event or events? Nothing floated to the top of my memory to provide a clue.

I waded through the old family photos, thinking they might provide insight into the origins of my yearning to travel, but not a thing of importance emerged. There was little to glean from listening to my parents and grandparents reminisce as they played pinochle around the kitchen table on Sunday evenings. No family lore about travel from the old country, or an uncle that was a rogue or pirate. Nada, no clues. There must be more to it.

My grandfather Hank frequently said his "boat was coming in," which I took to mean wealth from an unknown source. According to my grandmother Grannyo, our family was related to the infamous outlaw from the late 1800s, Jesse James. Grannyo further enthusiastically expanded our family tree to include the Hatfields of the legendary Hatfield-McCoy family feud. Questionable boats, outlaws, and family feuds weren't fertile ground to discover the origins of my travel fever.

The travel photos of Africa and the Pacific Islands in *National Geographic* grabbed my attention. I thrilled at my father's "short snorter": a string of foreign currency notes taped end to end that he collected as a World War Two fighter pilot stationed in the South Pacific. When I let it spill out of my hand, it was longer than I was tall. Much longer, as I was short for my age. Snorters were a hobby of sorts—some soldiers collected stamps, some coins, others only memories. Like soldiers, fighter pilots hoped to be stationed in places they would live long enough to remember. The short snorter currency notes were good luck charms.

I revered my father's snorter as a treasure, hidden in a carved wooden box on the credenza in my parents' bedroom. All by myself in the house, I ventured toward the box, grasping it in my hands and lifting the lid to be awed by the distinct depictions of people and places on each banknote. It wasn't my nature to snoop around, but I felt I wasn't, as he had taken care to show it to me. Like most veterans of that war, he didn't talk about it much, but looking at those notes gave him license to drift in his thoughts. The names of other pilots, the island names, and the air base names spilled into his storytelling. Each note portrayed people in peculiar attire, tropical jungles, and unrecognizable words and numbers in unusual languages. Those alluring descriptions of distant—and a little frightening—places beguiled my imagination. That, and the focused attention from my father, stuck with me.

Trains sped into my life at a young age and captivated me. Passenger trains, in particular, intrigued and engaged my imagination and all of my senses. They roared, the ground trembled, and they shook the air with fury. Voluminous smoke billowed out from the depths of the engine as thick as thunderclouds in a coming storm, hanging in the air, unwilling to dissipate, evidence of surging energy. The train's approach began with a subtle rumble and a more and more clamorous and pressing horn, both sorrowful and enthralling to my psyche. Like the pressure wave of air in front of the train, a stream of questions raced through my thoughts. Who was on that train? Where were they going? Where did they come from? As the powerful mechanical beast approached, the mournful sound of the train horn peaked, then faded with a clackety noise that left me with a seesaw of emotions. Questions about the origin, destination, and passengers of the train came after the anxious and worried feelings.

Then, in my early teens, the fascination with trains became a hobby. My father too became an avid HO model train hobbyist and financial sponsor for me, as one could spend a lot of money on building a train set. Our shared passion helped to dissolve the deep-seated hostility I had toward his frequent absences during my childhood. Holding that against him was selfish, of course. He was traveling to make a living for our family, but it still took time and experience for me to forgive him. To me, it was a tacit admission that I was taking my privileged life for granted. My point was made abundantly clear through my eventual travel experiences.

After much thought, I realized that my love for travel wasn't ignited by one moment or event, but an accumulation of unexpected and un-planned moments. Turning points in my life kept me on a path toward a pivotal event that forced my hand and put me on a plane to Europe. Those moments and those trains were the manifestation of my urge to travel. Without realizing it, I had accumulated some emotional baggage, which would need to be repacked as I began my travels.

• • • • •• • •• • • • •

Lonesome Express Train

He was gone...again.

It seemed like he was always leaving and never home long enough. He'd always returned before, but this time it would be two weeks or more, an eternity to me, his six-year-old son. Crying wasn't in the cards. He told me I was the man of the house while he was gone. And everyone knows, Men Don't Cry.

"Take care of your little sister and your mother," he said. But I felt like crying. I missed him, and I was angry too. But I had promised to take care of them, and it chuffed me to think he trusted me to do so. What else can a man do but keep his word? Loneliness wasn't a word to me, only a feeling that visited me whenever it chose to. Especially when the trains passed.

It was just me and my younger sister, Deré, who was a year and a half my junior. Our four siblings would come later. We were living in a small, rented house near the railroad tracks in Lees Summit, Missouri. Our father was on the road calling on accounts in the Midwest, selling hardware and painting equipment to feed his wife and young family. Like many World War Two veterans, he was full of ambition and drive. But his frequent and long absences took a toll on me, and I'm sure on our mother and my sister as well.

I accepted that assigned role from my father wholeheartedly, as much as an overwhelmed child can. But in my private moments, I was lonely and afraid. Confusing everything were the other emotions I experienced during those train moments: excitement, curiosity, and lots of questions.

A pleated aqua-blue heavy brocade curtain acted as a wall, dividing the living room and kitchen. It muffled some of the noise from the frequent trains as well. In the snug living room, next to the curtain, was an overstuffed 1950's sofa. The right arm of the couch was huge to my inexperienced eyes and extended outward and was level with the bottom of the living room window. The place provided an ideal vantage point for observing outside activities. When the first faint moan of a train horn was discernible, I would jump on the arm of the couch so I could stare out of the window. The view was unremarkable—a tree-filled backyard partially obscuring the railroad tracks. My perch on the couch was a front-row seat to the familiar sequence of events. The poorly constructed house with thin plaster walls vibrated and shook from the air pressure created by the train's kinetic energy. The arc of the sound, distant at first, then increasing to an urgent crescendo, would fade away, acknowledging the speed of the mechanical beast's passing. I felt a vague ache in my lonely self after the noise ended.

Sadness was there, but also a sense of wonder and excitement. I wondered where the train had come from and where it was going. Fear and excitement stirred my thoughts: *Maybe I should run away from everything. Get on one of those trains and escape my unwelcome responsibilities.*

How in the world could I even do that? I had seen the trains up close at the RR crossing and they were huge, incredibly complicated, and fast! The answer was beyond me. But the intrigue remained and surfaced in due course.

My mother told me years later that during that period I had threatened to run away. Having departed with a small bag of something or other in hand, I shortly returned to the front door. I knocked, and when she answered, I informed her of my departure using a child's logic and limited understanding of word meanings. "Goodbye for never." It was my best shot at obstinance. The thought of dinner approaching cut short my brief hiatus.

Mystery Train

During my twelfth year on planet Earth, I found myself standing alone in the immensity of the Kansas City Union Train Station. Massive, vaulted ceilings and the expansive marble floors amplified the sounds of both humans and machines. Trains maneuvering on the tracks created loud echoes, which invaded the cavernous space. The ebb and flow of energy gave a cadence to the noise. The people exiting and boarding, most in a rush, added confusion, with my anxiety reaching a fever pitch. I loved it.

My parents said, "Wait here," as they ventured off to find the Boy Scout group from the Kansas City region. I didn't know any of the other scouts, so I paid no attention to finding them. I was going on a trip to Valley Forge to attend the National Jamboree. It was my first solo trip. I was both frightened and thrilled.

I wasn't much taller than waist high to most of the people. The engrossing activity above and around me was electrifying. I became a passenger enmeshed in the crowd and had to flow and move as a grain of sand in the surf. Our train had a morning departure, and the station was busy with business travelers. The current swept me toward a set of tracks where I was fortunate to find my anxious parents and a group of Boy Scouts. Had my parents not been so relieved to see me, I would have been in trouble.

In any event, I was too eager to be bothered. Although the frantic activity of the scoutmaster's attempts to get us organized and on board was humorous, I noticed that most of the boys were older—early teens, or even late teens. That usually meant a young guy like me getting shoved around, ignored, or worse, but there was none of that so far. Philadelphia was the destination, and then a transfer to Valley Forge.

It was an overnight train with sleeper cars, but I was high on adrenaline, so I wandered around. I settled into my assigned seat after several hours, exhausted. I got up to look for the bathroom and encountered a crowd blocking the aisle, cheering on some kind of activity in one cabin. They were the older guys, and I could tell they were doing older guy stuff. I needed to get through, so I asked what was going on. One of them chuckled after looking at the innocent child Boy Scout and then paused before he smiled and said, "Jerking off contest." I knew what a jerk was. I knew several at school, but I didn't know about a contest to get rid of them.

"Oh," I said, "good idea," thinking my response would show I was savvy to the contest. I expected an acknowledgement, but he only gave me a quick glance. I passed on to the toilet. It was a few years before I reached puberty and understood what was going down back then.

Duane boy scout with Duke the dog

●●●●●●●●●

Epic Journey

My childhood dream of travel and adventure was vague and stitched together from imagination and scraps of information gleaned from books, magazines, and by pestering adults. Genuine analog experiences. The life lessons learned from travel were in the future: the opportunity to observe, consider, and compare the many human conditions with one's own realities. Often those were stark comparisons, exposing personal mores to reevaluation.

Five decades ago, there was only one option to get off your butt if you wanted to travel and seek adventure: the physical act of doing it. Nowadays, many consider the digital equivalent of getting off your butt an Instagram post. An enhanced photo of a destination substitutes as an exciting travel experience. Imagining yourself there stands in for the experience and the viewer can check that box on their copy and pasted bucket list. Humans are an adaptable species, as our survival attests. But old-style travel—the kind that takes effort to organize, has inconveniences, and involves some risk—has fallen victim to the adage, "You can't miss what you never had."

I agree that traveling, especially abroad, can be transformative. However, it is not a given that one receives that level of benefit. Like most worthwhile things, you need to invest significant time and effort, apply good intentions, and stay the course when confronted with customs or beliefs that differ from yours. Travel can deliver you to exotic and distant places where you encounter strange and fascinating things and people. The standard-issue human resembles you, with a head, two arms, two legs, and a mouth. With further scrutiny, you may notice visible differences in skin, eye, and hair color. What distinguishes people from another is when they open their mouth and speak unfamiliar sounds, new societal values, different ways of thinking with different opinions, and surprising points of view. You are on their home turf. It is your responsibility to listen and learn. Also, to keep an open mind and not prejudge. If you project a nonjudgmental mind, you are likely to be welcomed—or at least tolerated—while they size you up. The underlying premise here is "What you give is what you get." Travel is a rewarding experience, but it also has its responsibilities.

All the foregoing is entry-level stuff—International Travel 101. It's surprising how many people must have failed that course.

Scott, Dave, and I thrived on a wild journey and survived hair-raising close calls with our destiny riding shotgun from Amsterdam to Kabul, Afghanistan. Details await you in the following chapters. We encountered a diversity of human characters who generally exhibited generosity and goodwill. That's not to say our Guardian Angels weren't busy. We fully acknowledged our karma but didn't comprehend exactly what that meant. We considered "good luck" a sufficient explanation for our survival. Our destiny be damned, we were bent on having fun.

Decades later, with a lot more accumulated road dust and Guardian Angel interventions, I felt there must be a deeper connection between events and the intervention of those angels. There was more. What about destiny? How did it figure into the big picture? My thoughts kept circling back to two common expressions in the vernacular—*vibes* (good or bad), and *karma*. They routinely depicted a result that was affected by obscure forces outside of one's power. My consideration expanded to include instinctive emotions and intuitive feelings. Phrases that have assuredly crossed your lips, like:

- Gut instinct

- I felt that...

- I knew I should have...

- I had an intuition...

Not to overlook luck and coincidence as intertwined elements of the above list.

Collectively those feelings are like Dots to be connected. My thoughts and considerations strengthened into a hypothesis, and then became what I call the *Theory of Dots*. If you want a sneak peek, you can explore my theory on the website https://ctdbook.com.

Although there is little daylight between the theory and the story, I analyze the Theory of Dots in the Interludes. The events of the story are told in the chapters.

Let's hit the road!

Chapter Two

Calling a Bluff

Rolling Stones: *Satisfaction > Lyrics*

The fall of 1970 was the start of my junior year at university. I was living in a fraternity house because that was the only way you could avoid living in a men's dormitory, part of the rigid and stifling college rules in central Missouri. It turned out to be the last months I spent there, and the beginning of the end of my formal education. But it was also the beginning of my enrollment in the "school of the road"—international travel.

Attempting to pinpoint the exact moment that the transition began is difficult, as I cannot recollect accurately how that happened. The catalyst was a guy named James. I vividly recall that he emerged out of nowhere early in the fall. I didn't know him, know of him, or know anyone who knew him. He just came on the scene as if he belonged and like we'd been friends for a long time. It all appeared natural, without need of further explanation. Interestingly, nobody else in my orbit of friends or associates intimated anything strange, either.

James projected an aura of worldliness and claimed to have traveled extensively, especially in Europe. He bragged about having been there before (I imagined that he meant many times), and it jolted me when he said he was going back in a few months!

Europe—a vague and exotic place that lived in classroom history books. Romans and the Greeks came from there somewhere; I thought they rode in chariots and slashed their way across vast distances. Later, World War Two was fought there as well.

It's possible that some of my distant relatives originated from there. Cows grazed on mountainous green slopes, wearing huge bells around their necks. Men in leather shorts called them by blowing into long horns that curved up from where they rested on the ground. And there was a place, Holland, where they ate a lot of cheese and ice-skated in winter on frozen canals as windmills lazily turned in the distance.

Europe barely registered in my consciousness, but resonated in my hind brain and intrigued me big-time. The idea of visiting engulfed me in a surge of intrigue unlike anything before...besides cars and girls.

James spewed a constant stream of European experiences that were fun and way cool, and even some risky adventures. He created a convincing web of excitement that pulled me in, with no resistance or skepticism. I was hooked and decided that I was going to Europe with him when he went back. There was no hesitation. He would be a fun guide, and I took it for granted. I announced my intention to everyone with absolute confidence and enthusiasm that I was going to Europe. A particular destination was not important. I was going to Europe!

He was my constant wingman for what seemed like a very long time. In those days, a month seemed like endless weeks. He lingered for two full moons, and then he vanished. One day, he wasn't there anymore. Gone, disappeared, no goodbye, no explanation. I found out he was a fraud. He'd made it all up, and when he was about to be discovered, he bolted. Somehow, it didn't shock me. It almost seemed logical. Still, it pissed me off because I had told anyone who would listen that me, the man about town—as I imagined myself—was going to travel to Europe. I had to save face and go, but now I would go alone. *So what? It'll be fun! I hope. I think. I'll be OK and meet people. Sure, no problem, nothing to be worried about—I'm a man, a traveling man.*

Even then, albeit in a private moment, the strange unexplained appearance and then disappearance of James was a confounded puzzle. Why then? Why me? I chose the convenient explanation that it was merely a coincidence, not anything more. This book relates the situations that accumulated along the road and were labeled as "coincidences." Decades later, I reached a different conclusion, resulting in a hypothesis I call the *Theory of Dots*.

Suddenly, but with no fanfare and in the nick of time, a savior appeared—Jack. His father was a TWA airline pilot, which allowed Jack to travel anywhere in the world that was serviced by TWA for the cost of only the tax on the ticket. It was very cheap. Jack journeyed—a lot. He had some medical issues and got a special dispensation from school, as well as a medical deferment from the military draft so he could take full financial advantage of the TWA arrangement without fear of being drafted and sent to Vietnam.

Cassette tapes were the rave in those days to make record album music portable. They were high priced in the US, and the selection of brands and quality were narrow. Hong Kong was THE place to source the best blank cassette tapes, and Jack would fly there just to buy a bunch for him and his lucky friends.

We had a mutual friend, Bobby, who had introduced Jack to me the previous year. Jack had hashish and exposed me to getting high. Smoking marijuana was the norm in the US then—at least, where I was—and I smoked my share as time passed. But I was spoiled by hashish and preferred it to pot from then on. I instinctively related it to travel by the association with Jack's frequent trips to international destinations. Hash was compact compared to weed, and had a flair of mysterious origin in distant lands: Lebanon, Morocco, and somewhere called Afghani [sic]. Hash had an intense flavor, with a thick and complex aroma. The mystique was ancient, with deep cultural ties steeped in tradition, and gained stature from history.

I imagined marijuana was a new thing, coming from California, or maybe Mexico. It was bulky and had to be cleaned up and rolled into a joint before one could smoke it. It had a sharper taste but wonderful aroma, lighter but distinct. The buzz was good. No doubting that, but I thought it fell short in the exotic department. As far as I knew, it didn't have the credentials of Jack's travel.

I concluded that my early introduction to hashish was fortuitous. It wasn't a mere coincidence, but rather a sign of forthcoming events. How else could I explain Jack's arrival at a critical moment to pick up the pieces of my shattered travel plans and allow me to save face?

Jack was an avid snow skier and quite good. I got word that he was going to Switzerland for Christmas, and he invited me to join him there in a youth hostel in Zermatt, Switzerland. That cemented my trip! My excitement caused me to overlook important details...like the location of Zermatt, Switzerland, and the airport I should use.

I had a destination, and it was in Europe—I would figure it out when I got there. So I bought an airline ticket to Zurich—the only city name I had heard of—understanding that they spoke German there. Good enough! After my arrival, I purchased a map and realized that Zermatt was on the opposite side of the country from my destination.

As a complete novice, I didn't understand how international airline travel functioned. What I failed to grasp was that the flight to Zurich would land at the first international airport in Switzerland, which is Geneva. Passengers and their baggage would clear immigration and customs, then continue to Zurich. I deplaned in Geneva and didn't follow the process to recheck my baggage and myself to continue to Zurich, which turned out to be another stroke of luck. Had I continued on to Zurich, I would have missed my eventual route along the shore of Lake Geneva and passing through Montreux, home of the world-famous jazz festival, and on to Visp, the train gateway to Zermatt, which was car-free.

I claimed my backpack, cleared the arrival formalities, and exited the airport. Everyone was speaking in a language that didn't sound like German. It had a softer sound, like I imagined French would have. Oh well. I stuck out my thumb and immediately got a ride. I got as far as the edge of the airport proper before I was let off near a tobacco store—a place for all things useful for travelers. Cigarettes, of course, but also postcards, stamps, and maps.

An English-speaking local confirmed my suspicions by explaining that French, not German, was the local language. I bought a map and scrutinized the area around Geneva. Ah-ha! There it was, jumping out at me like an old friend—the Matterhorn. An anchor, something familiar, a place I'd been to before. Well, at least the Disneyland Matterhorn bobsled ride version in Anaheim, California, that I loved as a kid. But wait, there's more: Zermatt, my destination to meet Jack, was right there at the base of the Matterhorn! Destination found; adventure begins.

Although Zermatt didn't look very far from Geneva as the crow flies, there was the not-insignificant matter of the Alps. They're an extensive mountain range of high, snowcapped peaks that are fairytale beautiful—snow being an important descriptor. It was December and I was hitchhiking. The weather was gorgeous, even at higher altitudes, with the direct sun creating a welcome warmth. But in the shade, it was a different story. The thought of being stuck between rides on a mountain road in winter was not a cheery idea.

That same English-speaking local suggested I take the route to the north, arching over Lake Geneva and hugging the lower-elevation shore-line—likely to be a fertile road for getting rides. It was the right choice. Geneva Airport is north of downtown and not far from the shore of Lake Geneva. The tobacco shop was on the airport road, which connected directly to the N1 highway, the picturesque route that I intended to take. My hastily fashioned sign from a discarded cardboard box read "Visp," my ultimate highway destination. From there I planned to take the train to Zermatt.

I shouldered my backpack and snagged a ride. In short order, I got my first glimpse of the real Switzerland. I had imagined it to be beautiful, and it was. The dazzling blue of the lake complimented the brilliantly clear blue sky. The white caps of the mountain peaks amplified the shaded blues of the alpine slopes nobly guarding the far shore of the lake. I was awestruck by nature's artistry and the pristine Swiss buildings.

The 100 km (60 mile) drive to Montreux raced by. My early morning flight arrival in Geneva and the quick foray through arrival formalities allowed me to be on the street with my thumb out by 0900 hrs, and I was in Montreux by 1100 hrs. I was keeping track of time, as I wasn't sure how late the train ran from Visp to Zermatt. I made it in plenty of time for the hour-long train journey.

My ride from Geneva, a university student returning to school in Bern, took me to Lucerne He was quiet but knowledgeable of Switzerland's multicultural unification. From Lucerne, I got a ride all the way south to Martigny. Fortunately, my ride was a youngish couple who had lived in Montreux, and they suggested we drive into town and they'd give me a quick tour. They were fun to talk to, as both spoke English with a UK accent, having done a stint in London. They diverted to the lakeside road, passing the casino and the Château du Chillon. Montreux has a mild microclimate, with Mediterranean trees and grand Belle Époque buildings. The brief journey only heightened my desire to return. If the drive along Lake Geneva was stunning, Montreux was breathtaking.

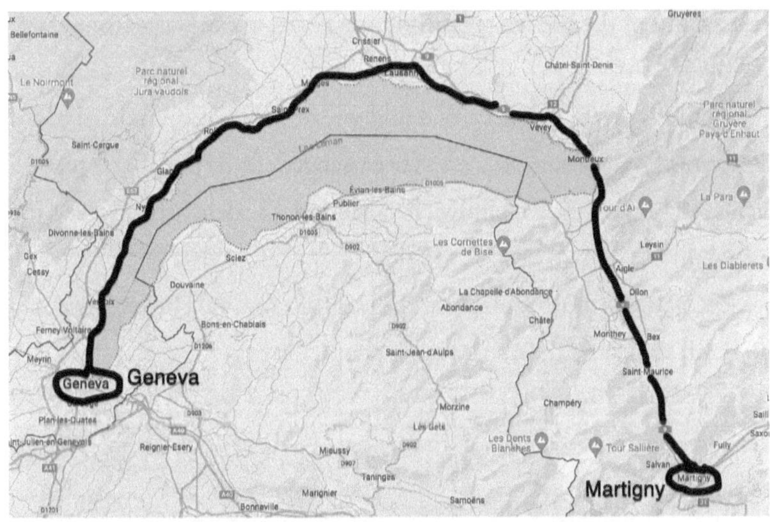

Geneva to Martigny. Map data ©2024 Google

We merged back onto the national highway and drove the remaining 50 km (31 mi) to Martigny. While traveling on that section of road, the Alps loomed in front of the car and the lake passed on our right. It was an exhilaration to drink in visually. Reluctantly, I said goodbye to the engaging and fun couple in Martigny, bidding them, *"Au revoir."*

Time to move—I had a train to catch. My cardboard sign was nearing the end of its usefulness, but I still had about 70 km (43 mi) up the Rhone Valley to Visp. The couple had taken me to what they said was the best spot to catch a ride to Visp. The road hugged the south side of the Rhone River, which carved a wide valley with alpine mountains on both sides. Vineyards were visible on the mountain slopes on the north side of the river. The winter sun's radiant heat, lower in the southern sky, melted the snow in unshaded areas. A scenic drive, but in December, the true beauty of the Alpen fields was missed. After less than an hour, I snagged a ride, as promised by my departing friends. The drive in the log hauling truck took about an hour—he was hauling ass, err, logs, so to speak. He arrived at a warehouse that was near the Hauptbahnhof in Visp. We had broken out of the French region and were back in the German language region.

I figured correctly that I could find one of the large pretzels I'd heard about in the train station. Another passenger cut it in half and made a ham and gruyere cheese sandwich. The food was delightful. So was the liter stein of German beer.

Several trains were available in the early afternoon. The trip was only an hour, so I chose the one leaving about 1530 hrs.

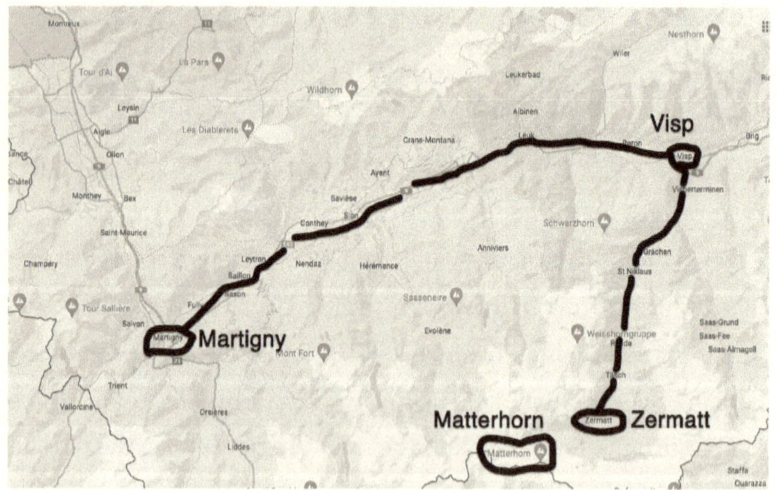

To Visp, train to Zermatt. Map data ©2024 Google

The train pulled into the Hauptbahnhof in Zermatt at dusk. The snowcapped Matterhorn was cast in a golden glow as the sun was retiring for the evening. Families, couples, and friends exchanged joyous greetings, creating a festive atmosphere. The deep snow muted the lights and shapes of the buildings, like a scene from a Hans Christian Andersen fairy tale.

I was alone and beaming as I did a double take—a horse-drawn sleigh was evidently the local equivalent of a taxi. The sleigh driver had the reins in his hand and waved me over. I was on a budget, yes, but this was too much to pass up. I climbed aboard with my backpack in tow. In the snow of the Christmas season, we lumbered off, with the horses shaking their heads with snorting breath freezing in the air. We chanced upon Jack, fresh off the slopes, as we made our way down the Hauptbahnhofstraße to the youth hostel.

I was on a roll. A fortuitous sequence of events had brought me to a ski resort in Switzerland and the start of life as a traveler. Adventure was unfolding with little effort on my part—I was digging it. A trend emerged, but I was too caught up in the fun of being a traveler to notice. Coincidences, lucky breaks, and interventions pointed me toward the East. But that's for later chapters.

I was a backpacker on a modest budget. A budget I would stretch to the limit to stay as long as possible in Europe! Jack could hop on a plane for a weekend of skiing in Switzerland if he wanted to. He was about my age, but even his youth dictated he stay longer than a couple of days. Jet lag didn't discriminate between age groups, and Jack knew from experience that a longer stay would be much easier on his body. An excellent skier, he was nearing the end of this trip when I caught up with him. I, however, was not a skier and only entertained a vague idea that it would be an excellent place to hang out and meet girls. My intuition proved correct—youth hostels were in fashion and there were many girls of many flavors. English, being the lingua franca, made communicating easy. I could arrive early at the youth hostel's fireplace and bar and greet the ladies when they came back from skiing.

I only caught glimpses of Jack, but I am profoundly thankful for his help in my successful escape. Escape from what, I wasn't exactly sure. Boredom with "higher education?" Wanting to escape the monotony of American life? Avoiding being trapped into a predictable life path? Yes, but there was more to it than that. I wanted adventure and change, and so travel dangled as bait, but without details. Where to go, what to do? No matter, do it! And Jack was the catalyst.

It was cold and the snow was deep. But in the sun's warmth, at that high altitude, you could take off your heavy winter coat and be comfortable in only a shirt. I walked toward a bench in the warm sunlight with a stunning view of the Matterhorn. I noticed two elderly women with an appearance straight out of an Alpen storybook. They were walking down the mountain trail, each with two pails full of fresh milk, one on each side, suspended between an ancient, curved piece of wood. As I approached the bench, I could smell hashish—excellent hashish, in my modest opinion. It had to be from the guy sitting there. That was Scott, and he would become my best friend to this day.

I approached with deliberate casualness, slowing down to give me time to assess the believed source of that fine aroma. The pipe confirmed my suspicion, and he was concealing it with practiced behavior. As a seasoned smoker, I detected it immediately. *OK, that's good.* My attention turned to his appearance and the likelihood of him offering some of that smoke to me.

He was wearing an army field jacket, but it was more than a typical hippie fashion choice. He looked like he was wearing an old friend, something familiar with a patina only time can produce. Likely he was a Vietnam vet. But his hair was medium long. *He's been out for a while.* Lots of kids also wore "jungle boots" along with other military garb, like field jackets. Scott was wearing regular American style hunting boots with a lot of wear—more evidence that he had been a civilian for a while.

I suspected he was part of the program that sent GIs to Germany from Vietnam to "decompress" before returning to the US. The Vietnam War was still raging in the early '70s, and the war machine was chewing up a sizable chunk of the Baby Boomer male generation. The boy-men were young and strong, dumped like cannon fodder into a surreal war of hidden enemies in a hot tropical jungle. Most were ill-prepared, mentally or emotionally, to fight a war they didn't understand. Countless of them accomplished what had to be done while getting high and listening to music, attempting to make sense of it and merely surviving.

When the standard tour of duty in Vietnam ended, the military command structure deemed many soldiers were too wild for an immediate return to the United States. The transition program[1] enabled volunteers who met the criteria to end their Vietnam service early and become prepared for life in the real world. Germany received a deluge of young American men with raging hormones and a lot of time on their hands. The GIs found themselves in another foreign country, speaking another foreign language. At least they weren't being shot at. So they found the release that you would imagine—party time!

All of that raced through my mind as I got closer. His long hair, mustache, and nonchalant behavior, like he wasn't doing anything against Swiss law, cinched it!

"Hey, dude, mind if I have a toke?"

I was scrutinized, apparently passed, and we jelled. Two guys of the same mind, if not the same background, rapping at the base of an alpine mountain on a sunny day in the Swiss Alps. Yes indeed, travel is all it's cracked up to be.

We engaged in a comfortable, increasingly stoned dialogue with undertones of testing each other. Scott had been traveling longer than me, so he had the upper hand. The conversation gravitated to where we had traveled so far—Scott had drifted down to Switzerland from Amsterdam. I'd heard about Amsterdam; it was at the top of my list as a must-go destination. Hitchhiking around the Alps in December wasn't appealing, even to a novice traveler. With that in mind, I throttled my enthusiasm and, with the air of a seasoned traveler, referenced how cool Amsterdam is (careful not to say "must be").

Scott said, "Yeah, it is. I've been hanging out there for a while." His stature and road savvy needle pegged in my nascent traveler eyes. "Ever smoke Moroccan?" said Mr. Traveler.

I wasn't sure if I had or not. "Sure," I said. "It's OK."

Scott said, "The best Moroccan is from Ketama, in the north part at the base of the Rif Mountains."

I was in no position to question him, as my world geography sucked at that point in time. But it ticked boxes that heretofore hadn't crossed my mind. *Morocco, holy shit! That's in freaking Africa!* (I was pretty sure.)

Before that day was over, in the sun on a bench at the base of the Matterhorn in Switzerland, we agreed to hitchhike to Morocco. But not before we smoked most of Scott's good black hash in the Swiss Alps.

Before you get the impression I had entered a fairy tale, let me share a bit of knowledge learned soon thereafter. Scott was one of those Vietnam vets who volunteered for the early out transition program. No wonder his clean-shaven, mustachioed face hid an undercurrent of seriousness and determination. His Vietnam service had fostered a controlled and patient man. That tranquil patience, which I didn't fully understand, exasperated me occasionally. Like those worn hunting boots, for example. He had a procedure to put them on—it didn't vary even if I perceived we were in a hurry. I won't reiterate the whole damn process—an accurate description would be lengthy and probably irritate you. But the last part—the lacing up—was the crowning delay. One eyelet at a time, then tug tight. Repeat for sixteen eyelets. Then the last step: a careful tying of a bow...twice.

Of course, I didn't have any annoying habits like being spontaneous and jumping into something with little thought.

Despite our different backgrounds and age difference—Scott was three years older—we became comfortable traveling companions and lifelong friends.

Zermatt - (L to R) Me, Unknown & Jack

Malaga, Spain – Scott

Chapter Three

North Africa

Crosby, Stills & Nash: *Marrakesh Express > Lyrics*

Africa, holy shit! When I signed up for this trip to Europe, that itself was venturing into the exotic and the unknown. But Africa? That's a leap beyond the pale.

I referred to my trusted map of Europe that guided me to Switzerland, the Matterhorn, and the introduction to Scott. Looking more closely at the very bottom edge of the map was a sliver of geography that illustrated the northern portions of Morocco, Algeria, and Tunisia. I noticed the larger and bold word *AFRICA* just before it cut off the rest of the continent.

It clearly indicated that our destination was far from being a quick trip. The distance between Zermatt and the tip of Spain, the crossing point from the European continent to Africa, spanned 2,000 km (1,243 mi).

Scott said, "Morocco has some excellent hash, but it's hard to find, even there. If we can make it to Ketama, we might get lucky."

I trusted Scott's word, lacking the experience to form an opinion. But the shot at adventure sealed the deal and we hit the road. I hadn't been in Europe for even two full weeks and now was moving on to Africa. That was cool, but I knew that there was plenty of adventure waiting for me in Europe when I returned. And Amsterdam was at the top of the list.

The journey to Morocco from Switzerland resulted in not only a progressive change of weather (warmer), but also a radical transition from the calculated tolerance of Swiss governance to that of an authoritarian dictatorship. We serendipitously splurged and took a train through Spain, avoiding the potential wrath of Francisco Franco's supporters while hitchhiking. We endured a 12-hour train ride in second class on a crowded train to Madrid, followed by an overnight train to Malaga. The crowded train was not a fond memory rerun of the train to the Boy Scout Jamboree. The crowded cabins reminded me of the "jerk contest" on that trip, and I made a point of avoiding sleeper cars.

There was an upside. The unpleasant body odor, stinky socks, and unwashed clothes in the crowded train cars provided a perfect cover for the smell of the hash that Scott hid in the rolled-up cuff of his field jacket.

Fellow travelers further informed us that Spain had a nasty habit of coming down hard on drugs. *Generalissimo* Franco was the reality in Spain, and his stranglehold on the country personified itself in extreme views on what qualified as acceptable social behavior. Having long hair like mine was a step too far.

We arrived in Malaga a couple of days before January 1. We planned a normal day or two as tourists, enjoying the warm sunny day (compared to that of northern Europe) and a New Year's celebration at the tip of the European continent. Instead, we faced a steady stream of taunts and near threats about our appearance, meaning our long hair and youth. We spent New Year's Eve holed up in a cheap pension, eager to get the hell out of Spain and into friendlier territory.

Long before the internet, we depended on news and travel alerts that emanated from word of mouth. Word on the street from travelers along the way, and confirmed when we arrived in Spain, was that you couldn't get into Morocco with long hair. *No problem. Buy a short hair wig!*

Scott's hair was borderline long. When he tucked it behind his ears, we deemed it passing length. Mine was a different story. I bought a cheap short hair wig, and it looked the part. It also looked ridiculous on me.

We took the ferry to Ceuta and crossed into Morocco. The customs agent looked at me in the short hair wig and my passport photo with shoulder length hair, then I heard the soon-to-be familiar sound of the bureaucratic *whomp, whomp!* The official government sound of approval stamped on paperwork, then my passport. I was in Morocco. We laughed with a sigh of relief. It soon became apparent that long hairs were everywhere, and short-haired wigs were easy to come by at youth hostels.

We hitchhiked south from Tetouan with the intention of a visit to Ketama, a small village on a slope of a mountain range in northern Morocco famous for its hash. Ketama was in the Rif Mountains, a region with a long history dating before the Romans and long settled by the Berbers. A rugged region with rugged inhabitants. During our journey to Ketama, we stopped at Chefchaouen, where the old town's pastel blue walls were a sight to see and later became an Instagram trend. However, we heard rumors of the military blocking the road to Ketama. We weren't having any of that, but the news was consistent among hippies and, well, it also rang true. Ketama and the Rif Mountains region were usually under guard by military patrols and checkpoints. To have the military close access off was something more serious.

Our immediate attention switched to Marrakesh, so we continued south to Fez, then over to Rabat, skipping the tourist routine. Low-price accommodations kept us within our budget, the idea of which was to live as cheaply as possible. We lingered in Rabat, then ventured due south to Casablanca—a beautiful city with lots of our people around. We took the train, the Marrakesh Express, to its namesake destination. And yes, like Crosby, Stills, and Nash sang, there were chickens, ducks, pigs, noise, and lots of locals in *djellabas*, not to mention a motley throng of tourists.

We were with our people! No one hassled us for our hair or appearance. Everyone got along and we relaxed and melded into the hippie scene of the early '70s in Morocco. It was a fabulous transition from the haggard feeling back in Spain of an uptight, myopic society. That was more generational—not the people our age, but the political environment put a lid on the freewheeling "love, peace and Woodstock" vibe we enjoyed. The train ride was joyous, if not crowded, and the cars seemed to rock and roll serenely as we *click-clacked* along the rails toward our destination. I didn't encounter any "jerking" on this train ride, except the sudden application of brakes from time to time. The railroad tracks in the desert were a collection point for animals and humans. I don't know if those jerks involved any fatalities.

Marrakesh! Damn, here we were in the fabled city of rock 'n' roll lore. We were out of smoke, sure; of course it was easy to come by, but of disappointing quality. We persisted and eventually scored some sweet blond Moroccan—soft and resiny with a promising aroma—and surprisingly cheap. We hung there for a couple of weeks and found our share of adventure while avoiding the authorities.

Even in the distant past, as far back as the era of this book, most people knew the Sahara Desert is in Africa. And quite a few of those folk realized places like Morocco, Algeria, and Tunisia bordered that enormous and desolate region. Even I imagined that reality, but hadn't situated it within my immediate surroundings.

Formally, the Sahara Desert is several hundred kilometers south of Marrakesh. It holds the title for the biggest desert with a "hot" climate (not all deserts are tropical) and covers 9.2 million square kilometers (3.5 million sq. mi)—slightly smaller than China. However, the Agafay Desert is a small regional desert, only 50 km (31 mi) from the center of Marrakesh. We took a local bus, seeing oases with palm and date trees, people in white robes and turbans, and many animals, both wild and domesticated. Donkeys pulled rickety wooden carts upon on which were animals in cages, or tied over gunny sacks of farm produce that was to be sold at the market. And sand, lots of sand. If you were far enough away, you could observe the heat shimmering above the sand, warping the distant signs of human life and conjuring mirages stirred by one's imagination... And, in our case, by hashish smoke.

Have I mentioned camels? Lots of camels. Without these very fascinating creatures, desert dwellers would have a harder life. Camels did it for me. Just their presence made me confront the reality that I was in the freaking desert! They also smelled cool. Some might call it a stench, but smell signals authenticity. They were big, and too many ugly creatures that were chill while living in a hot and threatening environment.

Scott and I decided we needed a couple of those. We could cruise the desert in search of cool stuff—go places you couldn't hitchhike to. Be part of a camel train. See the real Sahara. We were kinda high, so the idea wore off rather quickly. The smell brought us around to reality. Can you buy a camel? Yep, you sure can. Do you want to own one? Nope, definitely not.

By nature, most are docile, but they are very large and very strong, and they also know how to defend themselves. Camels can bite with sharp teeth, kick in all directions, spit large quantities, and run faster than you. They often develop an affinity for their owners and handlers, but if they develop a dislike for someone, you need to be cautious. They recognize people and have long memories.

A word of caution: Stoned humans with a curious nature who come too close to an irritated camel will find evidence that they can indeed kick in all directions. I still have a crooked nose from a camel's kick. Known as Ships of the Desert and Beasts of Burden, they deserve respect, as they don't take any shit from bothersome humans. I came to know them as Beasts of Hurtin'.

As the weeks passed in a blissful stoned state, we lived frugally. However, one day, with even less to do, we discovered we had about US$80 left between us. We were living on oranges, Moroccan green mint tea with sugar, and the occasional bowl of couscous. It's low in calories and rich in protein. Nowadays, it's often included as part of a weight loss program. Our weight loss department didn't need any help, but the protein was critical. We had to be careful and stay away from lamb. Trouble arose early on due to our sensitive digestive systems, quickly transferring its aftermath through our intestines with scant warning. What was more concerning was the balance in our travel fund account. That was a bit of a shock, but not much of a worry to the savvy travelers that we fancied ourselves.

Nonetheless, we thought it a prudent idea to head back to Europe, where we could replenish the bank. We packed up (having gifted my short-haired wig long ago to someone in need) and started hitchhiking from Marrakesh in a northeast direction. The plan was to pick up the coastal road east across North Africa, with not a thought about the fact that the next country we would enter was Algeria, an ally of North

Vietnam. Scott had fought on the opposite side in Vietnam, and I was a long-haired American that likely offended Allah in all possible ways.

We blitzed through Morocco and discarded the remaining hash we had as we neared the Algerian border. Algeria was a world apart. It was common knowledge that Communist countries took harsh measures against people having fun. Possessing even soft drugs, or indulging in them, was dangerous and resulted in stiff prison sentences. Private automobile traffic had considerably decreased, making it more difficult for hitchhikers. The vehicles were also much older and not well maintained. Algeria was a socialist country and lacked the benefits of capitalism that we were used to. We were fortunate that an Algerian university student picked us up hitchhiking and took us several hundred kilometers toward the capital Algiers. But it shocked us when he pulled over in the middle of bloody nowhere and said he couldn't take us any farther. Our Arabic was nonexistent, and his English was as bad. He seemed nervous, which further alarmed us. Even more concerning, we were in a hostile area with no town in view, and it was already dark. Great.

Do Guardian Angels operate in Communist countries? The answer would come soon enough. The reality of our situation fully realized, we began walking with no other obvious alternative. We had just walked past an unpaved road, not much more than a trail, when an ancient farm vehicle of unknown variety lumbered to a stop behind us. The driver appeared to be of the same vintage as the vehicle. With a full-on Arab beard and ragged clothes, there was also a reserved smile on offer. He motioned us to climb in back—a flatbed with side rails similar to a pickup truck bed—and we did so with some hesitation. We had no other options, so we decided to ride it out. He backed up and turned right down that dirt path. We bumped along, going farther and farther from whatever bit of civilization we may have been near on the coastal highway. Despite the beautiful star-filled sky, apprehension prevented us from enjoying it. Were we headed to trouble, or to a safe harbor for the night? Our uncomfortable bumpy ride seemed to last much longer than it did. We could only judge by the stars and the enveloping darkness. Our decision committed us, regardless of the outcome.

The vehicle topped a small hill and we could see the outlines of some huts. Starlight glinted off the smoke emanating from one of them. We pulled into the compound and an older woman greeted us. We thought her the wife of our driver. Both warmly welcomed us into a mud brick hut with greetings in Arabic and a little French. I remembered from my days as a Vietnam War protester and the related reading of counterculture books that Algeria achieved their independence from France in the early '60s. Such an important event only a decade ago would loom large in the memory of these people.

There were only two rooms. The one they led us into was obviously the main sleeping and eating area for the family. The outer room had a firepit in the center. It conjured up a resemblance to the often-portrayed medieval scene, with the pot hanging over a fire being stirred by an old woman. The smoke from the fire hung in the room before escaping through a round hole in the arched, but low ceiling. Goats roamed the room, while straw covered the sandy floor. A mixture of odors wafted through the space; not unpleasant, but definitive. Odors that were rich in layers of time. Even the smoke from the fire was complex, like they had deliberately aged it before being allowed to escape. The small space concentrated the air, imbuing it with a vintage scent. The elements of human life were prominent, with their animals contributing nuance. It felt welcoming and safe, the result of our arrival in a secure location for the night. The pungent odors were therefore much easier to accept.

The smell of mint tea was also inviting, as was the small portion of couscous that was offered. We felt humbled and honored at his outpouring of hospitality. In due course, we retired into the adjoining room, where an old gentleman, the elder of the family, was sitting on a raised platform—a bed of sorts. His smile was genuine, and you could feel his sincerity and glee in meeting us. Our appearance and likely national origins were a nonissue with him, as well as our hosts. Conversation was not in the cards, but communication by tone of voice, body language, and a few scattered French words created a warm and friendly engagement. The elder had a few scraps of newspaper in French, with headlines about the end of the successful Algerian revolution. He then showed us his rifle. Scott and I each held it with appreciation, and he nodded to each of us when we handed it back. The reverence was clear without words spoken.

With that, he rose and gestured that he was leaving the room, and the resting platform was ours to use. He parted with *"Bonne nuit,"* then *"Allah akbar."* They had so little to offer us, but gave us everything they had. It honored us to be their guests.

We slept well and rose early the next morning. They were firm that we were to be driven back up to the highway, which allowed us to view the area: the land was barren desert scrub. We noticed subsistence farming of grain crops, sheep, and chickens before we left the compound. We arrived at the highway in short order—the trip back seemed to go much quicker—as Scott and I were in a contemplative mood. We said our *au revoirs* and watched them drive away.

Guardian Angels don't need passports, can speak all languages, and do not heed the predilections of humans, like political beliefs. Ok, that's settled. But are Guardian Angels assigned to a human to oversee? Do they cover a zone, like in sports? Can they disown an assigned human for unacceptable behavior? Are they independent contractors, or do they have an employer? They have no need for compensation. It seems like there's a link, or at least some kind of relationship, between karma and good or bad vibes. My intuition informs me so. Therefore, we add Guardian Angels to the growing collection of subjects to consider in my hypothesis to explain Dots.

So, we started the day back at the same location on the road we left the night before. We were some unknown distance west of the capital, Algiers. With thoughts of gratitude and having gained an inspiring knowledge of human nature, we began walking and sticking our thumbs out at the occasional passing car or truck. Eventually we got a ride, and about an hour later, we were passing through the capital. Even though we were in an Arabic country, it had a Communist government. The official buildings and many others had that same unimaginative, dull look of Eastern European Communist architecture, with an Arabic twist. We were happy to be let out on the eastern edge of the city. It was about 2,300 km (1,429 mi) from Marrakesh to Tunis, where we intended to catch a boat to Italy. We were now about two-thirds of the way there. It would be another 1,000 km (621 mi) from Italy up to Munich, Germany. We'd have to improvise—we couldn't carry enough oranges to last the distance.

Travel is the best education. It's higher education, university level all the way. No age limitations and no entry exams, but no diploma awarded to hang on a wall. The reward is a cornucopia of experiences and exposures to vastly different cultures and points of view. It's a life-changing series of studies that lays a foundation for personal growth and encourages one to challenge the norms of their birth country. In the short time that had elapsed since I joined the school of the road, I'd absorbed enough to set the wheels in my head churning.

One never graduates from travel if they're fortunate. The number of improvised classrooms, countless subjects, and exam equivalents is vast and thrilling. The lessons learned are not just memorized; we absorb them like vitamins and sunshine. It feels good in the moment, then sinks in over time to nurture wisdom and knowledge.

Travel can throw a lesson in your face, like being discriminated against because of your color, appearance, clothing, religion, or nationality. Lesson learned—not everyone thinks or looks like you. There's always more than one side to a story or situation, and you learn by asking questions without harboring a hidden bias.

However, there's a particular branch of street schooling that is easy to get into, but tough and treacherous to survive. It's a school that millions are born into without choice. They hold classes in inner cities, third world countries, and poor rural areas throughout the world. Students are ill-prepared for the curriculum and not given second chances. *Smart* is not the same as *intelligent*. You need both attributes to survive that school, and only the sharpest thrive. Each of us has no say in who our parents are, or where we are born. People understand this well. I consider travel a privilege that carries a responsibility to respect those who were not born with the advantages many of us take for granted.

In the bazaars of Morocco, I witnessed youths approaching tourists and shaking them down with a glance. The way they dress, their shoes and walk, and the language they speak tell the young people where they're from. A polished casualness in their approach effortlessly transitions into a greeting in the foreigner's native language—more times than not, they're spot on. In the following second or two, if they sense they've used the wrong language, they switch to the next best guess. I've heard them start with German, then Russian, Hungarian, Finnish, Dutch, and Afrikaans. Some of these street kids can't even read or write.

So is that intelligence or being smart? I believe it's both, with a survival component. Their instincts are honed early in life, driven by hunger and desperation, and eventually the tough edges are worn off and they become perceived as educated. Like all animals, humans' first order of business is survival. Most people on Earth do not begin with the advantages with which I and many others have had. I learned that a little compassion toward those on the street is in order. Appraise the person and situation before responding to a hand reaching out from dirty ragged clothes. In countries like Algeria, even travelers down to their last few dollars, pounds, francs, or marks are wealthy compared to most with their hand out. While there are exceptions, acknowledging my good fortune is a humbling reminder.

· • ● • ● • ● • ● • ·

In Algeria, governmental policy attempted to restrict—or at least discourage—contact between locals and visitors. The metropolitan areas were the most controlled. Our ride took us through Algiers and let us out on the eastern edge of the capital. We were grateful for that and avoided most of the city, figuring it would have been tough to thumb our way out of downtown. However, we were in a bleak and rather dingy part of town—the wrong side of the tracks, so to speak. We walked, since no other option presented itself. We approached a group of young guys just hooting and laughing, taunting each other and posturing, in case a girl was watching. Even though that was not likely in an Arabic country.

Their attention shifted to us and they absorbed the unexpected sight of long-haired Westerners striding down their street. Either they accepted the Communist doctrine that foreigners were to be suspect and reported to the authorities, or they were just looking for some trouble. Scott and I were veterans of this situation, and knew that engagement would only egg them on. We reshouldered our backpacks, walked a little straighter, and moved past. None spoke a foreign language, except we could make out "heepy." It was mildly tense, but they didn't challenge us.

Traffic was going by in both directions, so that helped us to get out of their sight and attention. We got a series of rides in the back of trucks, watching the scenery change from urban to rural to full-on desert. It was warm, but not overbearingly hot. We made it about 300 km (186 mi) that day.

As night approached, the temperature dropped, as it does in a desert, and our last ride let us off as close to nowhere as you can get. We needed to secure a place for the night and were delighted to find a culvert that ran under the road. Apparently, it only served a purpose in the rare instances when it rained. The night was clear and star-studded, the desert an empty expanse, bereft of any human presence except for the desolate highway. We settled in for the night, thankful for our goose-down sleeping bags and some oranges.

With a new day beginning after a cold night, we checked that the area was as empty before, hoping to catch a ride before the sun became too hot. After being picked up, we rode for hours until we reached a roadside stand in a small village owned by our driver's friend. We enjoyed some delicious mint tea and couscous, courtesy of our ride—another unsolicited act of kindness that we were very grateful for. As a bonus, the little village was a rest area for long-haul drivers. There was a lot of traffic (for Algeria), which buoyed our spirits further.

We then figured out that we were close to the Tunisian frontier, and the border between Algeria and Tunisia. The next ride could be tricky, we knew, as we'd been down this road before, so to speak. If the driver let you out before the border to avoid any hassles for themselves, then we would have to approach the customs area on foot. That would inevitably lead to more scrutiny, more bureaucratic hassles, and a long wait.

Not long after, a sedan with only a driver—no passengers—stopped and gave us a lift. He was a Tunisian doctor on his way back to Tunis and spoke some English, so we had a pleasant conversation as we approached the border. Our driver reassured us there would be no difficulty with the formalities. He crossed this border frequently for his work—just let him do the talking. Scott and I mentally exchanged "No problem there" glances. It went down just as the doc said. We expressed our gratitude and Scott and I promptly dozed off. When we woke up, the good doctor informed us we were nearing Tunis and asked what our intentions were. We did our best to say we wanted to get a boat to Italy. He correctly understood our desire, and not long after, we saw the port come into view! He dropped us in front of the ferry terminal. We were effusive in our praise and thanked him for his generosity. We bought tickets aboard the Tirrenia ferry to Naples, Italy, leaving the next day.

Travel—at least what had become our extreme kind of budget backpacking—was really cheap. In our case, it was "practically free," to quote the street hawkers. Our 10-day journey had covered over 2,000 km (1,243 mi), and we still had some (not much) money in hand between us. Enough to buy the cheapest class tickets to Italy. We achieved such a feat only by the generosity and kindness of many people—none of whom knew us, and most didn't speak our language or even share the same cultural background. It's a safe bet that the little money we had was more than the average person of Algeria, Morocco, or Tunisia would earn in a month. We were blessed and shown kindness throughout our journey.

• • • ● • ● ● • • •

Specifically, we covered a distance of 5,000 km (3,107 mi) by land from Zermatt, Switzerland, to Tunis, Tunisia. We walked (not much), hitchhiked, took trains and buses, and rode a ferry from the southern tip of Europe to the northern tip of Africa. Then we hitchhiked across the breadth of North Africa to the eastern limit of Tunisia.

Hitchhiking to Europe was not an option from Tunis. We switched to water transport and boarded the ferry to Naples, Italy (600 km, 373 mi), and then hitchhiked from Naples to Munich, Germany, about 1,000 km (621 mi). It was a helluva a good time, and Scott and I made it without any major issues between us. We proved to be excellent traveling companions.

We departed Africa, arriving back in Europe nearly broke financially, but rich in experience. At least, that's what we used to rally us into recovery mode.

Marrakesh, Morocco

Discarding hash at Algerian border

Interlude One

We've All Done It

Led Zeppelin: *Ramble On* > *Lyrics*

I have great news for you. You were right! And you knew it all along, with a gut feeling about it. But why did you end up making a bad decision—again? Thankfully, it was a minor thing. You knew better, but chose wrong.

Who am I to rub it in? I live in a glass house, so I shouldn't throw rocks—right? It's not only me and you who have gone against our intuition, but every human also born in the last thousand years, or more, has done it.

Intuition isn't the same as instinct, but we instinctively seem to dismiss intuition.

The Merriam-Webster Dictionary defines *intuition* as "the power or faculty of attaining to direct knowledge or cognition without evident rational thought and inference." It defines *instinct* as "a largely inheritable and unalterable tendency of an organism to make a complex and specific response to environmental stimuli without involving reason."

The issue is a human thing. It makes little difference where you were born, what language you speak, or your religion or ethnic origin, intuition is shared by all. Everyone has said or heard someone say phrases like, "I should have listened to myself," "I had a gut feeling," "I knew better," or "I had bad vibes about it, him, or her." Usually we learn this after an outcome that was not what we desired.

Which statement occurs more often: "I'm glad I followed my instincts" or "I wish I had listened to myself"? Surely, it doesn't matter. Either phrase acknowledges the same fundamental reference to intuition.

Human intuition was already in place when we were still foraging for food on the savanna. Ignoring an intuition then could prove fatal. Now it's commonly believed that disregarded intuition is frequently accurate, but it's rarely a matter of life and death. Ignoring intuitions that have proven reliable is close to the definition of insanity: doing the same thing repeatedly and expecting a different result. Perhaps that's strong, but can we lay the blame on societal conditioning? Why do we habitually disregard our instinctive feelings?

Intuition is hardwired into the human brain. By that I mean it's included in the DNA of *Homo sapiens*,[2] and perhaps our forbearers, *Homo erectus*.[3] It's a shared mammalian characteristic that humans needed to survive before we developed reasoned decision-making.

Did intuition atrophy as humans became more societal and gained knowledge and intelligence? Did genetic code edit intuition in humans?

Time is distance, and distance allows opportunity for change. The period from the emergence of *Homo sapiens* to the 21st century is about 300,000 years—about 15,000 generations: enough for genetics to have its way.

Malcolm Gladwell wrote an immensely popular book, *Blink* (published in 2007), about intuitive decision-making. He reportedly "drew heavily" on the research of Gerd Gigerenzer, a German psychologist and director of the respected Planck Institute For Human Development.[4]

We're talking respected authors here, and bona fide scientific research. Some feel the path to understanding intuition taken by these and others veers from the traditional principles of rational decision-making. Although that's a respected opinion, it's not reason enough to dismiss alternate explanations out of hand.

The Interludes in this book explore my nascent hypothesis that a causality connection exists between inexplicable events or situations and human instinct and intuition. I should clarify, out of respect to science, that I'm advancing a hypothesis, not a theory. But *Hypothesis of Dots* sounds clunky and boring. *Theory of Dots* sounds, well, like science. Let's go with "Theory."

I further consider the pursuit of scientific knowledge to be the most beneficial form of adventure. So I ask for forgiveness from the scientific community as I continue using the word *theory* throughout this book.

It took time and distance for me to reflect on the events in this book and how they relate to my theory. The process was jump-started by looking through photos of my journey. I literally have thousands. When I began digitizing the selected analog images, they transported me back in time. As I assimilated the visual information, the story in front of me emerged.

I became engrossed in my photos, drawn into the scenes with memories swirling. Each gave me clarity, with a hint or a suggestion to identify this event, person, or place, connecting later to other situations, which fueled my theory. I had a gut feeling there was far more to discover.

Some photos resembled a reflection in calm water that emerged after someone threw a pebble into a pond and the waves dispersed. The adage, "Still waters run deep" applies here. The inhabitants of my still water pond grew as I continued to search. I saw human emotions and feelings created by intuition and instincts. Inexplicable timing of events and fortuitous happenings. Also, Guardian Angels preventing disaster or coming to the aid of someone (usually me), good or bad vibes, gut feelings, luck, and coincidence. But I had a feeling that coincidence and luck were perhaps not in the same league as intuition, and needed closer scrutiny.

I explored the Guardian Angel interventions, coincidences, good luck, and timing of unexpected meetings. I felt they were not all independent events. The relationship was becoming clearer, though still hazy. A conundrum, for sure.

Destiny loomed large in my thoughts—the idea of life events being foreordained was intriguing.

Karma was a recurring explanation. Is it the water in the pond?

There is still much to learn about intuition, gut feelings, vibes, and Guardian Angels, and their connection to reasoned decision-making.

The pond is deep and has more secrets to share. We'll dive to greater depth in the following Interludes.

Chapter Four

No Question About It

Van Morrison: *Into The Mystic > Lyrics*

Long before the internet existed, people had always communicated, albeit in a more relaxed time frame, whether in person, or by postcards, letters, and telephone. Telephones had the tightly curled cord attaching the handset to the telephone device with a rotary dial, which was used to place the call. You put your finger in the numbered hole in the round dial and rotated it all the way to the metal stop. Then you waited until it leisurely returned to its original starting place so you could repeat the process for the next of seven numbers for a local call. Each numbered hole also contained three letters of the alphabet. For example, a phone number could be *LA4 5746* (524–5746). Perhaps that painfully slow (in hindsight) process was a feature designed as a cooling-off period, allowing some callers to forego embarrassing calls. A similar delay feature on today's smartphones is only now available.

Travelers had to visit a local post office, queue up, and prepay to use a telephone to call internationally, and that was bloody expensive. Mostly people saved time and money by sending postcards and letters via a government postal system. The efficient national systems delivered within their borders in days or weeks. Internationally, longer. Inefficient postal systems, maybe never.

You could also pick up mail using an international system called *poste restante*. You would go to the designated window in the local post office, show your passport, and ask if you had any mail. Or, if you were a savvy traveler, you could buy American Express traveler's checks. Owning at least one that was still valid allowed you to receive poste restante mail at their offices in select cities around the world.

Travelers like me and many others used this system to allow friends or loved ones a reliable way to send a letter. You picked a city that you intended to be in and provided a time range—the weeks or months that you would be there to collect mail. As I recall, American Express had a three-month time limit before they destroyed uncollected mail.

The letters, or even just a postcard, that I mailed to my family and friends were scant.

When Scott and I arrived back in Europe from North Africa, we traveled up the length of Italy and over the Alps to Munich, Germany. Apparently, I had mentioned to family and friends that I expected to be there, and it was a minor miracle that a letter sent by my brother and four sisters was waiting at the American Express office in Munich when I drifted in.

As mentioned earlier, we were rather low on money when we arrived in Germany. Zero wouldn't be far off.

When I opened the letter, I was so surprised I had to sit down. In the letter included US$50! That was a sizable amount in 1972 to a backpacking traveler, and an incredible amount for my young sisters and brother to accumulate.[5] Such a warm, thoughtful, and loving thing to do for a wandering brother they seldom heard from. I was humbled and thankful. The onslaught of experiences and accumulation of impressions from travel and adventure are prone to obscure the bonds of family. That letter brought financial relief and reconnected me to them, and it couldn't have arrived at a more important time or place. It catalyzed my extended stay in Europe and facilitated the adventures that followed.

We walked out of the American Express office a short distance to a nearby park to gather our thoughts. We looked like typical long-haired backpacker travelers: Scott in his army field jacket and I in my bell-bottom jeans, long hair in a ponytail, and full beard. We gazed absentmindedly at an older man dressed all in black playing with a young child near a merry-go-round. He looked our way and walked toward us. As he approached, he extended his arm to shake hands with Scott and said, "Hello! I'm Johnny Cash," followed by, "You boys in the military?"

We knew who he was, and he caught us off guard with the silly question. Neither of us complied with military appearance guidelines, looking as we did. The child pulled on his pant leg, wanting attention, so Johnny Cash left, saying, "You boys take care." The sound of his voice was unmistakable, and he seemed genuinely friendly.

Nearby was a cart vendor. Scott and I treated ourselves to one each of the huge Munich pretzels that are warm, crispy, delectably salty outside, and nice and soft inside. They were fresh. A proper Munich pretzel cannot be over five or six hours old. We washed it down with a liter stein of delicious lager German beer. It left enough money for us to make our way the following day (hitchhiking) to an army base near Heidelberg, to stay with some of Scott's GI buddies off base.

But we didn't want to spend more money, so we spent the night in the labyrinth of tunnels under the München Hauptbahnhof (Munich Central Train Station). They prohibited sleeping in the tunnels; we had to keep moving or risk being harassed—or worse—by the *Polizei* who patrolled at night. An ominous feeling filled the air. The walls were a worn ivory color tile, clean but dingy looking. The lighting was the blueish-green color of sodium lamps, which gave the impression of desperation and loneliness. We had a bit of the former, but none of the latter.

The surreal train tunnels took a toll on us, so the bright sunshine that greeted us as we left early in the morning was a jolt. We shouldered our backpacks and walked to the nearest federal highway (no hitchhiking on the Autobahn), stuck out our thumb, and immediately got a ride. He was an army noncommissioned officer and a "stoner," which classified him as someone that indulged in drugs as opposed to a "lifer," or officer, who likely abstained. Our ride was going to his base near Heidelberg, and Scott gave the driver a piece of paper with his friend's address before nodding off. We awoke to find ourselves very near our destination. Tired and disoriented, we failed to thank the driver for his kindness. We realized it inconvenienced him taking us so close to our destination—one of many gracious acts we experienced on the road.

Germany was littered with army and air force bases. Most of the military were returnees from Vietnam, as I described earlier. Everyone Scott knew lived off base. They went to "work" on a regular schedule. When not working, they partied hard. Scott had stashed some money and hash with his friend. True to his word, both were there when we arrived.

After a week of friendly hospitality and nonstop partying with the decompressing Vietnam vets, I begged off and made my way to the

Zurich Airport and a return flight to the States. Germany was all in with the Woodstock-style music festivals that were underway in the US. The American GIs contributed to their increase in numbers in Europe and Germany, and Scott made use of them. He was a busy guy frequenting the festivals, and I heard all about it upon my return to Europe.

The several months I spent in the US flew by. I focused on getting my shit together and returning to Europe. I was working a job, keeping expenses down and saving money. Scott and I maintained contact, as mail delivery between the US and Germany was quick. You could count on less than a two-week turnaround time for sending and receiving a letter or small package. I attributed that to the huge number of US military stationed there. It facilitated our ability to coordinate supply with demand at the German music festivals.

· • • • ● • ● ● • · •

The *clunking* sound that a commercial airplane makes when the landing gear activates and then locks into place woke me up. From my window seat, I could see the enormity of the Frankfurt Airport. The Rhein-Main Air Base was also still there, and in full operation—busy sending soldiers to war and then tending those who survived back to a civilian life. Despite the air base's bustling activity as a transition point, it played a minor role in the grand scheme of the Vietnam War.

It appeared I was picking up right where I left off, the intervening months in the US a distant memory. Determined to continue the quest for the best hashish and to have some fun upon returning to Europe, our first destination was Amsterdam.

Scott met me at the baggage claim. We went to a lower level and took the train to Rüsselsheim am Main, where he had secured a living space.

Small but livable, it was in the same neighborhood as his current military buddies. Scott was a popular guy. He'd been to Vietnam, knew what the guys had endured, and knew his way around a military base. Scott also had the best hashish connections. I repeat myself by saying it appeared I was picking up right where I left off. A couple of weeks flew by, and then we were on a train for Amsterdam.

Arriving in Amsterdam felt like a long delayed but inevitable journey. We assimilated quickly. I didn't know that Amsterdam would become an intimate part of my life from then on.

It wasn't a letdown, except the weather sucked most of the time. But the culture, the old buildings, the music, the women, the coffee shops, and the hash were every bit as amazing as I had hoped. We started hanging out at the Branderij Bar and Youth Hostel. Rock 'n' roll music and a pool table felt like familiar territory. Most of the clientele were not tourists, but travelers calling Amsterdam home base—eclectic and wild human specimens. It was a vibrant scene to hear news from the travelers' word-of-mouth network.

Our circle of friends and acquaintances bulged with eccentricity. There was a continuous ebb and flow of people moving on to somewhere else, and those returning. It was an accepted fact that everyone returns to Amsterdam. Our circle came into contact with Dave and his friends in the Vondelpark. It was Hippie headquarters, a counterculture scene, and all around a beautiful park with few police where most anything went. Scott and I gravitated toward Dave, as his friends were a bit too amped, even for us.

Dave was my height, 1.83 m (6ft), with dark-brown wavy hair and a stocky build, but not overweight. His striking blue eyes had a twinkle with undertones of decency. A chuckle in his laugh was genuine and tinged with a little hesitancy. His mustache extended beyond his lip, then plummeted over both corners of his mouth. He was working on a beard, but not all parts of his face were cooperating with the growing process, leaving some sparse patches on the cheeks. Not every guy sprouts a thick full beard, but it didn't detract from his good looks.

He always wore hiking boots—the original kind, before they were fashionable. The boots looked fully broken in, but I didn't know if he carefully and deliberately laced them up like Scott—I don't remember ever seeing him without 'em! He even wore them when he was wearing shorts, with the same wool socks drooping down (before that was fashionable too).

To some, Dave appeared unyielding in his personality. A man-of-few-words kind of guy who deliberated his thoughts before speaking, devoid of shyness. He had a dry wit and brought some of the brusqueness from the oil fields with him. On the outside, his persona said, "Don't mess with me." Underneath, he was a good guy.

Scott and I were getting restless. We clued Dave into our desire to go to Afghanistan. He listened and nodded his head. Dave was the quiet type—intelligent, and little escaped his quick eye and keen senses. His sturdy constitution let him smoke as much hash as almost anyone else we knew. After a long night, he was usually the last one standing. He was all in for a road trip.

• • • ● • ● • ● • • •

It was time to head east. Summer in Amsterdam can be nice, but more often than not, it's *slecht weer*—shit weather. I've seen bicycle riders struggling to pedal their bikes against the wind in driving rain. When you think it can't get any worse, it does. A gust of wind will blow the rider backward. As is common in Holland, the spring of 1973 was cold and damp. The leaden skies day after day were a good reason to smoke a lot of hash and drink beer. Let me be clear—Amsterdam is a fabulous city with plenty to do, and when the sun is shining, it's the place to be. But those days were few and adventure beckoned.

We spread a road atlas of Europe out on the floor of our apartment. The top floor, of course, because everyone we knew lived on the top floor. It was the least expensive and therefore where most young people lived. Buildings in Amsterdam were narrow, and the stairs rickety and dangerous.

The map was useful up to the eastern boundary of where Western countries agreed Europe ends and Asia begins, and that included Istanbul, Turkey. After that, we were on our own. Examining maps of Turkey, Iran, and Afghanistan, our options for eastward roads were limited. "Looks like about 7,500 km (4,660 mi) to Kabul," we agreed as we smoked a chillum.[6] That was an alternative to rolling hash reefers, or a pipe. Made of clay and shaped like a long funnel, it came in many sizes. The most common size for personal use held 3–5 grams (around 1 tsp) of hash mixed with tobacco to keep it burning evenly. A chillum is not for the casual smoker. When the cloud of hash smoke cleared enough to see the map again, we agreed it was time to hit the road. Fortunately, we had no schedule, with wads of money and a bit of boredom to motivate us.

We were adamantly opposed to driving a car with Dutch license plates. Every customs agent from the border of Holland to Afghanistan knows Holland is where you go to buy and consume drugs, and it would take a lot of hash for us to drive that far.

So, we did the logical thing. We flew to Frankfurt, Germany. Those license plates had a more respectable reputation among government officials.

We exited customs and immigration in Frankfurt, grabbed a taxi on the curb, and told the driver to head into town. We spotted a rental car agency not very far from the airport and urged the taxi driver to pull in. He gladly dumped us and our stuff and drove off.

We were at the Autovermietung Schultz GmbH. I can't say it thrilled the agent at the rental desk to see us—three rowdy longhairs, probably Americans (good guess)—but we didn't ask the cost and we paid cash in advance. They became a lot more accommodating and were all smiles when we left. The mood was different many days later when we brought the car back.

The VW Type 1, or *Käfer* in German, but Beetle or "Bug" in English, is a diminutive car by most standards. The space was cramped with us and our belongings, so it instantly became disorganized. And it got disorganized on the outside too, after we had a few too many German beers, drove a little too fast, and ended up high-centered on a country road near a tiny *Dorf* (village). We walked a short distance to an inn seeking some help and some beer. Our German seemed to get better as we drank. It and making noises and gesticulating arms convinced some new drinking buddies to help us get the car back in action. Apparently, we humored the folks in the inn and crashed there for the night in one of the guest rooms upstairs. We were relieved that the exterior damage was only to the bumper and some cosmetic scratches. No damage to the undercarriage or mechanical functioning. We drove back into Frankfurt and got a proper room at the InterContinental Frankfurt Hotel. They, too, didn't seem thrilled to receive us. Cash to the rescue once again.

But I digress. The condition of the VW Bug from dear old Autovermietung Schultz GmbH was atrocious upon its return. We had damaged the front of the car when we went straight instead of turning—it wasn't severe, but certainly noticeable. Filth, mud, and dust coated the exterior and interior. The windshield was opaque except where the windshield wipers had smeared the mud enough that one could see to drive. We were oblivious to all of that and delivered the car back to Herr Schultz in a despicable state. They must have been relieved to get the car back, and the settlement for damages was acceptable to us. We were eager to get out of there as quickly as possible.

While driving back to Schultz to return the rental, we passed a used-car lot. A particular automobile caught our eye. On the front row of the lot, with those strings of little colored triangle flags stirring in the breeze, we stopped and knew we had found our vehicle. It also was a VW, but a larger sedan. Finding something we liked so close to where we would drop the rental car was a godsend. We had one of those moments where you intuitively know you've found what you want. We all had that same intuition, so it must've been right. After dropping off the rental, we would return, buy it, and head east. We did exactly that and there was a surprise waiting for us in the glovebox of the car.

Chapter Five

Afghan Primer

Bob Seger: *Hollywood Nights* > *Lyrics*

Amsterdam had us primed for Afghanistan. We had imagined the trip there many times while sitting in the Vondelpark, smoking a chillum of hash with travelers who had just returned. Despite knowing some of them might have embellished the dangers, we were aware the journey would be long and as perilous as one would make it. It wasn't a train ride—unless you considered the Siberian Express to be a direct route. Public transportation was doable, with a minimum requirement of extreme patience and no deadlines. Commercial air travel was an option, but no way for a real traveler to get there, and expensive for the Europe on $5-A-Day type. The Magic Bus was the dream of dirt-cheap travelers on a shoestring budget. The bus's planned journey was Amsterdam to Goa, India, via Afghanistan, Pakistan, and Nepal. Passengers had to pool their money and do repairs when the bus broke down, but it always made it to Goa.

We had graduated from the U of H (University of Hitchhiking) and would take the high road—or at least a road of our choice—to get there:

in our car and our itinerary. That's not to say we studied thoroughly, mapped the route, and primed diligently for the trip. We were having a blast in Amsterdam hanging out, and weeks just slipped away. Life was good, and we were a little reluctant to move on. So we lingered in Amsterdam—not much of a hardship.

Amsterdam operated on a higher level of adventure travel expertise than any other city on the Continent. It was the ultimate hippie destination, a traveler's clearinghouse for the exchange of pertinent intel. News, useful tips, and potential threat warnings for the Continent and all destinations east were as up-to-date as was then possible. The Dam Square was crawling with experienced travelers and interesting people from everywhere. It also harbored fakes, scoundrels, people on the run, and police and Interpol undercover agents. They were easy to spot. You only had to look at their shoes. If they had laces and a shine, smile and move on.

The coffee shops, bars, youth hostels, and the street were the places to glean useful info...if you took care to apply common sense to what you heard. A traveler's experience was their street cred—how long they'd been on the road and where they'd been. The longer the better, and a CV that included Nepal, India, and Afghanistan put that person in the top tier.

Amsterdam had it all—cool vibes, tolerant authorities, and millennia of history as a merchant center. It was world headquarters for travelers. Dave blew into town about the same time that Scott and I arrived. We hung out at the Branderij Bar near Nieuwmarkt, at the corner of Koningsstraat and Kromboomssloot, near the Red Light District.

Scott, Dave, and I had all traveled independently in previous years and we each had encountered contrasting spheres of travelers. We each gleaned useful knowledge and applied it when the opportunity presented itself. That was the way things worked on the road. When the three of us gravitated together in Amsterdam, we did the same thing among ourselves.

The universe decided it was time to introduce another important player. Hawk was both personable and engaging—knowledgeable but not overbearing. He'd been there, done that, but was circumspect in talking about it. He was the quintessential traveler and personification of Amsterdam's reputation as a trading country. Hawk was a merchant of the ancient tradition disguised as a hippie. A deep thinker but quick to action, and a get-things-done kind of person.

Hawk helped to open the Sapsalon fresh-squeezed juice bar up on the Koningsstraat, only about 50 m (54 yds) from the Branderij. Hawk was a decade senior to us, which automatically gave him higher standing in the travel pecking order. He was ostensibly American, and his friend, PK, was Canadian. They had a bus and had been doing the back and forth from Amsterdam to Afghanistan, India, and Nepal for a couple of years. The profitability was marginal, but Hawk and PK had alternative motives in wanting to prepare for a more lucrative operation. In later years, Hawk enthused to me that he supplied nearly all the best Afghani hash to the North European market via Amsterdam in the 1970s. His methodology was inventive and effective; he never lost a shipment.

They knew the route and hazards for the drive to Afghanistan by heart—there was no internet to Google! We lapped that info up while smoking Afghani hash.

We learned Afghanistan was a loosely organized country of many tribes, ruled by a king. It was desperately poor, with little opportunity for individuals to climb out of poverty. Despite that fact, some did well for themselves. Education was the key, as is often the case, and being born into a situation that allowed schooling overseas was at the top of the list. There were also exceptionally intelligent youths with a knack for languages and took advantage of it. Cleverness, drive, and opportunity were the steppingstones for this group of people. They were the ones we were most likely to meet, as they gravitated to where the money was—tourists.

The landlocked kingdom had resisted invaders for centuries, from Genghis Khan to various European powers. Afghanistan was a poor third world country, but wealthy in undeveloped natural resources. A nation of tribal origin rich in culture and human character and long in history, it had a storied past of explorers, adventurers, invaders, and evaders. It was a place to respect and be on your toes, with the best hashish in the world.

But hearing so much for so long about Afghanistan ceases to be a thrill. Enough time had passed—we were finally ready to hit the road and see for ourselves firsthand.

Hawks pet python freaked out border guards

Costa del Sol sexy boat

Hawk's bus in the Desert of Death

Sail Away

Interlude Two

Pebbles in the Pond

Crosby, Stills, Nash, & Young: Almost Cut My Hair > Lyrics

Interlude One introduced the visualization of a reflection in still water disturbed by dropping a pebble into a pond. Questions are like that pebble: They often disrupt the status quo or open the door to new insights and new opportunities. For our purposes in this analogy, I'll use questions as the pebbles to seek a connection between intuitive feelings and the circumstances that lead to inexplicable situations.

The pond is a metaphor representing one constituent of a developing theory to explain the enigmatic events described in my narrative. The theory began to emerge as I was digitizing my travel photos, some of which are included in this book. Early thoughts and recollections simmered as I went from photo to photo. Questions arose, but went unanswered. The more photos scanned, the more questions surfaced. The mystifying events that evolved into a focus in this chronicle needed a core explanation. It became apparent that none existed, at least not within my very limited range of knowledge. It was clear that my theory involved tackling many questions and making some conjectures. Research was required, and science was the logical place to start. Put on your propeller hat as we explore physics, metaphysics, and quantum mechanics. But we'll also dive into areas that are seldom considered related, such as cosmology and genetics. Fortunately, we can rely on science to have addressed many of the questions we need to ask. But we'll have to broaden our thinking with some established scientific understandings.

The inhabitants of the pond are themselves mysterious, elusive, and often ignored, to one's detriment. They are familiar passengers of human thought and decision-making. They include Guardian Angels, intuition, instincts, gut feelings, karma, vibes, luck, and coincidences. Others will surface as we stir up the pond, including the term you may have noticed already, *Dots*. The *Dot Matrix* will refer to the pond inhabitants in my theory.

And what is a Dot, you ask? A Dot is a person. It can also be a moment in time, a place, an event, or a thing. But always you or another person is involved. Think about something unusual that happened in your life. Meeting a special person is top of the list. Finding a unique place, stumbling upon a new way to solve a problem, remembering an event that turned out to be significantly more important than was apparent at the time—those we can also refer to as Dots. However, lingering fingerprints from contact or association with a person's Dot Matrix are always present. The occurrence of Dots often passes without notice—something that happens in the stream of events in one's life, realized later to be important. They can even be a momentous occasion, something you remember for the rest of your life.

My theory posits that the Dot Matrix inhabitants' impact how and why your life intersects with Dots. Does a Dot materialize because of luck or coincidence? Does your karma or vibes attract or repel a Dot? Is it possible to influence the timing, the location, or the type of Dot that you encounter?

More pebbles thrown, more to come...

The consideration of my Theory of Dots, née hypothesis, will span the breadth of human existence. Serious investigation relied on common sense, philosophy, astronomy, and ancient sciences of thousands of years ago. Without leaving those useful tools behind, the Interludes hitch a ride into the future with modern science. Along the way, they stop to pick up physiology, metaphysics, cosmology, astrophysics, and quantum mechanics. The ride is thrilling, but honestly, much of the conversation goes over the head of many people. Fortunately, I only need to ferret out details that are well-documented on the internet, thus avoiding most of the boring stuff.

The vehicle used in the following Interludes is scientific study—from the infinitesimally small to galaxy-sized elements of the fabric of space-time. Strange concepts are discovered, such as the phrase "Spooky action at a distance," voiced by Einstein when referring to quantum entanglement.[7] That describes the infinitesimally small, quantum-entangled particles that react simultaneously regardless of the distance between them. Given the vast distance of the cosmos, an instantaneous reaction would travel faster than the speed of light. And Einstein's special theory of relativity[8] concludes nothing is faster than the speed of light. Therein lies the dilemma. Lightspeed is indeed fast, but an action traveling over light-years of distance instantly is faster. A clue may be discovered in quantum entanglement—how a gut feeling, or a vibe, can bridge a distance using none of the five senses.

The Theory of Dots aims to explain the existence of a connection between a person and significant people, events, places, or things—a Dot. My theory considers how we can connect to Dots, why there's a connection, and if there's a reason for a connection. Dots are encountered in the "now," but what has to transpire to allow a person to be in the "now" at the precise moment and location in time to connect with a Dot?

The out-of-the-blue appearance of James described in Chapter 2 is a fitting illustration. Rather than spooky action at a distance, James was spooky action up close. He materialized without prelude, as if a longtime member of the cast of friends. Even my friends accepted him as if he had always been around. His tales of Europe were captivating and seemed real, though I couldn't verify their accuracy. His constant presence and enthusiasm built to a crescendo, then he disappeared without a word of explanation. As if on cue, Jack stepped in promptly to fill the gap and my trip to Europe was on. A coincidence? Even so, it seemed as if a Guardian Angel had intervened. My theory allows for coincidence, yet the abundance of related factors reject this explanation.

I explained the two back-to-back spooky events with a familiar adage, "The universe must have had a plan." If so, it was an elaborate plan for my benefit. And why did a plan even exist? And why me, and why then? I don't know where James came from or where he went. Jack materialized as if on cue. Significantly, he was the catalyst that launched my first trip to Europe and led to more unexplained occurrences. The Interludes examine these as Dots.

The Theory of Dots (TOD) includes a commonsense application of knowledge derived from human experience. But that's not enough to explain the more complex relationships within the Dot Matrix, or how they may contribute to a connection between Dots. A more thorough analysis requires digging deeper, using scientific studies. In the following Interludes, we'll dive into quantum physics and confidently navigate metaphysics. I understand that's likely to cause some to roll their eyes and exit stage right.

Don't leave! Consider these familiar phrases as your comfort food and physics as the digestive enzymes to absorb the science.

- Guardian Angels

- I had a feeling

- I knew I should have

- I had an intuition about that

- Gut feeling

- In the nick of time

- Gave me bad/good vibes

People resolutely anchor these phrases in the human psyche. Intuitive responses were essential for human survival on the savannas long ago. Scorned or derided now, the underlying message is critical to the Theory of Dots. That message is: Your intuition and intuitive responses are more important than you think.

So, what is the origin of these intuitive responses, and how are they received in the mind of a human? For example, how does a gut feeling materialize? It's often triggered by a recalled situation or experience, or a scent, a sound, or a tactile or taste sensation vaguely associated with the immediate situation. You can sense a gut feeling by simply thinking of or imagining a scenario.

How do those triggers access your brain if not detected by one of your five senses? It seems likely that there's a medium or network that transmits those feelings over time and distances. As a self-acknowledged layperson, I posit that karma is the network connecting Dots, and karma is the water in our pond.

Karma is a Sanskrit word meaning "action." It refers to a cycle of cause and effect that is an important concept in many Eastern religions, particularly Hinduism and Buddhism. In its essence, karma refers to both the actions and the consequences of the actions. Importantly, karma is not set in stone, is not out of our control, and is not indirect. By this I mean, you don't do good things with hopes of getting a randomly good outcome—in other words, karma is not doing your chores this week in hopes of winning the lottery. Instead, it means that the steps of your life, your spiritual development, and your personality are directly molded by your thoughts and actions. "Present you affects future you."[9] This definition of karma will be embellished in future Interludes. I don't believe in karmic concepts made up to benefit oneself, or the counterculture use of the term *karma* by the Baby Boomer generation.

I admit, karma was not in my forethoughts while I was near the place of its conceptual birth in India. It has its roots in all three of the major religions of the region: Hinduism, Buddhism, and Jainism. Afghanistan is overwhelmingly Islam, which does not recognize karma but includes similar concepts. Thankfully, karma doesn't appear to recognize religions or national borders. Spoiler alert: the dramatic appearance of the merchant in the empty desert near Kandahar after the car accident was a slam-dunk example of a karmic event.

Writing about that incident 50 years later, it still looms large in my mind and memory. The merchant was a Dot—more accurately, a DOT—and was the catalyst that energized me to write this book and start down the path to clarify what meaning it has. On a human scale, it's a far piece to travel to the desert in Afghanistan, with untold alternate paths that could have been taken. Instead, all of us—Scott, Dave, the merchant, and I—arrived at the same time and at a critical moment in that specific place in the desert.

I posit karma plays a big role in the connections we seek to understand.

Chapter Six

The Road East

Steppenwolf: *Born To Be Wild* > *Lyrics*

The VW two-door sedan we had previously discovered in the used-car lot in Frankfurt seemed cavernous compared to the Schultz rental VW Bug. One owner, excellent tires, clean condition inside and out with an exterior color of sky-blue, representing the open road that we were about to embark on. As you might imagine, it didn't stay clean, inside or out, for very long!

We had a collective intuition that the VW sedan was the right car the moment we saw it. We still felt that way when we returned to buy it. It could've been that we were desperate to get on the road, but the fact that all three of us sensed it made an impact. And our due diligence inspection supported our initial conclusion. That kind of intuitive reaction is something everyone can relate to, but there was something else. That "one owner" detail involved karma and would surface later with a vengeance. No spoiler here, but was our intuitive decision to buy the car related to the karma that manifested itself and came back to us in due course? Intuition, instinctive behavior, and karma are all human reactions to events that fall outside of mental reasoning. They appear to be connected, but in what way? What would that look like?

We'd seen karma, as I define it, illustrated in the many kind gestures that benefited Scott and I during our journey between Europe and Africa. Karma was also apparent in the interventions of Guardian Angels. Similar to my assertions that your behavior, good or bad, toward others as a traveler will stitch the fabric of your travel experiences, so too with karma.

We liked the VW. It was solid, and we were eager to get on with it—didn't even haggle over the price much. We paid in cash and eagerly waited for the paperwork to be processed so we could hit the road. We brought little in the way of personal effects—we figured we'd be dressing like Afghanis soon, anyway. What was most important was the Sony portable cassette deck to blast tunes as we left a trail of hash smoke across Europe and Asia. We calculated and brought as much hash as we figured we'd smoke before we could replenish the stash in Afghanistan.

Our music selection reflected our state of mind (besides being stoned): young, restless, and eager to move. We didn't even want our shadow to keep up with us, and it was rock 'n' roll all the way. We hung each speaker from the clothing hook on either side of the back seat—crude, but effective. We blasted everything from Van Morrison to Edgar Winter. Loud and fast. Like us, usually.

Tot Ziens[10] Europe

We bolted out of the used car lot in our tricked-out VW sedan. That's a generous description. The exterior looked like an automobile your grandmother would love. We liked that about it too. A nondescript vehicle that would not draw attention to itself. I thought of a dorm room when I looked at the interior. The mechanical aspects of the sedan were good, and the heater and windshield wipers were about to be tested. The weather was typical in that part of Germany—cold and rainy. We dragged mud into the ride while getting it ready for departure, and the dirty interior soon reeked of illicit smoke. Before we roared out of that secondhand car lot, we rigged up our Sony cassette player: speakers hung from the coat hooks over each rear door, wires tucked in along the window frames, and the player resting in the front seat. Scott pressed the Play button and Van Morrison launched into "Glad Tidings." We were on our way to Afghanistan! The Autobahn was nearby, and we were soon passing the Frankfurt Airport. Dave, Scott, and I were alert for any potential scrutiny, especially when we passed the US Rhein-Main Air Force base on the south side of the airport. The area was swarming with police and security personnel.

The facility was bustling, as the headquarters of Military Airlift Command was coordinating transport for military personnel to and from Europe. The C–5A Galaxy airplane was one of the largest military aircraft in the world, and they were prominent—the damn things were HUGE.

Commercial flights and military planes sometimes shared the taxiways near the air base. If you had a window seat in a Boeing 707 that was taxiing next to a C–5A, a giant tire—one of the 28 required to handle the weight of the plane—filled your vision. Crane your neck up and up, looking through your window to see the fuselage underbelly. The monster C–5A was fascinating to watch. I couldn't believe that it could get off the ground.

This was Scott's point of entry to Vietnam; he had lived in this area, and around Heidelberg. Like many Vietnam vets, he talked little about his experiences there and not much about his time "decompressing" around here—except for all the partying. He was happy to drive right past the airport on the Autobahn, barely glancing at it as we drove on to southern Germany, the gateway to cross the Alps as we sped toward the East.

Music festivals in Germany were prestigious events. Woodstock may have been bigger, but the festivals still had big-name headliners. We skirted Heidelberg, with our sights set on the Black Forest and then Stuttgart. We passed near Germersheim, where the British Rock Meeting Festival took place in May of '72. The bill at that time included Pink Floyd, The Faces, The Kinks, Humble Pie, Buddy Miles, and The Doors (sans Jim Morrison, who died the year before). Scott recalled the organizers acknowledged his contribution to the party atmosphere over the festival public address system as "good stuff."

The German Autobahn did not have a speed limit. Drivers of fast cars loved it; the fainthearted feared it. We, of course, occupied the former group and drove the wheels off that VW. It was a novel concept to drive as fast as you wanted and not worry about a speeding ticket. There was an unofficial limit—drive within the operational safety margins of the automobile and your personal driving skill. It only took a time or two to be going 120 kph (75 mph) and have a Porsche flash past at 220 kph (137 mph) to realize that you needed to stay alert... Don't drive in the far-left lane, it's for passing only. Look for flashing headlights in your rearview mirror; you're about to be passed by a vehicle at high speed. Get out of that lane quickly.

The Black Forest intrigued us, so we jumped off the Autobahn south of Karlsruhe, avoiding France, to the west, and Switzerland, farther south. We spent some time marveling at the dense forest of nearly identical trees. When we pulled over and turned off our stereo and the car, we found it to be quiet, intriguing, and worth exploring farther. But we hadn't been on the road very long and wanted to get some distance between us and Germany.

It's important to note that France had a thing against smoking Mother Nature, enforcing severe penalties for possession of hash or marijuana. Switzerland was much the same. There was a reasonable distinction between small and large amounts of drugs in both countries, and throughout Western Europe. However, we were hailing from Amsterdam, which had skewed our perception of the difference between large and small amounts. We grasped the difference between kilos and grams, but our daily usage of hash was considerably greater than most typical tourists—or even the locals. We smoked a lot of hash over quite a long time and our tolerance grew as we smoked ever larger amounts daily. When we talked about quantities among ourselves, we referred to a "chunk" or a "slab." We left Amsterdam for the flight to Frankfurt with a sizable chunk of superb Afghani hash. Enough, we thought, for us to get close to the hashish motherland.

I digress. Hence, we didn't want to cross into France and absolutely not Switzerland, as they were at the apex of technical ability to detect contraband at their borders. They were quick to enhance their border points with the latest and greatest tech X-ray, dogs, scales, and even mirrors that rolled under the car while the agents watched on a screen. This was prior to computer capabilities, but they had ledgers with vehicle weights, dimensions, and chassis specs for the most popular cars, trucks, and buses. If it rolled, they could compare the specs with what they were looking at and determine if there was a discrepancy worth pursuing. They were very successful at discovering double doors, altered vehicles, and even spaces in boats that were being towed. However, for unusual vehicles—vintage military trucks, World War Two vehicles, military ambulances, expedition vehicles, and large construction machinery—they were less successful. That gap in the vehicle ledgers was a convenient area to use when selecting the transport of many varieties of contraband.

The Black Forest, designated as a "mountainous" area, was beautiful, but from where we were, it seemed more like high hills. There was the odd pointy hill, so we ignored the details. The genuine mountains, the Alps, were on the horizon to the south, and there were snowcapped peaks that gave full definition to their designation as mountains. However, they were clearly in Switzerland, so we stayed to the north, veered east in southern Germany through Austria, and then swung to the south.

The secondary roads we drove took us through picturesque villages, where we had time for a beer or two and a smoke. We concluded that the Black Forest earned its name from the thick pine trees that cast the lower elevations into perpetual darkness. While the cool scent was refreshing at first, it soon became stifling. No wonder the cuckoo clocks make that crazy sound time after time! When night was approaching, driving on the Autobahn was easy, as it was well lit. These tiny rural roads were not. We found a little inn and called it a night.

We were more than a week out and less than a 1,000 km (621 mi) from Amsterdam, but it was never very far away from our actions or thoughts.

After a good night's sleep, we rose early and hit the road, keeping to the north of Switzerland, driving east on the national highway toward Austria. We had traded the superfast German Autobahns for the narrower, slower, but more scenic roads of the other European countries.

We had relentlessly played hard driving rock 'n' roll music as we left Frankfurt and sped down the Autobahn. The hours of driving in that atmosphere left little space for quiet contemplation. Rolling Stones, Led Zeppelin, Jimi Hendrix, and The Who were right on and matched our mood. Slower-paced national roads would favor Crosby, Stills & Nash, Van Morrison, and Grateful Dead. They fostered, at least in me, time to think and mull over thoughts and questions fermenting in my brain. Or maybe it was being stoned and absorbing all the unfamiliar sights, smells, and sounds of travel to new places. Probably both.

We motored eastward, more or less parallel to the majestic and beautiful Alpen mountains. The real Matterhorn was several hundred kilometers south, but as I drove, I considered the importance of the miniature theme park Matterhorn ride in my life and how it connected to my current situation, immersed in the majesty and beauty. Lots of questions were bouncing around in my head. All of us seemed to be lost in our thoughts as we drove ever closer to the end of Western Europe and the beginning of Eastern Europe—Communist countries that suppressed and controlled their populations. No doubt there was little fun to be had there by guys like us.

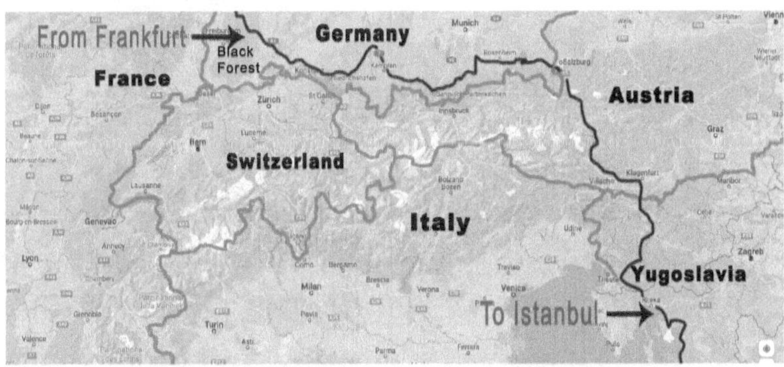

Frankfurt to Istanbul. Map data ©2024 Google

That passage hugging the Alps was the first time I took advantage of the lull in action and allowed questions to surface that had been lingering in the recesses of my brain. For the last couple of years, I had been running fast, enthralled by travel, peddling fast to absorb and respond to new cultures, languages, and perceptions. It was a heady time for a young man from the Midwestern United States. I was a student of the road and loving it all.

Travel profoundly changed everything for me. My perspective of the world and my place in it took on new meaning. I saw and accepted reality with a much broader input of information and experiences, which evolved effortlessly with time and distance. Travel provoked a deeper curiosity in myself and the concept of time and space. But it wasn't only travel that launched deeper thought.

When Jimi Hendrix released *Are You Experienced,* in 1967, many thought the songs were a reference to LSD trips. Allegedly he hadn't dropped acid yet. Nor had I. But popular culture made him and his music an anthem for LSD and psychedelic art. My experimentation with LSD didn't happen until years later, but it was definitely a catalyst for expanding my thoughts.

We had to drive around 800 km (497 mi) through scenic but slow routes from our location near Freiburg, Germany, to reach the stunning lakes and woodlands of Klagenfurt, Austria. The surroundings were bucolic and retained the charm and architecture of an old city from nearly a millennium in the past. A few dozen kilometers south from there was the border with Yugoslavia[11]—a Communist country.[12] We didn't know what to expect. And even worse, we were low on hash!

We crossed into northern Yugoslavia without incident and hustled 200 km (124 mi) south toward what we hoped was a sunny and warm coastline.

It was pristine and majestic! We were on the Dalmatian coast of Yugoslavia (now a region of the Republic of Croatia) and winding our way south. The road rose and fell along the narrow two-lane highway, where vehicle traffic was scarce. The crystal-clear waters of the Adriatic Sea were stunning. There were pockets of beach here and there, but mostly the water sparkled as it met the vertical cliffs, producing a marvelous symphony of sound. Pure harmony with the azure-blue of the afternoon sky, the drifting cotton-ball clouds hiding the sun momentarily as they scurried off to gather force so they could water life farther inland.

The air was fresh and invigorating. The Black Forest's somewhat stifling nature made the unexpected contrast all the more welcome. We embraced the feeling of adventure and the absence of humans, imagining ourselves to be balanced on the brink of danger as we skirted disaster careening around every corner. In fact, we drove slowly to enjoy the scenery, stopping often.

Countless islands lay offshore. Some had spectacular structures, built like medieval castles that seemed to rise from the stony surfaces into edifices that mimicked the rocky geology.

We were amazed to find that the Communist country had managed to maintain its ancient buildings and renowned history, contrary to our expectations. However, as we entered the city, it presented us with the unimaginative architecture we labeled "early penitentiary"—dull, ugly utilitarian designs that matched the hardships in life endured by the "comrades" living the drab life that they were born into.

Was it the simple misfortune of being born there? Surely, they did nothing to deserve this life. Are there alternate realities in which those unfortunate people could have been born, but by chance or design, they were not? Thoughts and questions like those circulated through my mind. Were they triggered by my hallucinogenic experiences, blurring my reality with an expanded sense of the self? Was I experiencing a flashback that was touted as one danger of LSD? Nah, I didn't think so. I was just letting my thoughts run free—a harmless and interesting pastime.

Yugoslavia was uncharted territory to us—there was little tourism then and very little information trickled into the scuttlebutt knowledge base in Amsterdam or elsewhere. The country was under the hardcore fist of Josip Tito as president of the all-powerful Communist Party.

Yugoslavia was an outlier in the bloc of Eastern European countries. Tito threaded his way between the Soviet Union, Western Europe, and the US. He did not include his pragmatism in politics in his social policies. He crushed political opposition and fostered a stark life for most citizens. Our experiences with the people we met—only a few of whom spoke English—were fine. They warmly welcomed us with understandable curiosity, but kept at a distance. As Western visitors, we were obliged to stay in hotels designated specifically for us. We were hoping to pull into one of those castles and stay a while. Not to be, though. We enjoyed our drive down the shoreline, staying one night in Split, the other in Dubrovnik, but we didn't enjoy the architecturally bankrupt cement edifices or the unimaginative cuisine.

It had been a spectacular drive down the Adriatic seaside of Yugoslavia. The rugged coastline was dramatic and reflected the character of the people, while the clear and inviting water of the sea calmed our souls and spirits. The shift to a different reality from Western Europe was effortless. The sense of adventure propelled us forward like a friendly hand in the middle of your back. We weren't reluctant, just a bit cautious.

We faced a decision just past Dubrovnik. Should we take the most direct route to Greece and clip the northern part of Albania, or the longer way around by jogging up and around Albania but staying in Yugoslavia? We lacked any knowledge of Albania, yet assumed it was more Communist than Yugoslavia. Maybe the coastline was equally beautiful or not. We were eager to pick up the pace, so we went up and around Albania, dropping into northern Greece in a day or so of driving.

That part of Greece was a region known as Macedonia. It had been a part of Yugoslavia, so we could hardly tell the difference between where we were then and where we were now. Does that make sense? We did the logical thing and took the most direct route through Greece to the border of Turkey.

Boom! We left Europe—where we knew the people, roads, and signs well—and were about to enter Asia, where everything would be completely different. We didn't see it as any big deal at all. *Let's go, pedal to the metal!*

Another question was drifting around in my thoughts: How could religion—Christianity of Europe and Islam of Asia—cause such a difference in social traits? Was that the right question, or was there more to it, as there usually is with anything to do with humans? Traveling seeded questions that created new patterns of thought, forcing me to think more deeply. Some kind of shift was brewing within.

Dag[13] Asia

We crossed some risky borders in Europe, into and out of both Western and Communist countries. And we had knowledge from reliable sources that there were two to be very careful with—the one we were approaching, Turkey, and the following country, Iran.

Some think the bridge over the Bosporus is the border between Greece and Turkey. Not so. It's the point of division between the two continents, Europe and Asia. We crossed from Greece into Turkey about 250 km (155 mi) before that defining bridge.

Both Greece and Turkey were notorious for meting out harsh punishment for drug use. The infamous movie *Midnight Express*, which didn't come out until 1978, was about the jail in Istanbul, Turkey's largest city. We drove past Sağmalcılar Prison (later called Bayrampaşa Prison). Unbeknownst to us, it would become famous and shine a harsh light on Turkey. However, the location we saw was not the prison depicted in the film. They used a more imposing location on the island of Malta.

Once in Turkey, it was a long haul across the mountainous backbone of the country. From Istanbul to the eastern Turkish border with Iran was close to 2,500 km (1,553 mi), with the capital, Ankara, about a quarter of the way. The road was narrow, two-lane, and often treacherous, with small villages along the way. Snowcapped mountains lurked to the north, and the rural population was tolerant of our appearance. Although Turkish is the predominant language, Islam is the predominant religion. Turkey, like Arab countries, has a history and responsibility to provide hospitality to travelers. Only on rare occasion were we escorted out of a village among a rain of rocks, encouraging us to move on.

East of Ankara, the weather turned cold and windy. After slowly motoring through a small village, we came upon an old man bundled up and carrying his few possessions in a sack. We had been blasting Edgar Winter on the stereo, and we all noticed the man at once. Someone turned down the tunes and asked if we should give him a ride. The nods gave a consensus so we pulled over and opened the door, motioning him to get in. He scrutinized us, seemingly comparing the warmth of our car to the chilliness outside, and grinned. He got in. We turned the tunes back up and cruised. We were quite curious to see how he would react. Within a few minutes, he was nodding his head and making a few movements to the beat of the pounding rock 'n' roll. It was brief and not overt, but he responded, and not negatively. I doubt he had heard Edgar before—and maybe not R&R—but we all smiled as he departed, and he got a ride to the next village.

As we approached the border with Iran, the imposing Mount Ararat loomed over us on our left shoulder. Scott and I would view it from the air when we winged west on a Pan Am flight from Kabul to meet up with our Afghan carpets in the US.

Our route would cross from Turkey into Iran in the far northeastern corner of the country, skirting Mount Ararat and what is now Armenia.

The Shah of Iran was still in charge and holding court, although we doubted he would invite us to visit. It's a big country with an ancient history and beautiful scenery. Tehran was called the "Paris of the East" then and was home to an educated population—Persian, not Arabic. The contrasts were astounding. The architecture was beautiful and extravagant, hosting a variety of vehicles and pedestrians. Compared to what we had seen so far, the city was up-to-date, with a strong Western feel. Foreigners were welcome, and hordes of young people thronged the streets. All fascinating, but we had a destination in mind, so we hit the road. Tehran was 1,000 km (621 mi) from the border with Afghanistan.

We were rocking and rolling unabashedly in our mobile sound studio...or, more accurately, the VW sedan that had safely and dependably propelled us across Europe and into Asia. We had traversed Turkey, and then the breadth of Iran to the border of Afghanistan. Herat was just across the Afghan border—a welcome sight, or so we thought. Ahead of us lay the final 1,000 km (632 mi) stretch of road to Kabul.

What we didn't know when we left Herat was that about halfway there, our rolling would nearly cost us our lives.

Near Kandahar - dashing out of a poppy field

We stopped for a Buzkashi(14) match. Click photo for video

Chapter Seven

Afghanistan

Jimi Hendrix: *Highway Chile* > *Lyrics*

We entered the Afghan government customs facility at the border near Herat, crossing from Iran. A white late model VW bus with prominent Swiss plates was pointed in the opposite direction and leaving Afghanistan, or attempting to leave. We could make out several Western tourists in the typical clothing of people who had been hanging out in the country for a while. Several guards had them grouped together, away from the bus. The place was abuzz with activity. The commotion around the bus was punctuated with Dari (an Afghan dialect of Persian) and Pashto chatter from the Afghanis, with only occasional muttering from the foreigners. A group of onlookers milled about, peering and pointing at the activity. They were likely the customs area occupants and hangers-on, but distinguishing the tourists from the guards proved to be a challenge. The rest of the crowd were Afghan, some of them with the look of authorities. The vibes we picked up were intimidating, and it definitely had the makings of a bust.

To describe this place as a "facility" is much too generous. The squalid, dirty, smoky encampment housed the dregs of officialdom. Discard any thoughts of competency, release mental images of an organized entry procedure to Afghanistan, and think near chaos, bloated bureaucracy, and unbridled graft. As the scene around us further unfolded, the main attraction was the group of unfortunate former occupants of the VW bus. We weren't even on the playbill as we slowly drove forward into the abyss of that scene, unsure of what to do.

Time slowed as we watched in fascination at the growing melee. However, our focus snapped into clarity when the man unmistakably in charge froze the action with his arrival. His enormous smile belied his complete control over the destiny of those foreigners. His uniform was sharp, but only compared to the slovenly look of his subordinates. We could clearly see the masked look of menace he harbored, even though he was 10 m (33 ft) away from us. His perfected look of composure scarcely disguised it.

At that moment, one of the throng noticed our car—apparently a customs official based on the sidearm that he was wearing. He waved us over to a parking place and motioned for us to wait. We certainly weren't going anywhere, now trapped in a compound with a crowd blocking the exit. The unfolding drama enthralled us, anxious about its outcome and what it might mean for us.

As the dark man advanced toward the vehicle, the crowd split, and we could spot the partially disassembled bus. The doors were open, and they had pulled the door panels off. Men were lying under the car, tapping here and there; the attendant was finger-pointing and shouting at the discovery of the hidden hashish. Like leaf-cutter ants, a procession of ragtag workers removed similar sized parcels from the car and piled them on the ground a few meters away. The boss glanced in that direction as he approached. Four foreigners, with looks of despair and an obvious sense of foreboding, stood together in a group, guarded by armed men in uniform. Their furtive glances toward us were telling—they had indeed been busted.

Each of us solemnly took stock of the situation. We were "clean," but our appearance and a cursory check of our car's interior would surely uncover plenty of evidence that we had only recently shed some of the natural substances that those guys a few meters away had in abundance. These crazies could easily set us up and deal with us in any fashion they thought appropriate. Allowing overt actions on our part to look around or otherwise appear concerned would likely only worsen our fate.

So we turned our attention back to the movie-like show outside our car just in time to see the dark man walk toward us. The look of satisfaction was still there, but now supplemented with a smile like you've seen on a crocodile's face.

He waved us out of the car and said, "Come, come, gentlemen, to my office," with an impersonation of a British accent.

The border and frontier were indistinguishable in this part of the world. A country's border demarcates the officially registered and protected line where one country stops and the other starts. The frontier is the undefined zone on either side of the border. In this parched and sparsely populated desert, you could be in Iran or Afghanistan and not know the difference. That's exactly the way the nomadic populations considered the entire country. They divided it up among tribes, with feuds and unsettled grudges having more sway than governmental regulations. It was impossible for a visitor to identify the tribal area they were in.

It became evident now that the petty mindset and perceived authority of our host, Mr. Croc, authorized him to declare and execute the local laws and regulations.

We were several kilometers into Afghanistan proper and about 75 km (47 mi) still to go to Herat. The buildings were little more than shacks, built with sun-dried mud bricks from the not-too-far-away muddy creek that passed as a river in this desert. The interiors were poorly lit and had open fires for cooking, and in the winter, heating. Animals also commonly shared the tiny, cramped living spaces, which had a particular odor that we would soon become familiar with. We'd been in deserts in North Africa, and now in parts of Asia—they all shared a common trait. You would be in the middle of nowhere with no living creature in sight, but do something, make some kind of noise or distraction not common there, and suddenly, there would be people... Lots of people. It was eerie and abnormal to the Western psyche. You got used to it, though.

We, of course, accepted the invitation to the office and walked at our own pace. It seemed we were unguarded, but guessed we were being watched and behaved accordingly. Back in Amsterdam, Hawk had stressed that we should accept any offers of hospitality graciously. To insult a local that was abiding by the age-old custom of hospitality to passing travelers was a huge faux pas, and dangerous.

Mr. Croc greeted us at the door and showed us in. In comparison to the typical hut, this one had electric lighting and an old ramshackle desk. A gesture was made for us to settle on the sand floor, on top of Oriental carpets. He sat cross-legged, so we did too.

He introduced himself as Chief Custom Inspector of the Herat Region. We were ceremoniously welcomed to Afghanistan and asked for our passports. As he set them aside, we wondered if we would ever see them again.

His continued dialogue gave us some reassurance, but his smile made our wariness gauge needle peg at maximum.

We were intensely curious about what had transpired in the customs area and what might be the fate of those guys. I think our host knew that well and let us simmer about it.

He segued into his authoritarian government persona and said, "You should know that possession of substantial quantities of hashish is illegal. Our neighbors (in this case, Iran) are quite upset when it passes from our country to theirs. Therefore, it is our duty and responsibility to see that doesn't happen." Another practiced application of his OK British accent. At that he smiled, followed by a chortle. "As you saw, the visitors we welcomed into our country attempted to exit with about 100 kilos [220 lbs] of our excellent hashish." He shrugged his shoulders and scolded in a nonchalant tone, "Unfortunately for them, we knew of their pending departure from our country and knew where to look. But you gentlemen are arriving and can expect to be treated well."

With that, he waved his hand and one of his underlings brought him a chunk of hash, at least 100 grams (3.5 oz). It also looked like excellent quality—could be from Mazar-i-Sharif. A couple of other custom agent types entered and prepared a hubbly-bubbly (hookah) with a mixture of tobacco and hash.

All kinds of alarms went off for us. They had just busted a car loaded with hash, and presumably the occupants were about to spend some time in an Afghan jail—not a place one wants to visit, let alone serve time. And now they were inviting us to get high with them like old friends. Shit! This was too weird. But we were on a fast train going somewhere not designated and we had better make ourselves comfortable and enjoy the ride. Double Shit! The hash smelled excellent, which confirmed our visual appraisal. These guys knew their way around a pipe and could inhale like pros. They were imbibers, not just putting up a façade. When it was our turn, we knew we were being judged by a jury that had the power to treat us as they saw fit.

We clearly passed the test, whatever that was, because the Big Guy handed us that chunk of excellent hash, stamped our passports, and said we could leave.

Shit, shit, shit! Now we were really screwed. We were gifted a chunk of hash by the Chief Custom Inspector upon entering Afghanistan and smoked it with him. The same guy that had busted a bus loaded with it in front of our eyes. He, who told us those poor bastards had been set up and allowed to drive across the country only to be snared a few kilometers from freedom. Of course, they also had to pass through Iranian customs, which also could have spelled doom. The obvious deducement on our part was we too were being set up.

Should we politely refuse? Refusal was not an option in this part of the world. Accept and discard it later? Could work, but also a clear insult if discovered. If it was a setup, they'd simply plant the hash on us anyway.

But most of all, it was a chunk of excellent Afghani hash, and we were out. We weren't about to give it up!

"That's very kind of you, and we appreciate it greatly. Thank you for your gracious hospitality," we offered as we left the office. But we couldn't resist any longer. "What's going to happen to the people you just busted?"

The expected smile said it all, but he offered, "They will suffer the consequences of their poor decisions."

Questions lingered in our minds. Why was an educated and well-spoken man holding court in such a remote and dead-end location and job? Punishment or opportunity? What decisions led to the dreadful outcome of those guys in the VW van? Did any or all of that have anything to do with us?

And decades later, as I reflect, I wonder if their Guardian Angels were off duty, or otherwise not protecting them. Everyone has Guardian Angels, right? Was their karma bad? Was it simply bad luck? We had already prodded and pushed our "luck"—and our angels, no doubt. We also hadn't given due acknowledgement for their kind services. Time to pay more attention! We might not have fully understood karma, intuition, instinctive decision-making, or even luck or coincidence, but we certainly could see there was more to it than met the eye. How did all of that fit together?

We were thankful to get our passports back (mine had the visa with the car stamp, which meant I had to leave the country with the car). That was of no concern at the moment. We were free to drive on into the country that we had driven about 7,500 km (4,660 mi) to reach.

We apprehensively drove out of the customs area and headed south to Kandahar, concerned about what the next few kilometers had in store for us.

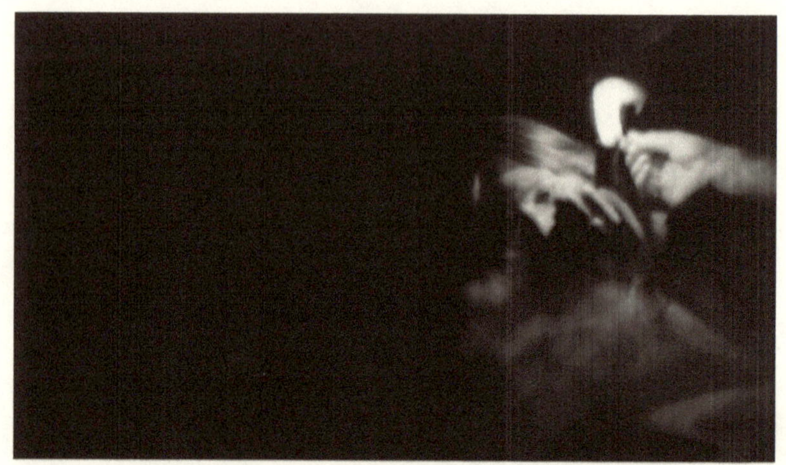

Herat Border - A friendly welcome to Afghanistan

Herat - Afghani customs people

Interlude Three

Questions Are Pebbles

The Doors: *The Crystal Ship* > *Lyrics*

I visualize questions as a flashlight. When switched on in darkness, it illuminates the area in the direction it's pointed. The once hidden becomes clear. An answer can then find its way forward. It might not be the correct path, but we are able to turn the flashlight in any direction needed. Answers are likely to emerge expeditiously, but sometimes they're only fleeting solutions. They may solve specific problems, create opportunities, and even save lives. But they often have a limited shelf life and are then discarded in the bin of time.

Questions, however, can be nuanced, restated, and repurposed with a word change or two, or even with just a slight tweak to the inflection of speech. By design or happenstance, prior queries can be revisited and reworked to address the current situation. Answers don't resonate as favorably with me—there are no wrong questions, but there are wrong answers.

One attribute of humans that distinguishes us from other living organisms is our ability to reason and arrive at a useful conclusion. Inquiries are fundamental to the process of how we've progressed as a species. Trial and error answered dilemmas on the savanna, where wrong answers had deadly results. As civilization progressed, elders answered village disputes, politicians answered city policies, scientists answered country debates, and societies turned to philosophers for deeper answers. The significance of questioning grew as societies evolved, and their asking alone became a disruptor of the status quo.

The Interludes throw questions, like pebbles, to challenge accepted explanations. They seek explanations for inexplicable events linked to Dots in certain aspects of science. Some of the pebbles to be tossed into the science pond:

- Toss a pebble: When you sense good or bad vibes from someone or something, how does that feeling traverse the space between you and the source of that feeling?

- Toss a pebble: Sometimes you have a feeling that someone or something is nearby without hearing, smelling, or touching them. How does that feeling span the gap of space?

- Toss a larger pebble: How can intuition and instincts integrate more deeply with the five senses in decision-making?

- Toss a rock: Did humans once have a greater capacity for awareness and communication that has diminished over time?

Conceptualizing our five senses does not require scientific explanation. Our bodies are immediately able to recognize the source upon hearing something. Smell something and the source is usually near at hand. Your eyes present that which is within a reasonable distance. Your taste buds detect flavors. A touch identifies surfaces. Not so with a "gut feeling," or a "bad vibe," or "I knew better." There is nuance in considering how these feelings arrive in our perception. Existing scientific understanding is inadequate to reach a definitive conclusion.

Some refer to these intuitive feelings as a *sixth sense*. The scientific term is "nonsequential information-processing mode."[15] Such descriptive language is sometimes revealing, but not so much here. This is more useful to us: "Intuitive decision-making can be described as the process by which information acquired through associated learning and stored in long-term memory is accessed unconsciously to form the basis of a judgment or decision."[16]

Intuition is a trait from the savanna, when humans had to rely on survival instincts. Intuitive responses diminished as life became easier, or were disregarded as inconvenient and most likely exaggerated. Perhaps individuals can rekindle those "lost" emotions and utilize them in their decision-making process. It is widely accepted that animals display similar intuitive responses to those clues that humans tend to ignore. A sixth sense is crucial for the survival of animals, particularly those in the wild. Birds, butterflies, and fish navigate by connecting to the magnetic field of Earth. Animals sense when there is a weather change coming. Many dog or cat owners will agree that their pets can sense when their human is angry or sad.

The subtle realization that a vague thought or feeling has materialized into something real is a shared human experience. Those feelings have names—*gut feelings, vibes, intuition*, and sometimes *déjà vu*. Can humans learn to communicate with animals by understanding how their survival instincts are transmitted? Perhaps the potential for communication already exists, but we limit our awareness to a small radius of perception. Does that medium for communication have a connection to karma, and is it the same medium that Dots function within?

The Interlude questions posed will range from space and dark matter to the human body and its secrets. Although many people are aware of the multitude of life that exists at the macro and microscopic level, we still pay little heed to their importance in our lives. There is a myriad of living organisms in and on the human body that are indispensable to a healthy life. The fact that they are unseen is irrelevant to their necessity. The interdependence of life-forms is a common thread up and down the food chain.

Life-forms communicate in a variety of ways. There's the familiar sight, sound, smell, and touch of humans and animals, while the chemical, sound, and electrical communication of plants and microorganisms surpass human perception. Nature's go-to solution for sharing information is a network that connects living organisms to each other and distributes important, life-sustaining nutrients efficiently, and with little waste of energy. They exchange information over great distances—the roots of trees in a forest, for instance, and over both microscopic and longer distances for fungi via mycorrhizal networks.

My theory posits that a network is also the solution for transmitting human feelings and intuitions over great distances, and is the connector of Dots.

Chapter Eight

Rocking & Rolling

Cat Stevens: *Miles From Nowhere* > *Lyrics*

"Piss stop!" blurted out Dave. After driving about ten tension-filled kilometers from the customs area, we needed a break. We pulled over, relieved our bladders, and released some of our pent-up anxieties. We had expected to encounter a trap of some sort after leaving the frontier. What exactly that would entail, we could only let our fertile imaginations run wild. Around every corner and over the crest of every hill could lay the trap. Military emplacement, roadblock across the highway, or air strike? Over only 100 grams (3.5 oz) of hash? Not likely.

And since there were few curves and fewer hills on this narrow two-lane highway with no shoulders, our view stretched far ahead, easing our stress a bit.

While standing on the side of the car in the middle of nowhere (we found ourselves there often on this part of the journey), with no humans nor beasts in sight, we made an executive decision. The chunk of hash smelled every bit as good as it did back in the Big Guy's office. It had a soft and resiny texture with a medium-brown color. Exceptional stuff.

We brewed up a chillum and smoked it. As each of us took our turn on the chillum, the exhale of smoke included our tension. We hopped back in our car and fired up the trusty cassette deck, turning up the volume on Van Morrison's *Moondance* as we set off for Kandahar.

Checkpoint! We hadn't noticed that a small hill we drove over blocked our line of sight. When we crested the rise, there it loomed, straight in front on the left side—a lone soldier with an ancient rifle emerging from the guard shack. Our unexpected arrival caught him by surprise, just like us. The guard shack, located nearly on the road, sported a red and white striped wooden bar attached to a large metal lever handle. It barred both lanes.

With no time to consider alternatives, I instinctively reacted when I heard "Run it!" shouted simultaneously by Dave and Scott. I nailed the throttle and hit the bar, snapping it off with a loud *crack*. It took a moment to register with the soldier, and in the rearview mirror, I saw him raising the rifle to his shoulder. It was an old British Enfield, a .303 caliber bolt action rifle—a decent marksman with a maintained weapon should have been able to hit us. The guard and his gun were neither.

I didn't know if he got off a shot or not, and we weren't going back to check. We had struck the barrier with the windshield, at just the right angle to break the wood and deflect it over the top of the car. There wasn't any indication of damage to the car. Adrenaline was coursing through our bodies, and we were laughing and whooping down the road.

Our spur-of-the-moment decision to carry on was sound, fortunately. It wasn't a trap. There weren't anymore soldiers, and we had no further concerns about a setup. And best of all, we had a nice chunk of excellent hash for free—courtesy of the Afghan customs department. We silently expressed our solidarity at the origin of the hash, which was likely in an Afghan jail by now.

Our dietary regimen for the last few weeks wasn't stellar. In fact, it sucked. Subsisting on beer and brats in Germany, followed by meager "sandwiches" in the remaining European countries, it only got worse as we crossed into Asia. Apparently, there isn't much protein or vitamins in hash smoke.

We were low on reserves and running on fumes. Our normal resistance to stress was toast. But we were young and adventurous, and on a mission. We were close to our destination, Kabul, and nothing was going to get in our way. Call that naïvety, hubris, or three young guys full of piss and vinegar. That was our modus operandi.

We drove the rest of the way to Kandahar and felt like shit when we got there. Whatever we had picked up, it got all of us equally. We were fevered and dehydrated...and shitting with abandon. We got a hotel, and it was a miserable night. There were no Western-style medical facilities in Kandahar, and we were told that there was no pharmacy in the town. We lay in bed, stinking, fevered messes. We could drink water, but nothing else would stay down. Besides that, the food was inedible, and even if we were healthy, it wouldn't have stayed down either. We were close to, or already, delirious, and through exchanged groans agreed we had to get to a Western health facility or we could die. That would be in Kabul—500 km (311 mi) from where we lay desperately ill.

To say that the road to Kabul was through a lonely desert would be true, but lacking adequate description. There was virtually NOTH-ING resembling modern (1973) amenities until reaching Ghazni, a very long 350 km (217 mi) drive. No towns, no gas stations, no hotels, no restaurants—nothing. Petrol was had by chance at ramshackle roadside outposts. It would be a grueling and possibly dangerous drive—even in good health.

While suffering in the filthy accommodations of Kandahar, I had a momentary lapse in sickness, or was deeper into deliriousness than I realized: I announced I could drive. We dragged ourselves out of the hotel and into the car, which was now a virtual ambulance, and off we went on the only road between Kandahar and Kabul.

When I was a Boy Scout, I went to the National Jamboree when I was 12 years old. I boarded a train with a group, so I wasn't alone, but I didn't know anyone else. The train deposited us in Valley Forge, and shortly after that I found myself in a US army field hospital with pneumonia. I was delirious with fever, and I remember very little. I recall walking into the nearby tent where the doctors were bivouacked. It was later revealed that despite being only 12 years old, I had a remarkably sensible conversation with a doctor. I thought I was normal, but in fact I had a very high fever.

In Kandahar, I fell back on that episode.

It was a weird experience driving; the desert conjured up images and thoughts that were almost like tripping on LSD. A couple of hours into the drive, I saw a flash of something, or someone, dash in front of the car. I wasn't driving fast. Staying on the road was difficult, yet I had a vivid image of a person I would collide with if I didn't take evasive action. I swerved to the left, and we hit a ditch. The car pitched into the roadside ravine, then launched itself skyward, rolling like a whale and doing a belly flop, finally landing on its side.

Seat belts were nonexistent, so we rattled around inside the car, as did our belongings. We created a mini desert dust storm, scattering a debris field that stretched out about 20 m (66 ft) in diameter from the overturned car. The extent of our illness may have saved our lives, as it is with drunks in a situation like this. We rolled with the punches and survived with only bruising.

But our stuff was scattered everywhere and we were in a daze, although we all quickly scrambled out of the car. A crowd (out of nowhere) formed, and the vibe was threatening and foreboding. A woman held a child in her arms, wrapped in a filthy blanket. She was rocking it back and forth, and I think she was crying. There was a lot of movement and hostile stares in our direction.

Assorted parts of the car were strewn about in all directions. The windshield had popped out when the roof buckled. At least one tire was flat, and the accident damaged every surface of the car that came into contact with the hard-packed desert sand.

There we stood, having the delirium literally knocked out of us, not knowing what exactly had happened, and now quite aware that we were under threat from an angry crowd.

Then a Dot drove up in a Mercedes sedan. It was clearly a well-off merchant with two of his servants in the car. He stepped out of the car and, inexplicably, I vividly recall his attire. He wore a karakul hat typically seen on wealthier Afghans from the city. Islam and local tribal custom mandated that men have a beard—mostly they were unkempt, but this gentleman's was neatly trimmed and groomed. The brown tweed sport coat was over a wool, loose knit sweater with red accents woven into the chest area. His trousers were Western cut in a style matching his other garments, with leather lace-up dress shoes that were polished.

They descended on the scene, rapidly evaluated the situation, and the man began issuing orders to his servants. He hastened to the woman holding the child and engaged the menfolk in a one-sided conversation. We noticed the reaction from the locals to this intruder, to his body language and gestures. The desert people clearly respected him as an authority figure. Or perhaps, a lucrative source for negotiation.

The two servants were a flurry of activity. They rolled the car upright, gathered up our belongings, bent out the bashed in body of the car to clear the tires, used the spare tire and did something to the remaining flat tire to make the automobile "drivable."

We were stunned, but came out of it and helped gather up what we could salvage. Our precious cassette player, speakers, and cassettes were unscathed. And so too was the chillum and hash on the person of Dave.

The merchant's generosity continued. He gave us a large water bag—a lifesaving gesture in the desert, and we eagerly quenched our thirst on the spot. While we were overwhelmed with all that was happening, we remained alert to the rapidly changing vibe of the situation.

In short order, the car was back on four inflated tires with the roof pushed back up so it would hold the windshield in place. Our stuff was back on board, and the car engine running. A miraculous effort by those two manservants.

I saw the Afghan DOT—angel, savior, and heaven-sent messenger—passing out afghanis in handfuls to the desert people. He paid special attention to the crying woman holding the unmoving child in her arms. With that, he turned to us, waved us into the car and, looking into the wreck that we were about to depart in, said, "You must leave immediately. You are in grave danger."

His body language, the enraged crowd, and the alleged wounded infant were overwhelmingly convincing. To top it off, we strange and very foreign travelers who had intruded into the peacefulness of their desert meant no further consideration was needed.

In a cloud of dust and sand, we were back on the road. We'd had enough of rolling and were not in the mood to rock.

After several hours of driving, we stopped at the first suitable hotel in Ghazni. We had consumed most of the water the good Samaritan gave us, and we felt better. Rehydration eased our woes, but we were precariously close to the edge of disaster—not just the car wreck, but also the effects of dysentery and the dehydration we had suffered.

We gathered our strength for a couple of days, not wandering far from the hotel. We hesitantly ate nan, melons, and whatever fruit we could muster, washing it down with chai. That and our youth was enough to rejuvenate us and get our traveling shoes back on.

The car was a sight to behold. It attracted a crowd of gawkers, but no one would touch it. We had few remaining possessions, but our music and our hash were still with us. Traveling lighter was good—we needed little anyway. Belongings left inside the car were visible and easily taken, yet nothing was stolen.

We departed Ghazni in our moving disaster area of a car, dubbed the *Flying Wreck*. It was like riding on a motorcycle—we were open to the world with wind in our hair. Off we drove, with Kabul as the next stop.

Dave piloting the Flying Wreck

Smoke break

Arrival in Kabul

Chapter Nine

Kabul, Afghanistan

Lynyrd Skynyrd: *Don't Ask Me No Questions* > *Lyrics*

We were certain that the doorman must have seen us coming, and what a sight we would have been! The InterContinental Hotel in Kabul is where the diplomats and government muckety-mucks hung out. It was expensive, and not the normal hotel of choice for hippies. We had little in the way of luggage, but we had plenty of money. We quickly bribed the doorman and made our way to the front desk before anyone could react to our presence. All three of us needed a transition from the trip and its chaotic excitement, and this would do just fine.

The hotel staff were quick to remove the mobile wreck from the hotel's grand front entrance, but clearly, it was the center of discourse for the extent of our brief but purposeful stay.

The hotel, only four years old, boasted a swimming pool, a tennis court, and several restaurants. The restaurant on the top floor, the Pamir, had a view of the snowcapped Hindu Kush mountains nearby, and the cocktail lounge, the Nuristan, was popular.

We availed ourselves of everything the facility had to offer, and it was an essential step in reclaiming our health and energy. Several luxurious days of good food, clean bedsheets, daily maid service, and the full-service bar and nightclub made a world of difference in our disposition and energy.

We hadn't savored the ambiance of a hotel of this stature since we left the InterContinental in Frankfurt—nearly 8,000 km (4,971 mi) ago.

The InterContinental and other Western-style hospitality establishments ceased to do business when the Soviets invaded Afghanistan in 1979. Clues of the eventual Soviet dominance gaining strength came to our attention during our stint in the country. Like most, we ignored the signals. The Afghans had handily played the Soviets and the United States for decades, and one could see evidence of that success in the country's infrastructure and the royal family's bank accounts. The clever manipulation of foreign invaders was a hallmark of the Afghanis for centuries.

Kabul was not like being back in Europe, but head and shoulders above what we had passed through since leaving Istanbul. It raised our spirits further, stimulating an eagerness to dig in and find out what was happening in this town that we had long lusted after.

The arid Afghan desert we drove through transitioned to a higher plateau. Kabul is located 1,800 m (5,905.5 ft) above sea level in a narrow valley, wedged between the Hindu Kush mountains. Although they are impressive in their own right, the Himalayas reign supreme to the northeast of Afghanistan.

The area, dubbed the "Roof of the World," contains over 100 peaks exceeding 7,200 m (23,622 ft) in height. This is one of the prime spots where humans learned what *rugged* means. And *rugged* truly describes the life required to survive the area's harsh conditions that Mother Nature regularly conjures up.

Kabul didn't just spring up. It has been a stopover along many trails for centuries. The Silk Road was an overland trade route that spanned the Asian continent from China to Europe from about the second century BCE to the eighteenth century CE. It ran east and west, just a little to the north but not so far that Kabul missed the action. The Hippie Trail,[17] which traced the old Silk Road in this part of Asia, passed directly through Kabul. The Great Game[18] was a rivalry started in 1830 between Great Britain and Russia over dominance in Central Asia. Afghanistan was center stage in that spy game as well.

Some of the prominent early visitors included Darius the Great, Alexander the Great, and Genghis Khan. Genghis was also great, but he settled for emperor. They made a mess, doing what they wanted, where they wanted, and staying as long as they wanted. If you could stay out of their way, avoid getting slaughtered, and didn't mind their strange habits and dress, the locals could tolerate them. Not much different from the current crop of crazy hippies of the 1970s, except the Western "freaks" were peaceful types.

Some travelers referred to Kabul as the "Paris of Central Asia" in the decade of the '70s, with some merit. I'm more inclined to suggest "Saloon of Central Asia." If you're not familiar with the term *saloon*, it's an American term for a watering hole, or a bar with benefits, popular during the *Wild West* era.

"West" refers to the North American continental geography west of the Mississippi River during the period of expansionism, which spanned the 1800s. "Wild" is self-explanatory.

Ordinarily, a saloon was a combination bar, brothel, casino, and eatery. There was little else to choose from in the towns that sprang up like mushrooms after a rain along the wagon trails plied by settlers, grifters, priests, traders, and desperados. These were hardy souls looking for adventure, running from trouble, or searching for that pot of gold.

We departed from the InterContinental Hotel in a stylish manner and the relieved hotel staff bid us adieu. They had parked the *Flying Wreck* out of sight in the employee parking area. With a flourish of assistance from several bellmen to place our "luggage" on a cart, they ushered us out through the revolving lobby door and down the sidewalk to the parking lot. It took us a moment to collect our thoughts as we walked up to what remained of our car, realizing that it was a minor miracle that the vehicle made it to Kabul.

We had largely recuperated from our various afflictions and were full of bravado and ambition. That's not to say we were in excellent health—I don't think we ever fully recovered our stamina and full vigor while in the East. Our dietary systems were constantly trying to distinguish between what was good for us and what was not. Mostly, they decided that was futile and just did what they could to extract nutrition before the food passed through our systems and out quickly. Often, in more of a liquid form than solid.

Chicken Street was the gathering place for Westerners in Kabul. If you wanted chickens, you needed to continue toward the airport when it became Flower Street. If you wanted flowers... Well, I'm not sure. But Chicken Street had most everything else. It was approximately in the middle of Kabul, near the royal palace and close to the foreign embassies, all of which were not very far from the airport. We figured Chicken Street was a solid choice for checking in with travelers and getting intel on an excellent hotel in which to set up our base of operation. We intended to stay as long as needed to get our finger on the pulse of town and plan a program.

It's a good thing we didn't have a time crunch because we—or, more explicitly, me—weren't leaving Afghanistan without the car due to the stamp on my passport. And the car was in no condition to sell, or even give away. But the purchase of our car, that rocking then rolling jukebox from the used-car lot in Germany, was a sound decision anyway. The car and the music got us to our destination. In due course, it would also reveal the concept of karma as a component in the Theory of Dots. However, in the interim, it was quickly becoming a pain in the ass. It would prove to be more than that.

Our criteria for a long-term hotel included convenience to downtown, small, comfortable, and affordably priced, with a staff that would tolerate us smoking a lot of hash. Our prioritization was in reverse order of the criteria.

We were attracted to a small hotel near Chicken Street and the Royal Hotel like a magnet. Maybe it was the vibes, or the gut feeling we had about it. The hotel would qualify as a Dot. Scott or Dave knew the name, but I don't think I ever really paid attention. It was easy to find. We checked it out, then checked in. Easy-peasy. Serendipity flowed, as the first hashish we scored through the staff was excellent and at a good price. It didn't take long to train them to adhere to our high quality standards. On one occasion, "Boy," a self-named staff member—he knew we'd never get his name right—brought a bag of pollen to us instead of handpressed hash. We already knew about *bat pressing*, so we went to the bazaar, found the vinyl sheets, scavenged a leather cord, and fashioned a bat. It was magical. The effort needed by at least two of us working in tandem to beat the pollen into hash made it more personal and, therefore, better. But we didn't need to dupe ourselves—the resulting hash was excellent. Pecking these words out 50 years later, I can see it and smell the intensely satisfying aroma. And we bat pressed hash nearly every day, at about 100 grams (3.5 oz) a time. We certainly weren't careless about the amounts we used, but we played with it as the smooth texture, warmth, and fragrant scent was intoxicating. Put a wad in your palm and knead it constantly, creating a special treat. Through the course of a day, between the three of us and visitors, it just got consumed.

We'd found a jewel of a hotel and were comfortable with, and trusting of, the staff. They took excellent care of us—fed us, provisioned us, and entertained us with good-natured banter. They even arranged for local musicians to play live in the courtyard from time to time.

We made exploratory excursions into town and wandered around, fascinated with the people and the local comings and goings. As one does in familiar surroundings, we habitually followed similar routes and developed routines. That's how we discovered Oriental carpets and the stores that sold them. We visited many over weeks, and one store welcomed us each time with chai and friendly hospitality, and no pressure to buy anything.

We didn't consider carpets as an opportunity then, but that would soon change. During our wanderings, we also saw familiar faces and noticed that the same people were in the same places—shopkeepers, street vendors, beggars, and child opportunists. They had spotted and tagged us long before as foreigners who could be entreated to provide a little something. The kids were sharp—street smart and quick thinkers. But it didn't take long before they realized we were long-term visitors and largely ignored us. We were not fertile ground for their monetary advances.

On a street near the river in what was best described as a traffic circle were several children in various states of distress lying about on the hard pavement. Even more troubling was an infant that was always swathed in dirty rags and crying. We consistently put some coins beside the child, as did Afghan passersby. One had to accept the reality if they planned to reside there for an extended period. Poverty was a fact of life and had been so for centuries or longer. The social support network was nonexistent. People gave what they could afford as an accepted responsibility for being fortunate enough not to be in that position. But something was not normal about that infant crying all the time. Yes, it had every right to be miserable—but that baby haunted our thoughts.

After some weeks of this, we hung around taking photos and observed the scene, looking for clues. The child's apparent elder sister was stationed at a distance of around 20 m (66 ft). Every so often, she went to the child and picked up the coins. While there, she rearranged the rags and did something that made the child cry when it moved. We had things to attend to but returned the next day. As the older girl's routine was about to start, we happened upon the scene and saw what she was doing. She was putting broken bits of glass in between the folds of the rags. Not touching the skin, but when settled, the pressure would press a sharp corner enough to irritate the child. A ploy to ensure greater sympathy and bring better results. It incensed us. As we started toward the girl, one of the street vendors wagged their finger, reminding us we were visitors, not police. This lingering dose of reality was deeply disturbing.

Questions were piling up—driven by cruel inhumanity toward a child, poverty, and what appeared to me to be a constricting religion biased against women. Inhumanity infers that humanity is normally good. Is that the case? *Why are so many—the vast majority, in fact—without a hope of improving their life? Not only why, but how come?*

We were lost in our own thoughts during the walk back to the hotel. We had scarcely any contact with Afghan women in Kabul. Women occasionally participated in the music nights at our hotel, but we never interacted with them. Conversation about religion or women or child abuse as a subject while hanging out on Chicken Street was not an option. Nor was it feasible to talk to Mohammed or Noor about our concerns.

Our attention drifted to matters at hand: *What are we going to do?* Meaning, *How long are we going to stay? Where will we go next? And what are we going to do about the car?*

We pulled out the maps salvaged from the car wreck. We considered both the European and Pakistan/Afghanistan maps a talisman and treated them with reverence. It seemed like a lifetime ago that we were looking at the maps in Amsterdam. It condensed the distance and time to make the trip into a folded-out piece of paper on the floor. The reality was much different, of course.

Beyond the map's limits, there were other interesting target destinations. Kabul was in the sweet spot for access to our also-ran contenders for the best hashish. Kabul to Chitral is about 400 km (248.5 mi). To Kashmir is 500 km (311 mi). Nepal is the farthest, about 1,000 km (621 mi). All were on our short list for follow-up visits after we got a program going in Afghanistan. The automotive rollover show between Kandahar and Kabul put paid to driving the *Flying Wreck* to any of those destinations.

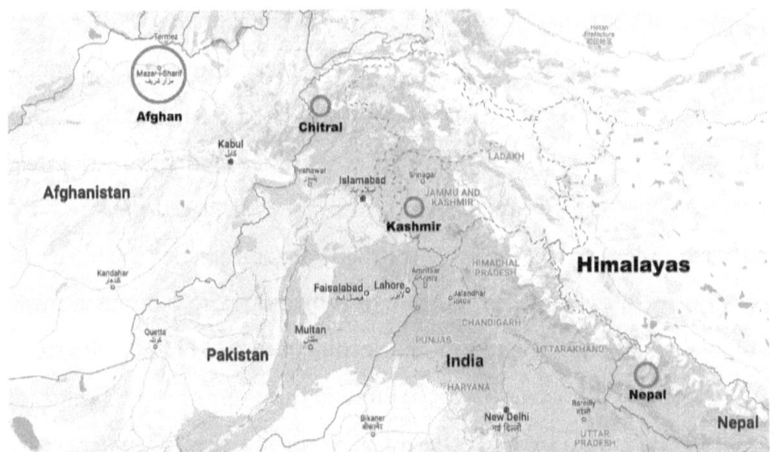

Mazar, Chitral, Kashmir, Nepal. Map data ©2024 Google

But it didn't extinguish the desire, nor the will, to visit all three. We put them on our to-do list for the not-too-distant future.

Kabul had a zoo. Compared to those in the Western world, this one seemed to focus on flora—not so much fauna—and it was short on exotic animals. It was more like the retirees from a circus took up residence. A lion, an elephant, some deer. Despite having a pretty good local fan base, the zoo needed better maintenance.

One of the featured animals was a pig. It enjoyed the status of a celebrity, but it didn't look special to us. Islam forbids the consumption of pork or pig products, so you'd think pigs would rush in there as a haven, but I think this might have been the only pig in Afghanistan. We got a kick out of it and found it humorous. It was the source of a new epithet added to our selective learning of Dari curse words and phrases. A good way to insult a local was to voice something related to a pig. You had to be careful that they saw it as good humor or a scene would ensue. Most of our naughty Dari words came from Boy at the hotel. No doubt he led us astray, loading us up with gibberish so we'd make a fool of ourselves in public. The fun was good-natured.

I'm confident that many considered the de facto zoo was Chicken Street and its immediate surroundings. No metal bars or fenced enclosures were evident; the animal species wandered freely in and among the spectators. There was no shortage of weirdness frequenting the area. Freaks, globetrotters, do-gooders, bureaucrats, displaced persons, and outlaws... All were out of place in a strict Islam culture, but tolerated out of curiosity or the ingrained custom of providing hospitality to visitors.

Chicken Street in Kabul was like Zeedijk in the Red Light District of Amsterdam. It drew every flavor of human, from very straight diplomats and bureaucrats to beggars, thieves, and our favorites—hippies. How can people peacefully share a small space but not cooperate on a global level? Do the equalizer and tolerance inducer allow a walk into forbidden areas of culture, religion, or personal ethos? A walk on the wild side? Or inquisitiveness with little risk?

Amid the sightseers, travelers, and locals, another subculture of adventurers was mostly obscure. These are the ones your mother tells you to stay away from—the dangerous ones who don't like rules and authority. Or maybe they just like to be different, follow their noses, and take life as it comes. Some are driven by money, some are risk junkies, and others just want to see what's over the next hill. And a few who have a specific goal and a plan.

Among the last group is a shared acknowledgement of rules that remain unspoken. Practicing accepted behavior is critical for those skirting the laws. In this case, those laws were regarding cannabis derivatives. A chance encounter with one of those passing by each other without a look or speaking. Often in an airport, a city or sometimes in a bar, but always because of a common thread of high-risk purpose or activity. That thread is the fabric of survival—a combination of hubris, bravado, restraint, and humility. The Credo of the Road, if you will.

Amsterdam, Kabul, and Kathmandu are prime examples of locations where this happens. AMS (Schiphol Airport in Amsterdam) is an enormous facility, but certain flights are prone to a chance encounter with someone known—recognized with a glance or fleeting smile. Sometimes it generates a flicker of worry, but that is often an inner alert system working in overdrive. It jump-starts your awareness with a metallic taste in your mouth, reminding one to be careful. All these helpful reactions make one feel intensely alive and in the moment.

Chicken Street was also one of those unique locations. Freaks were often in Kabul on their way to Kathmandu or Goa. Some had other intentions and stayed in Kabul for lengthy periods, coming and going with frequency. It was easy to tell them apart. Like looking at a tourist on Damrak in Amsterdam and knowing what country they came from by their choice of shoes or socks. Sneakers were most likely Americans, or Canadian. Black or white socks with sandals? Unquestionably German. People who were quick to start up a conversation were likely passing through on the Hippie Trail. Keeping their own counsel and alert, likely in Kabul for a reason. If you hung around long enough, learning to spot the quiet and alert types separated them like wheat from the chaff—then you strictly adhered to the Credo of the Road. Only time and circumstances allowed for a breach of that protocol. Scott, Dave, and I developed several of these kinships in Kabul, knowing that they could dissolve at any moment.

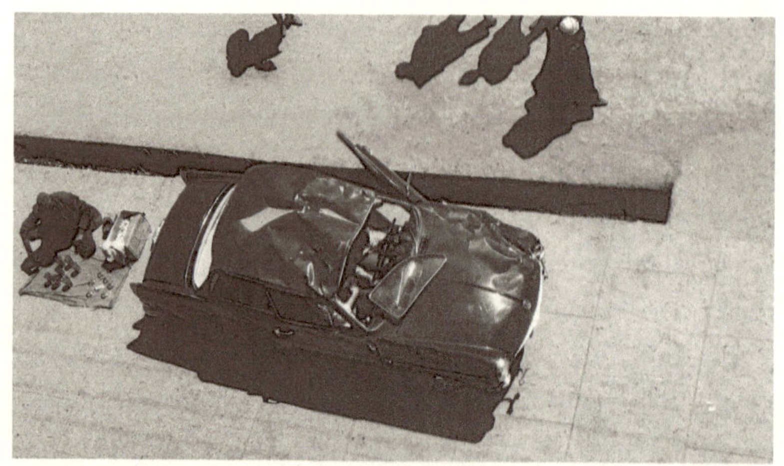

Curiosity and disbelief drew a crowd

Little brother of the infant in rags behind Scott

Chapter Ten

The Promised Land Delivers

Rolling Stones: *She's A Rainbow* > *Lyrics*

The folded-up map of Europe lying on the ground in the hotel's shaded garden in Kabul steered the stoned conversation back to Amsterdam, with lots of laughter and happy memories. While Dave and Scott went for a walk on Chicken Street, I opted for the shade instead. I'd just sit back and enjoy the buzz. I unfolded the map and refolded it so Amsterdam was front and center. Yeah, I'd finally made it to Amsterdam. And I wasn't a newbie traveler any longer. It was where I began, in a way.

Scott, Dave, and I were well aware that Amsterdam served as a hub for travelers coming and going to Europe and Asia. The crossroads of hippiedom, if you will. Travelers arrived with stories and souvenirs of their experiences and contributed to the collective pool of information or, just as often, disinformation. It was the analog version of what became *social media*. It wasn't uncommon for travel stories to be embellished, and the farther away the travels, the greater the liberties taken. At the top of the list for distant travels was Nepal, followed by Kashmir in India. Afghanistan was the principal transition point for the journey there and back.

We witnessed newly arrived or just-passing-through travelers to Amsterdam were more susceptible to falling victim to BS from mouthy know-it-alls on Dam Square or the Vondelpark. Some mistakenly assumed those buffoons had the same knowledge as veterans of travel based solely on bits of information they had collected. Scott, Dave, and I were immune to that bullshit, as we all had some road dust on us already. But it's fair to say that youthful enthusiasm and our privileged position of birth in a Western country jaded our collective attitude, and we probably laid on a bit more bravado than we had earned.

With my eyes closed in the shade, I visualized myself walking down the Spuistraat, away from Centraal Station in Amsterdam. I had an epiphany...or maybe just a stoner thought. Much of the travel souvenir stuff dragged back to Amsterdam found a welcome home both with the travelers and in the tourist market. And a lot of it—clothing, Oriental carpets, donkey bags, lapis lazuli jewelry—were all from Afghanistan. The Afghani look had become fashionable, and rock 'n' roll icons from the Beatles to the Rolling Stones adopted it. Millions around the world followed suit. And here we were, hanging out getting high in the epicenter of coolness. I didn't even need a pencil to connect those Dots.

• • • • ● • ● • ● • • •

A welcoming sense permeated from Amsterdam's hospitable approach to immigration. It was like an open bazaar offering sample tastes of Afghanistan, Morocco, Lebanon, India, Nepal, or any country that was on an informed hippie's short list of must-see destinations. Entrepreneurs in Holland opened restaurants, coffee shops, and bars with native language signage. The unperturbed Dutch adopted words from the languages, the styles of dress, and foods of those who'd taken up residence there. And, of course, some of those entrepreneurs offered the best varieties of hashish from each of those countries.

We had frequented the many coffee shops, bars, and music venues with parties, crazy nightlife, and youth looking for adventure day and night. Hashish was part of the currency. Harder drugs were there, but weren't a significant part of the mainstream—yet. I could forgive a reader if they had the impression that Amsterdam was the epicenter of hashish, but news flash: Westerners seeking adventure did not discover hashish.

• • • • • • • • • •

Records, or knowledge of cannabis as the source of hashish, go back as far as 6000 BCE in China, when they ate the seeds. In the 1980s, local farmers in the Xinjiang Uygur Autonomous Region, China, unearthed an ancient graveyard. A group of international archeologists excavated the ruins in 2008. They discovered a 2,700-year-old grave of a "Caucasoid shaman whose accoutrements included a large cache of cannabis, superbly preserved by climatic and burial conditions." The experts concluded that the cannabis was presumably used as a "medicinal or psychoactive agent, or an aid to divination." It's believed that those investigations are the oldest documented finding of cannabis as an agent to, in today's terminology, get stoned.[19] It's the first evidence of such use in a pre-Silk Road culture. In a revealing, if not unusual description of the deceased's remains, the scientists offered this observation: "The skeletal remains of a male of high social status of an estimated age of 45 years, whose accoutrements included bridles, archery equipment, a *kongou* harp, and other materials supporting his identity as a shaman."[20] Not too far from the description of a hippie on the Silk Road (Hippie Trail) in the 1970s.

Hashish was very popular throughout the Middle East in the early twelfth century. In 1526 CE, Babur Nama, the first emperor and founder of the Mughal Empire, learned of hashish in Afghanistan.

The consumption of hashish was controversial from the beginning. Some religions used it in their ceremonies, while others reviled it as evil and heresy. Certain societies promoted its use, while others implemented laws against it. Military campaigns used it strategically, often resulting in a double advantage: It generated income to help finance military conquests and pacified some of the conquered. A string of tyrants utilized the double advantage strategy effectively. That propensity for manipulation of a society increased as the value of hashish rose.

The potency and quality of the product made Afghan hash stand out. The *cannabis* species used for Afghani is of the Indica family, which is predominant in and around the Indian subcontinent, rather than the *sativa* species, which is more frequently found in popular Western marijuana.

The upward trend for increased potency sped up in the '60s and '70s by crossbreeding of Afghan (and other regions') seeds brought to Western markets. The new hybrid strains of cannabis resulted in a vast increase in potency; the best quality Afghan hash we were smoking during the period of this book had a THC content in the single digits. Hybrid varieties sold in Amsterdam coffee shops and over the counter in California since the 1990s can reach into the 90 percent range.

There's a story that Afghan seeds transported to Northern California started that process: "According to cannabis pioneer Wernard Bruining, who created Holland's first coffee shop nearly 30 years ago [Au:

quote from 2002], Western hippies collected Afghan marijuana seeds and spread them across the world in the 1970s, most notably to Northern California, where the seeds became genetic precursors for many of today's most popular cannabis cultivars."[21]

Here's my point of departure. It's not just potency or provenance that contributes to the mystique or desirability of hashish. Beyond those important factors, there's pedigree. That's true in hashish, breeding horses, musical instruments, or collectible cars. We enhance pedigree by how, when, and where it originates. All of those attributes enhance exclusivity. Walking into an air-conditioned dispensary and buying a few grams of hash with your American Express or Apple Pay is not the same as taking a risky journey to the source and smoking it with the people who made it. Or making it yourself at the source.

There are many production methods for making hash. The larger the quantity, the more mechanized the process becomes. That applies to Afghani hashish, and all other types as well. There's also a truism for all hash: If you start with better quality pollen, you usually end up with a better quality hashish.

The resin that is gathered from the Indica plant in the top regions of Afghanistan is called *char*. For the best quality, the pollen is handpressed into small balls measuring a few grams. Heat and pressure from the worker's hands transform the resin into what we call hash. After being in Kabul for a while, a few grams were not enough for even one chillum. If you want to speed up the process—make more in less time and be willing to lose a little in quality—there is a process. It's the one I mentioned in the previous chapter favored by Dave, Scott, and I, called "bat pressing." Our solution was to bat press about 100 grams (3.5 oz) at a sitting so we could smoke as much as we wanted, share with others, and not be constantly hand pressing a small amount of hash. It seemed like we were batting nearly every day. In celebration of the fiftieth anniversary of Afghan Bat Pressing, I share with you below the heretofore secret process.

We obtained a square vinyl sheet about 50 cm x 50 cm (20 in x 20 in). After laying the sheet on the ground, we placed a glob of char in the center and folded up the edges, so the char was in a ball shape. We twisted the vinyl, with the char tight in the center, and then tied the twisted part with a leather shoelace, leaving a length of the vinyl to use as a handle.

Then one of us would start the process. You took hold of the handle and placed the ball of char on a hard surface—like the wooden arm of a comfortable chair out in the hotel garden in the shade. Then you beat the char with a club fashioned from a tree branch with the bark shaved off and shortened to about half a meter long. We took turns—about 20 minutes per stint. In a couple of hours, we unlaced the vinyl womb and voilà! A hot, aromatic, soft lump of hash was born. The aroma was incredible, and the flavor was divine. It became a ritual that gave us tremendous satisfaction in the hunt for the best char—the preparation, execution, and results.

It was fascinating to witness the transformation from resin to hash—like baking bread. How gratifying it was to take that warm, soft, billiard ball–sized clump of hash out of the "oven." After beating it with the bat, you plopped it in the palm of your hand and continued to knead it to perfect the consistency and enjoy the sensation. We laughed at the suggestion (no insult intended) that it was like the devout Islam Afghanis that carried *subha* (prayer beads) around in their hands while absentmindedly caressing them...or so it seemed to the casual Western observer.

But really, there was some similarity. Whereas *subha* is a religious ac- tivity that many use to relax and take a break from "the world," smoking hash shares that relaxation quality with the additional pleasure of getting high. We didn't think of it as a religious experience by any standards, but there were rituals in smoking a chillum. We were just out to find the origins and the very best examples!

Baking our own bread, so to speak, was a special pleasure that entailed shopping for the ingredients, choosing the freshest and purest available, having the correct utensils, preparing properly, following a recipe, and patiently waiting for the results. We were hashish chefs! That process and shared experience embodied the spirit of a pedigree and were far more satisfying than walking into a store. And a helluva lot more fun—albeit risky. That too added to the satisfaction.

Dave and Scott wandered back into the garden and found me nodded out in the chair. They woke me by blowing smoke in my face. I was startled but smiling.

Tools needed: bat, vinyl, pollen. Not shown: repetitive beating with bat

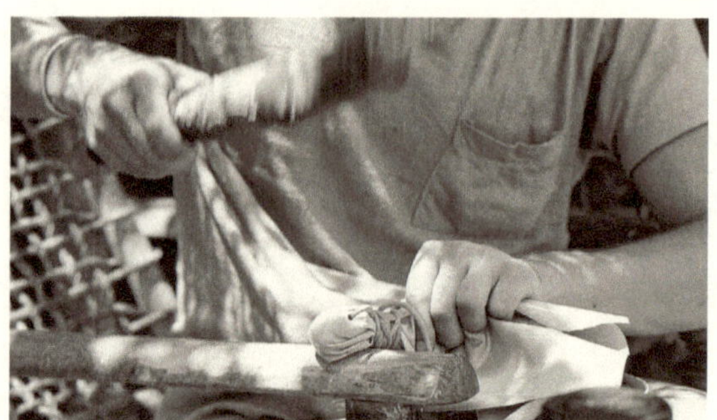

Wham! Wham! Repeat!

Voila! Warm resiny hashish. Delicious aroma.

Interlude Four

Networks Connect Life

Led Zeppelin: *The Battle Of Evermore > Lyrics*

Nature's network systems have evolved over billions of years to sustain life by connecting and nourishing organisms. Humans adopted nature's grid for communication, distribution, and government organization. We had a head start—the human brain uses a neural web to transfer information, emulating nature's preferred method of communication.

They're everywhere. In nature, we have the "wood wide web"[22] for trees, the neural network for humans, and the mycorrhizal network for fungi. Researchers speculated that slime mold was a member of the fungi kingdom. Despite the name, they are not molds. Though they exhibit characteristics common to fungi, they also share similarities to animals.[23] They too use a mesh-like structure for sharing information and nourishment. As we'll learn later, slime molds have been used to map dark matter. A network-derived system is a logical solution for connecting Dots.

As humans know all too well, things are not always as they seem. That phrase is often understood to have a sinister undertone, but with networks, it's a beautiful reality.

Fishlake National Forest in Utah is a prime example. It's beautiful, yes, with pristine lakes and gorgeous stands of quaking aspen trees. The golden leaves shimmer in the fall winds, giving them their name. The forests are breathtaking, with a hidden surprise: Pando. Not a cute bear, but a tree from a single seed that now has over 40,000 stems. One of the largest forms of life on Earth, it is often mistaken for a forest of trees. But it is one tree connected by a single root system—a tree colony network believed to be 80,000 years old. Standing at 43 hectares (106 acres), it is the heaviest living thing on Earth: a single, gargantuan organism. Yet it is deceiving to the eye and contrary to what logic would suggest.

An open mind is essential for the Theory of Dots. We now look closer to home for more evidence of hidden realities—the human body.

Where do you think your physical self, your body, begins and ends? Many would answer from the smallest cells in their body outward to the exterior of their skin. As science digs deeper into microbiology, many experts believe the current perceptions are too limiting.

I venture to say that most people feel certain that individuals are autonomous beings, disconnected at the surface of their skin from any further entanglement or connection to other organisms or materials. That definition would also apply to everything held inside their bag of skin, but that may not be accurate. Microscopically, our bodies host a myriad of symbiotic relationships with other living organisms. Additionally, the exterior of our skin also has similar arrangements. Humans are not unique in that regard—symbiosis exists and thrives throughout the animal, plant, and fungi kingdoms. Humans may not be aware of them, but those situations are still necessary and connected. Merlin Sheldrake's *Entangled Life* examines the fascinating dependencies inside and outside of the human body.

Our body and symbiotic organisms are interconnected at many levels, from the skin to the mouth, stomach, and bowels. To say the interconnection is prolific is an understatement. Changing the way we think about these realities is hard for individuals, but vital for all of us.

Sheldrake elaborates: "We [humans] are ecosystems, composed of—and decomposed by—an ecology of microbes, the significance of which is only now coming to light. The forty-odd trillion microbes that live in and on our bodies allow us to digest food and produce key minerals that nourish us. Like the fungi that live within plants, they protect us from disease. They guide the development of our bodies and immune systems and influence our behavior. If not kept in check, they can cause illness, or even kill us. We are not a special case. Even bacteria have viruses within them (a nano biome?). Even viruses can contain smaller viruses. Symbiosis is a ubiquitous feature of life."[24]

Adapting to the intricate relationships that challenge the belief that our bodies are only made of original human components can be hard. The human body develops original equipment organically, but also sources it from outside suppliers. You don't go to a Mercedes parts department to buy things for a Porsche. Both car companies use some components that are sourced from a third-party manufacturer, who will brand them with *Mercedes* or *Porsche* even though they're interchangeable. At the dealership, you receive factory-authorized goods and your warranty is valid. Your body needs the same reciprocity of human-grown parts working with those of other species that have formed a symbiotic relationship vital to good health. Your body will also give you warranted service for both.

Living networks come in all shapes and sizes. They perform many functions, but slime molds are a special case, and relevant to our interest in dark matter. The name is distasteful to some, but not to those who study them and find them fascinating.

Slime molds build complex filamentary networks in search of food, finding near-optimal pathways to connect to different locations. They communicate with each other via chemical signals. In the laboratory, slime molds have displayed the ability to navigate a maze to reach a food source. And after being fed on a regular schedule at one location, they can anticipate the reward of food at a future time. That's impressive for an organism without a brain.[25]

A NASA article in 2020 describes slime mold as being used to map dark matter. "The cosmic web is the large-scale backbone of the cosmos, consisting primarily of the mysterious substance known as *dark matter* and laced with gas, upon which galaxies are built. Dark matter cannot be seen, but it makes up the bulk of the universe's material."

It continues. "The existence of a web-like structure to the universe was first hinted at in the 1985 Redshift Survey conducted at the Harvard-Smithsonian Center for Astrophysics. Since those studies, the grand scale of this filamentary structure has grown in subsequent sky surveys. The filaments form the boundaries between large voids in the universe."[26] Astronomers have had difficulty locating these elusive strands. Researchers are using slime mold to map the gas in the local universe (within 500 million light-years from Earth).

Lead researcher Joseph Burchett, of the University of California (UC), Santa Cruz, wrote: "By using the slime-mold simulation to find the location of the cosmic web filaments, including those far from galaxies, we could then use the Hubble Space Telescope's archival data to detect and determine the density of the cool gas on the very outskirts of those invisible filaments. Scientists have detected signatures of this gas for several decades, and we have proven the theoretical expectation that this gas comprises the cosmic web."

The research team noted a striking similarity between how slime mold builds complex filaments to capture new food, and how gravity constructs the cosmic web strands between galaxies and galaxy clusters.[27]

"In shaping the universe, gravity builds a vast cobweb structure of filaments, tying galaxies and clusters of galaxies together along faint bridges hundreds of millions of light-years long. There is an uncanny resemblance between the two networks: one crafted by biological evolution, and the other by the primordial force of gravity."[28]

With Dots in mind, I call your attention to current microbial science research of fungi, which has revealed striking analogies to research in astrophysics, particularly dark matter. We previously assigned karma to dark matter as a potential substitute, or perhaps a constituent. The substance that makes up 95 percent of matter in the universe is called *dark matter* because its structure has kept scientists in the dark so far. That brings us back to the adage, "Things aren't always what they seem," which frequently drifts into a conversation.

Life has used networks for millions, if not a billion years. Fungi, perhaps the oldest life-form to employ networks called *mycelium*, are also among the largest of living organisms. Fungi use mycelia to explore, communicate, and exchange nutrients. These hidden branches are like a root system and are essential to life nearly everywhere. "These networks are the foundation of life. They create the soils that nourish all life on land. Without fungi, we do not have soil. Without soil there is no life."[29]

Human networks have fewer capabilities than those of other living organisms. For example, they cannot extract and move nutrients for food, like the naturally occurring tree roots or the mycelia of fungi. And they can only communicate with other systems of human origin. A natural nexus can handle communications while delivering nutrients, and those in symbiotic relationships can also support other living organisms.[30]

Research is making progress in connecting human systems to non-human systems. That will likely require a network interface based on human interpretations of natural systems.

The nexus of the human body carry sensory messages to the brain. Intuition often circumvents the sensory organs, yet the brain receives and processes that and other Dot Matrix messages. How is the message carried if body networks are bypassed? I've assigned karma, aka dark matter, as a potential answer. The connection to other Dot Matrix elements could be explained if karma is the medium that connects all matter.

Networks are the go-to mechanism for the distribution of energy or materials throughout the natural and human world. Few that are human-generated are simple, and all are energy inefficient. Nature holds great promise as a model for explaining the Theory of Dots. More on that in a later Interlude.

Chapter Eleven

Magic Carpets

Steppenwolf: *Magic Carpet Ride* > *Lyrics*

Brian was unusual by Kabul standards. He was clean-cut, intellectual, and only smoked a little hash. His outward interest was filming a Kabul/Afghani experience. He had a Sony Beta recorder, which was analog and recorded on tapes but was considered state of the art. It took a considerable amount of effort to configure it properly and achieve decent video and sound, and at least two people were needed—one on the camera and one on the tape deck to monitor the sound.

But what really fascinated me were his shoes. He had designed and overseen the handcrafting of a three-eye lace-up loafer made from Oriental carpets. I'd seen nothing like them before. Unique and awesome, they were distinctive—like his personality. We learned later that he paid as much attention to the details in his Afghan business as he did in designing and crafting shoes from rugs. He's one of those who drifted into our sphere of influence, filtered through the Credo of the Road.

Brian and his traveling friend Mark attended one of the live music nights at our hotel. Our chillum caught their attention at the small gathering. Neither Brian nor Mark had obvious traits that marked them as a particular nationality, but I noticed something that jogged my mental notepad for further investigation. Some laughter and joking opened the door to another chillum, which Brian offered to load up. He pulled out some handpressed Afghani, which was excellent. *Right. We're on equal terms.*

Through casual dialogue, we established Brian was most likely a Canadian, and Mark a Brit. Both had significant road dust on them after some months in Afghanistan. Brian, of course, had those exceptional shoes, which were a conversation starter. Camaraderie ensued, and they wandered into our hotel courtyard regularly. No invitation needed.

Mark was Brian's go-to guy as the subject of his videos. Our courtyard became a location shoot for the transition segments of the Kabul scenes. It was a good time, and we developed as friends. Lots of smoke, joking, and bullshitting, and a lot of respect. Brian was circumspect about his extracurricular activities, and we respected that. Lynyrd Skynyrd's song "Don't Ask Me No Questions, I won't Tell You No Lies" writ large. Scott and I became cameraman and sound guy. Dave was the master of ceremonies, overseeing activities with his signature grin, reflecting a calm consideration of events, and assuring a chillum was at hand at a moment's notice. As my first venture beyond photography, video captured my imagination and reared its head much later in my life. It also garnered a lot of unwanted attention from the locals, although I don't think it amounted to any kind of threat to whatever we all were up to.

Brian had the deportment of an intellectual who knew how to cloak it in convivial conversation and deprecating humor—a mark of a seasoned professional. He was good fun and provided us with a wealth of insight and useful local intel. He had extensive knowledge about Oriental carpets, which piqued our interest. In fact, he turned us on to one of his sources. It was a key development and cemented the position of Brian as a Dot in my life.

The carpet contact was Noor, proprietor of a well-established business of Oriental carpet importing and distribution, and a retail store with a focus on authentic Afghan carpets, handicrafts, antiques, and jewelry. His store was along the route of our Kabul walkabouts. We were stoked at this bit of good fortune, especially the fact that Brian recommended him.

• • • ● • ● • ● • • •

Collectively, we knew next to nothing about carpets (beyond that which we gleaned by questioning Brian). In addition, we had zero experience in legal importation to the US and had not identified our customers. Those facts were not a deterrent to our plan. Actually, we didn't even have a plan, but it felt like a good idea, and we proceeded—and drank more chai (tea) than we thought possible!

Finding carpets for sale in Kabul was as easy as finding sex shops in Amsterdam's Red Light District—no shortage of availability, but the quality of the goods varied dramatically. Fondling the merchandise in Amsterdam before you paid was frowned upon, but it's essential with carpets.

We channeled Brian's experienced counsel to us as follows: "It's a hands-on proposition—in fact, the first thing you do is turn it on its back and slowly caress the surface. You feel the texture, stiffness, materials, and look at the knots—the smaller the better, and the more per square centimeter the better. Turn it back over and look closely at both edges and both ends: Cotton warp or wool? Is the pattern familiar? Are the colors bright, or do they have a patina? Is the pile height mostly uniform? Only expertise and experience can delve into the more defining details like the dye used, the quality and type of wool, the provenance of manufacture, and the tribal affiliation—nomadic or regional. There is so much to know that accurate and reliable information is difficult to come by."

We appreciated Brian's patient and insightful guidance, but Scott, Dave, and I felt we had reached the limit of seeking any additional input from him without overstaying our welcome. We had to rely on Noor from that point forward. Hence the need to be comfortable and confident in his knowledge. Not having expertise or knowing our customer demographics in the US made it imperative that we got the best we could find and afford. Screening Noor got underway over chai—green or black tea. And lots of it!

Noor was a challenge to understand. A merchant in Afghanistan occupies a respectable place in the scheme of things, and must be a master of languages and foreign cultures. He must also skillfully maneuver among cultural and tribal realities while navigating third world bureaucratic obstacles. All of that while maintaining the liquidity to purchase product, keep the doors open, and cover expenses for and importing and exporting goods. A merchant capable of successfully executing those essentials demonstrates an admirable set of negotiation skills and application of clever thinking. Such a person is a highly gifted and intelligent human being.

But that doesn't mean they think the same as you. Gaining insight into what makes a person like that tick is important. Not only to negotiate for the best price, but to find out if he is playing it straight with you. A recommendation from Brian was valuable, but we had in mind to purchase a lot of carpets and accoutrements like donkey bags, camel collars, and a few other odds and ends. This sizable investment needed to be handpicked one carpet and item at a time, and that was only the basic proposition. Goods needed to be bundled, wrapped, and transported; customs formalities prearranged, fees handled, and other details attended to. Any errors or omissions along the way could jeopardize the shipment.

Most days, we could find Noor in his store lounging on a stack of Oriental carpets. He smoked Western cigarettes, and though we never smoked hash with him, I'd bet he would have agreed if it meant a sale. He was a portly man, always wearing a tailored suit, a dress shirt—but no tie—and stylish loafers. He sported a closely cropped full beard and black hair combed straight back—the style worn in Hollywood movies from the 1950s. Very un-Afghan! His accent in English was hard to place. Certainly not British or American. It's likely he was educated in Europe as he spoke many languages, including Russian and Chinese, with a well-honed ability to speak and understand English.

He was a very affable guy and interesting to engage in conversation. We needed, or at least wanted, to have a deeper understanding of his motivations. It was a challenge to navigate the fundamental cultural differences, especially without experience. Fortunately, it solved itself by us letting go of a determined effort and just engaging with and observing him.

Imagine walking toward the sound of music coming from a band playing in a park. You can't see them and didn't know there was a concert. At first you hear the drums, then the bass. As you get closer, you can make out the mid tones, then pick up the vocals. Before you can discern the song lyrics, you recognize the music—of course, that's Van Morrison! All the information comes together, recognizing the song as "Into the Mystic" by Van Morrison.

That's the way it went down with understanding Noor, and he proved to be pretty much what we saw from the beginning. He was a prime example of a Dot that emerges in stages, whose subtle progression of importance belies the depth of its significance.

Noor schooled us in more than Oriental carpets. His knowledge and experience of doing business in Afghan style was invaluable. Cultural insights, historical perspective, local customs, and skirting bureaucracies surfaced as a swimmer takes breaths between strokes. Investing several hours a day over some months was fun, enlightening, and put us in business. Easygoing, as honest as an Afghan carpet seller can be, and competent. We doubted we could do better. So, Noor it was, and we got serious about selecting carpets to ship back to the States.

• • • • ● • ● ● • • •

Walk inside a carpet store and it immerses you in sensory delights. Usually in stacks, the individual carpets flow into each other, but you can sense each one as a unique piece of art, handwoven in a professional tradition that has passed from one generation to the next. The air carries a musty scent of history and the inevitable passage of time, and a deep organic aroma, rich and complex, emanates from the wool. The blend of sensory pleasures creates a feeling of being grounded, much like a concert piece that relaxes you into your favorite sofa at home. Like the ghostly finger in early TV children's cartoons, the wafting of aromas drifts through the air, lifts your body into a prone position, carries you over to a pile of carpets, and beckons you to relax in their splendor.

Handwoven carpets are magical, a powerful touchstone for history and tradition, representing a heritage woven into pieces of art. They are essential elements found in every tribal tent or home.

It takes exceptional talent and sore muscles to weave no more than 10 cm (4 in) of rug in a day. Depending on the size, a carpet can take as long as six months to complete. Even a small prayer rug can take a month. It's tiring, repetitive labor, toiling day after day.

Companies built large industrial looms to increase the speed of production, making larger rug sizes possible. However, companies prioritized meeting market demands by sacrificing creativity for volume. The best carpets are made by hand. The inconsistencies in size, pile height, and color are proof of a masterpiece, far superior to machine-made items.

Oriental carpets is a term often used for handwoven carpets like those made in Afghanistan. As are many things in this part of the world, the phrase is steeped in historical allegory and biased by a Western point of view. The term *Oriental* comes from "oriente" and refers to lands in the "East," relative to Europe. The two prominent types of carpets in Afghanistan are Turkmen and Baluch. Turkmen are generally of higher quality. The Turkmen rug designs are specific to tribal groups in the same vein that Scottish kilts vary by clan.

• • • ● ● ● ● ● • •

Initially, entering Noor's carpet store felt like a mystical experience—a sanctuary embodying human expectations, hope, sorrow, tragedies, and success. Afghan carpets, a cultural icon, are an expression of the collective beliefs, aspirations, and values of a people—sometimes a tribal or family patrimony.

Noor would entertain us with stories of carpet hunters who braved treacherous mountain trails, bandits, wolves and, worse—government agents—while pursuing authentic antique carpets. Some of which, naturally, were in that carpet stack right over there! The truth was that Noor supplied the wool and other necessary materials to small groups of people in tribal areas, and even a few nomadic groups, so they would weave carpets exclusively for him. Many of these small carpet weaving operations used horizontal frames, with women and children doing most of the weaving.

We frequented Noor's store with regularity and soon a flow developed. Greetings, followed by casual chat, including local gossip updates from Noor, all friendly and engaging. His well-honed social and business acumen promoted a rapport of confidence and trust. In some cases, with some individuals, it would be an intentional grooming process. It didn't feel like that with Noor and we liked him, so we let it ride, and it gave us access to better rugs.

We spent time and effort to gain enough knowledge to determine what kind of carpet was best suited for our target market in the States. It was a tactile activity, involving full body contact. We crawled around on hundreds of carpets, like a cat turning around in a circle after circle before settling down on one in particular. We grasped the reason for always finding Noor relaxing on top of a pile of carpets. It felt good. It was an embodiment of comfort—physical and emotional.

Noor kept a casual eye on us as his store assistant brought over one carpet at a time, laying it on the floor for us to examine. We applied all that we had learned from Brian and Noor, carefully inspecting the design, dye, colors, cotton or wool, edges, and both ends. We flipped the carpet, analyzing the warp, weft, and size of the knots. By now, Noor knew what we were looking for and why. If we choose the carpet, it was left in place and another carpet was brought out and laid on top. If we hesitated over a carpet, Noor tactfully pointed out something we overlooked. In doing so, he added to our knowledge without causing us to lose face. That carpet was taken away.

Noor's carpet store was like a cluttered, overstuffed museum. Taking a break between carpet selection, we drank chai. One's attention might be drawn to something that had escaped attention before. One of his assistants stood at the ready to scurry over and climb, dig around, or jump to get the item spotted and bring it over for consideration. That's how we accumulated the tchotchkes we thought would be cool and, we hoped, would sell.

I likened the friendly atmosphere of Noor's store to the neighborhood bakery in Amsterdam near Van Eeghenstraat, two blocks from the Vondelpark. That was my neighborhood, and I liked to shop in the small family-owned stores. Most had a strict regime of closing on Saturday at 1600 hrs, not reopening until Monday at 1300 hrs. If you didn't get your bread on Saturday, you were out of luck! I often stood in line with the neighborhood *huisvrouwen* (housewives) in their blue aprons over their house dresses, some even wearing wooden clogs. They met my efforts to learn Dutch with a mix of patient responses and exasperation. I habitually bought a particular brown bread—you had to ask to have it sliced. After reaching the front of an unusually long waiting line, and having gained some confidence with my Dutch, I uttered, "*Een stuck bruin brood besneden.*" I was the only guy in the shop. The bakery broke into an uproar of laughter. There I stood, chagrined and confused, waiting for it to quiet down and hopefully receive my sliced bread. After she had stopped laughing enough to speak, the woman behind the counter said earnestly in English, punctuated with a smile, that I had just ordered a loaf of circumcised brown bread. I learned two new Dutch words: sliced is *gesneden* and circumcised is *besneden*.

After that, the shopkeepers greeted me with special regard, along with smiles from the *huisvrouwen*. I also received fresh bread from the back room instead of the front display counter.

Having developed a trusted relationship with us, Noor shared his insights into Afghanistan and its people. More accurately, its tribes. Afghanistan remains a recognized country in the United Nations and by everyday people. But the designated borders are utterly meaningless to its inhabitants. Noor explained he was a Pashtun, one of the major tribal groups, along with Tajik, Uzbek, and Hazara. Many tribes and subtribes exist in the Central Asian countries of the "stans"—Uzbekistan, Tajikistan, Turkmenistan, Kyrgyzstan, Pakistan, and Afghanistan. The political borders are porous; the various tribal members go about their lives based on tribal customs. All have a very interesting history and have existed since... Well, almost forever, as far humans are concerned. Naturally, the tribe of most interest to us was Pashtun. They accounted for nearly half of the Afghan population and maintained a strict code of conduct called *Pashtunwali*. Their appearance made them easy to spot on the street. They wore what appeared to be pajamas—*shalwar kameez* in the local lingo— and white pillbox hats, and had beards. They also inhabited parts of Pakistan and throughout the Hindu Kush.

Noor mostly described the tenets of Pashtunwali as a strict requirement to treat guests as royalty. They had to provide guests with the best that a host could offer, and they considered guests to be under the host's care and protection. That helped to explain the considerable graciousness that we experienced once we entered Afghanistan, particularly the Dot who appeared at the scene of our car accident between Kandahar and Kabul.

The hospitality Noor extended to us went far beyond customer care in Western habits. However, other tenets in Pashtunwali are not so friendly. I only learned of those in later years. Sir Winston Churchill, who was stationed in the Pashtun areas of northern India and Pakistan in the early twentieth century, provides an insightful description in his book, *My Early Days*: "...the columns crawl through a maze of giant corridors down which fierce snow-fed torrents foam under skies of brass. Amid these scenes of savage brilliancy, there dwells a race whose qualities seem to harmonize with their environment. Except at harvest-time, when self-preservation enjoins a temporary truce, the Pathan [sic] tribes are always engaged in private or public war. Every man is a warrior, a politician, and a theologian. Every large house is a real feudal fortress made, it is true, only of sunbaked clay, but with battlements, turrets, loopholes, flanking towers, drawbridges, etc., complete. Every village has its defense. Every family cultivates its vendetta; every clan, its feud. The numerous tribes and combinations of tribes all have their accounts to settle with one another. Nothing is ever forgotten, and very few debts are left unpaid. For the purposes of social life, in addition to the convention about harvest-time, a most elaborate code of honor has been established and is on the whole faithfully observed. A man who knew it and observed it faultlessly might pass unarmed from one end of the frontier to another. The slightest technical slip would, however, be fatal...\"[31]

With that description in mind, I'm reminded once again of my grandmother talking about the American version of familial feuds—the Hatfields and McCoys. Same theory, same closed-mindedness, same passing of feudal burdens from generation to generation. Afghanistan has existed as a region of civilization dating back to 3000 BCE. It both suffered and benefited from its location at a crossroads of trade along the Silk Road. Tribal influences were loosely aligned for centuries, and still prevail. Afghanistan was a kingdom when we arrived. It had been so for half a century before it became a republic during our stay. The king was a Pashtun, Mohammed Zahir Shah, who turned out to be the last king of Afghanistan. In July 1973 his cousin, General Mohammed Daoud Khan, overthrew him with support of the Russians. Another passing of feudal type burdens, with modern overtones.

· · · · ●· ● · ● ● · ● ·

Scott and I were constantly taking photos. For both of us, it was a passion and fun. It could also get you out of a jam, which would come in handy on one of our treks over in Pakistan. But that's for later. With carpets, it was fun and part of documentation for the future. Noor became accustomed to us snapping flicks in his shop. Doing so also let us keep track of the carpets we had selected and were to be kept aside for us in stacks between our visits to the store. To the best of our knowledge, Noor kept to his word.

Our photography continued out into the street. Our daily forays observing and photographing the mass of humanity, doing and acting as Afghans are prone to do, was bewildering and enlightening. Curious Afghans were constantly around us, sometimes begging for money, often trying to convince us to give them money, and occasionally becoming angry. The latter was not a result of anything aggressive on our part, but ignorance that our appearance was unacceptable to some of them. There were a lot of foreign travelers, many of whom looked like us. In the view of those who felt wronged, our attire was an insult to Islam. Long-haired men were not the norm, but could be tolerated with a proper cap in place and a beard that was long and not trimmed. We adopted some of the local clothing, but drew the line at the plastic sandals that were worn year-round.

The truth is, we typically came into contact with a broad range of Afghan social classes on a daily basis. Although not typical business travelers, we still encountered high society, diplomats, bureaucrats, and poseurs at the InterContinental Hotel, but our interactions were superficial. Had we the opportunity to mingle longer with that stratum, we would have opted in, at least for a while. Our preference was the street, where photo opportunities were abundant and far more interesting than the lobby of a five-star hotel—most of the time. We had our hands full of absorbing Afghan behavior as it was. Afghanistan is a fascinating, unruly, tribally dominated region that calls itself a country—at least on the international stage. I am pained by the dreadful circumstances it has endured for the past four decades, full of turmoil, strife, and destruction.

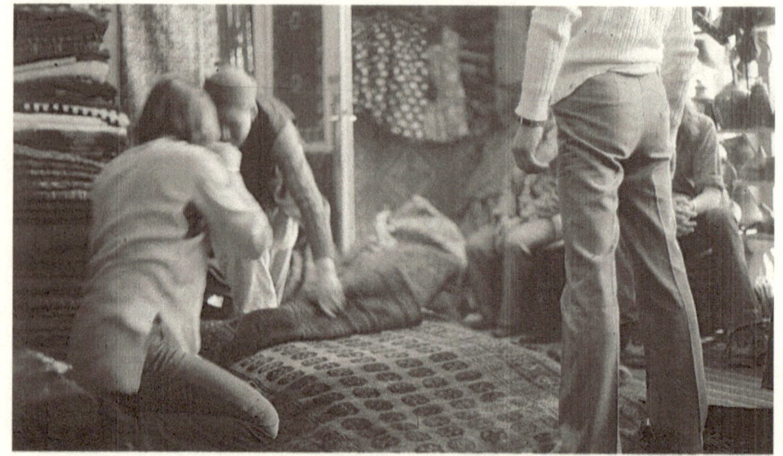

Photos for our records

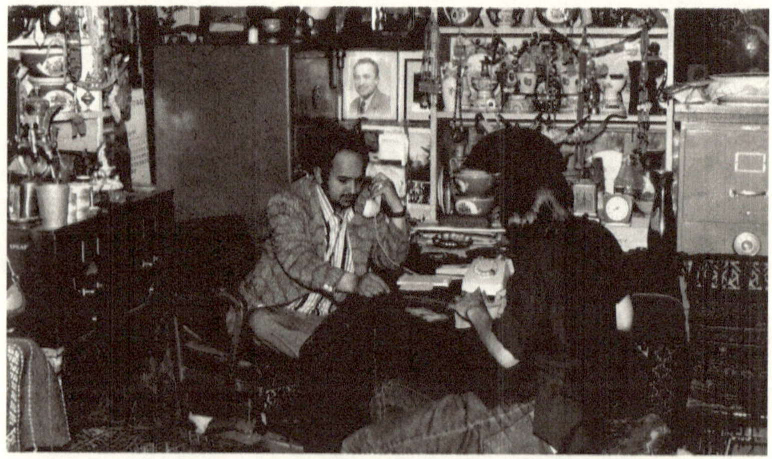

Arranging shipping

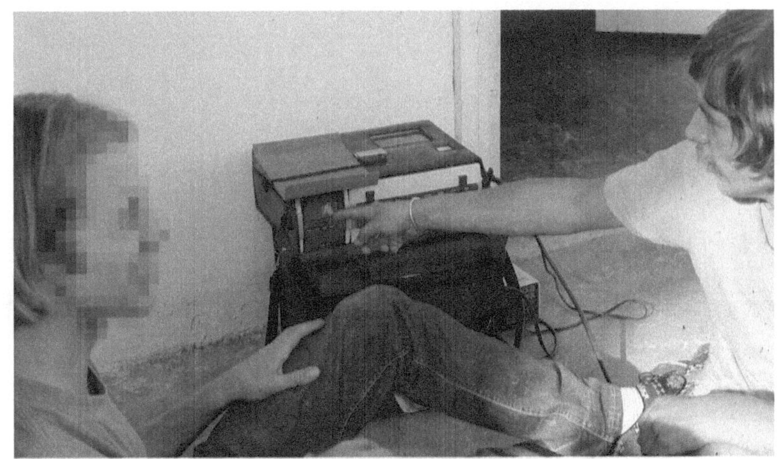

Brian, those shoes & Scott

Mark, Brian, Duane

Chapter Twelve

Flying Carpets

Grateful Dead: *Me & My Uncle* > *Lyrics*

Noor was a thoughtful man, a deep thinker, and not prone to hyperbole. When he spoke, we learned to pay attention.

"There are many things that can be arranged, many rules can be broken, and some laws that I can ignore in Afghanistan. I am at your service for those. But your automobile, that is different. You entered the country with a car, and you must leave with the car."

With those words, Noor elevated that stamp in my passport to a new level of concern. As we accumulated carpets and other merchandise to ship to the US, we now had to add the car issue to the top of our "to-do" list. As that bit of news sank in, we decided we would need to have some flexibility in our planning—which was nonexistent, anyway. Things would take longer, if nothing else.

The three of us decided that Scott and I would follow our carpets and assorted Afghani goods to the US, while Dave would hold down the fort in Kabul until we returned. Identifying and locating our customers, marketing and selling the merchandise—donkey bags, camel collars, prayer rugs, area carpets, throw pillows, lapis lazuli jewelry, and more—was left unsaid. We believed we had purchased a robust selection of goods to sell. Missing were the cool carpet shoes, but Brian had that option locked down.

Potential buyers would embrace the handwoven stuff, like bags, rugs, and donkey accessories. The camel collars were somewhat unusual—very cool, though, and would make striking wall hangings or unusual decorations for horse lovers. We only bought a handful of those. The higher profit items were the jewelry. Most of it was costume jewelry, but still genuine Afghani. The most exotic jewelry were the lapis lazuli rings, bracelets, and necklaces. Lapis lazuli is a gemstone mined in Afghanistan for eons, at least back to the seventh century BCE. They derived the name from the Latin and Persian meaning *blue stone*, and it has significant mentions in the Bible. The best quality is a dazzling deep blue with gold flecks; lower quality is lighter blue with white flecks.

Ours wasn't a brilliant reading of the generational cultural trends that prompted us to include goods that would appeal to that demographic. There was no marketing epiphany. We didn't even have a cohesive marketing plan. It was mostly being in the right place at the right time—Afghanistan. However, we did have a couple of factors in our favor. I had two acquaintances in the US in mind, one in the Midwest and one in Florida. I had their phone numbers, and if those didn't work, my backup was a mutual friend to contact for updated info on both. We had a decent chance that at least one of the two would be interested in our authentic Afghan merchandise, or turn us on to someone that was. It was all we had, but we felt our karma was good.

It wasn't as if we naïvely believed we would stumble upon a buyer—a little of that, probably, but more a sense of confidence. We knew how to work a crowd, had the street cred, and could punch above our weight in the US because we were coming straight from Afghanistan. We hoped to find a buyer who would pay cash for most of our goods and, if needed, finance the rest so we could quickly return to Afghanistan. Tsk, tsk, you are thinking— fat chance! Well, it wasn't exactly a speedy process, but our instincts, intuition, and karma ultimately prevailed during the trip.

• • • ● • ● • ● • • •

Rock 'n' roll music of this period glorified drugs, sex, and exotic cultures from the East. The Beatles get credit for putting a spotlight on that area of the world with a strong spiritual aspect. Not only the Beatles, but other R&R musicians took up the mantel and popularized a raft of societal, fashion, and political expressions. The Beatles shaped those trends in a spiritual direction—yoga, meditation, mind expansion, and inner reflection. The Rolling Stones, you might ask? A bit more of an in-the-moment expression of the above. Put simply, "sex, drugs, and rock 'n' roll."

The scene in Kabul intrigued us, and we were plenty knowledgeable about what was cool in hippiedom. We previously lived in Amsterdam, after all. Afghanistan's way of life was a rich and exciting experience, being immersed in those cultural artifacts overflowing in Noor's store. But we weren't that interested in the spiritual side of it, unless a girl we fancied was into it. Then we were experts who had traveled to the source and been to places they had heard of. That worked magic.

Our social life still centered around the music nights at our hotel and Chicken Street excursions. Brian and video filming were a welcomed diversion to business, and always a learning experience. Reports indicated more Russian interference with Western travelers, but King Mohammed Zahir Shah, educated in the West, remained calm. No worries.

• • • ● • ● • • •

Noor had been extraordinarily generous with his knowledge and with our many visits over a rather lengthy period. We witnessed others coming into the shop, gawking at the store overflowing with Afghan antiques, and then walking out. Some might buy a carpet, maybe two, and a trinket, then leave. I think Noor accepted we were going to be semi-permanent fixtures. He sensed we were serious and he went through all the necessary actions to prepare the carpets for shipment. He had many phone conversations with unknown persons and described the export process and how it would go down. He put the correct number of carpets in a bundle and arranged them by size and origin—Turkmen (Bokhara) or Baluch. He boxed up the other merchandise, segregating the handwoven from nonwoven goods, and making sure the boxes correctly identified the jewelry and trinkets. Those careful preparations allowed our shipment to avoid the worst of the capricious Afghan rules for export. Noor had other methods to further ensure the goods' safety and integrity, not to mention preventing the quantity of goods from shrinking—an additional expertise to expedite the process. We wished for similar wizardry on the US end.

Some of those phone calls were with Mohammed, the Pan Am agent who would pick up the responsibility for our shipment when it arrived at the Kabul airport freight area. Don't let those words create an image of a humming warehouse with forklifts and well-orchestrated movements! Noor proposed to take us on a reconnaissance trip to the airport, partially to demonstrate his knowledge, influence, and stature, and we were curious about how this shipment thing actually happened, so we were agreeable to the trip. The forlorn structure was more akin to an abandoned building in a forgotten strip mall. Dimly lit, with scattered sunlight streaming in from gaps in the walls and ceiling, with scattered clumps of goods unattended. Afghan men squatted on their haunches, attending to nothing at all. There was little to lend confidence that a shipment would actually leave, let alone make it to a foreign destination.

The deference Noor received in our presence proved he had leverage with the customs agents and airport authorities. That reassured us he could get the job done. In fact, considering our experiences in Afghanistan to date, had we witnessed anything resembling an efficient operation, we would have called BS and bolted. The only thing that raised a flag after the fact was that we didn't meet Mohammed there. When asked, Noor explained he was still negotiating with Mohammed for the lowest price he could get for us. That was not a reassuring thought. We filed it under "watch closely." With an asterisk of "benefit of doubt" to Noor.

• • • • ● • ● • • •

During our frequent visits to the carpet store, I questioned Noor about options to solve the car stamp in my passport problem. He stressed that it was a major issue, and to complicate matters further, it was impossible for a foreigner to sell a car in Afghanistan. So, what was the solution? Give it away? Not so easy, unfortunately. Noor had seen the car by this time. A typical used German VW sedan like ours made the Skoda, a Russian car, a comparative piece of shit. No number of strategically chosen words could disguise the fact that our car had rolled over, had no windshield, had no operating headlights, and was barely drivable. But it had a good engine! We could try to convince an individual with customs, or a customs police agent, to take the car. We could also pay someone to let us give them the car. As time passed and we neared the time to become carpet sales agents in the US, it seemed less and less a ridiculous solution.

Remember those cartoons when you were young? I'm talking about Rocky and Bullwinkle, the Roadrunner, and Bugs Bunny cartoons. You could spot a villain by a tight shot of his face (typically a male, except for Natasha). He would smile, one of his front teeth gleaming, and the brilliant flashing shine emanating from a gold tooth was proof positive that he was the one to watch.

The Kabul police captain in front of me had that gold tooth, and it shone brightly as he smiled the most disingenuous smile I had encountered since... Well, maybe back when we were at the customs area in Herat with Mr. Big. The captain's uniform was dowdy and had the dusty appearance of almost everything in Afghanistan. He was large in the belly and one of his uniform shirt buttons was precariously tilting under stress, ready to launch itself into space. His shoes were unpolished, but at least they weren't the ubiquitous plastic open-toed sandals. He mindlessly toyed with the prayer beads in his right hand as he told me of his authority and experience in situations like mine. He assured me there was absolutely no problem about taking care of that little inconvenient stamp in my passport. He would simply work with his associate at headquarters, and since we had agreed to give him our car in gratitude, they could process the paperwork at a reduced price.

There it was. Give him the car for free, and then pay him to take it off our hands. This was the first offer of help from an alleged authority, and it reeked of a scam. The US embassy wasn't much help when we visited to find out how to leave the country without the car. But they said that unless someone properly canceled the passport visa stamp, the immigration officer at the airport would likely catch it, and the cost and hassles would increase exponentially. Any proper solution had to be implemented by Afghan authorities in the immigration department. Meaning, not a cop on the take with the help of an associate in police headquarters.

Back to the drawing board.

The captain was the first of several "buyers" for our car that Noor sent our way. They visited the store, where our car was parked nearby with one of Noor's local urchins guarding it. Fortunately, we weren't paying for that service, but we wondered if we were paying a premium for the carpets. *El Capitan* must have shaken down many before us, as his English was pretty good. Then there was an alleged government official, followed by a local merchant, neither of whom spoke English, necessitating Noor to act as our translator. All visits ended the same way. Nobody wanted to buy it, but they were happy to take it off our hands for a "small fee."

We weren't critical of Noor about the scoundrels who showed up. We thought it reflected the difficult situation we were in with the car. No evidence showed that his purpose was anything other than helping to resolve the problem, and that fact was troubling. With all the connections that Noor had at his disposal, if he couldn't get it taken care of, we were in deeper shit than we thought!

Cars were expensive in Afghanistan; non-Russian or Eastern Bloc cars were rare, and in great demand. Our German VW qualified as one in demand, but it was a moving wreck and far from being classified as a good, or even a "used," automobile. We saw cars with far fewer body parts than ours in service as taxis, but most had windows. Of importance, however: The engine and drivetrain of the *Flying Wreck* was in excellent condition.

The farther removed from Kabul, the worse condition cars were in. In fact, some old US cars that slipped into the country years ago had the fenders removed so they could carry baggage in the recesses. The larger engine compartment in older cars also left lots of space for cargo, or people...if the hood was removed. We figured someone could simply cut the smashed top of the *Flying Wreck* at the four corners, making a sleek, open-air "sports wreck" with plenty of room for people, baggage, goats. Whatever. The Kabul locals didn't quite see it that way.

It was increasingly evident that disposing of the car would be a challenge. And a time crunch was closing in. The task had grown from selling it, or giving it away for free, to the current belief that we'd have to pay to get rid of it. Even that was proving difficult.

Our purchases of carpets and baubles were getting close to our budget limit, which meant that we would ship them soon. Scott and I planned to follow the carpets to the US, to work the sales leads (as weak as they were), then hightail it back to Kabul. Plans for our next program needed follow-up actions.

The general atmosphere in Kabul troubled us a little. Subtle inferences from Noor confirmed those feelings. However, the many tasks at hand kept us busy, so we paid little attention to Noor's comments or the subtle changes we noticed about the town. As apolitical visitors to Afghanistan, we had only a vague idea that trouble was brewing, including its extent or impact. Fractious political parties were vying for power, each stirring the pot of animosity among the populace from the devastating drought the country suffered from for several years. General Mohammed Daoud Khan was one of the extended royal family members, and first cousin and brother-in-law to the king. Daoud had previously served in government, but was abruptly forced out. He had connections and aspirations of his own and was making unwanted noises. Many political observers believed he was not one, given the chance, to make immediate and drastic changes to the status quo. The Russians, however, with ties to the general, had a different agenda.

We reached a critical point with the carpet program, as we needed to ship our purchases quickly. Our efforts to get rid of the car were floundering. We focused on the former and tabled the latter. We shifted into high gear to get the goods in the air so we could move on, eagerly anticipating a quick departure. Noor brought all the rugs—four bundles of carpets and three large boxes of other stuff—to the store and we inventoried our stock. Our photographic inventory of each item was probably adequate, but we also created a list, literally with paper and pencil, as it was the only option we had. We decided to establish pricing upon arrival in the States, determining them based on local demand. We had done no market research, no comparative shopping, and had next to nothing to base selling prices on. No problem. We had our instincts, karma, and enthusiasm to go on.

Noor had recently completed negotiations with Mohammed of Pan Am freight for an all-inclusive price for shipping services from "carpet store to customs storage in Cleveland, Ohio." The quote included Mohammed's oversight and management of the shipment, local transportation, export handling, export fees, Afghan customs clearance, and air-freight. Additionally, US customs clearance and the correct US customs paperwork to avoid additional import taxes, as well as paying all "fees" in Afghanistan, were part of the service. Not quoted was how much Noor received for guiding us to Mohammed. If there was a finder's fee, Noor had earned it, as our efforts would surely have resulted in nothing when leaving Afghanistan, let alone arriving in the US.

Within a matter of a few days, Mohammed arrived at Noor's store and we met him for the first time. He was relatively young, fairly tall for an Afghani, with a European flair in dress and a friendly smile. Notably,

Mohammed had an air of experience about him and spoke excellent English—a no-nonsense kind of guy with a can-do attitude. Noor and Mohammed greeted each other in a formal and professional manner that we thought showed respect, but contained no signs of collusion.

We sat around the store on our carpets and drank chai, discussing the shipment procedures. Mohammed enthused that our business, exporting carpets and related Afghani goods, was a routine matter and the process would flow easily unless there were unexpected items in our shipment. It was a question posed as a statement. Mohammed was a pro.

Dave was first to respond. "Only the goods described are in the shipment." (*This time*, each of us thought.)

"There will be many mouths to feed, and I must attend to each," said Mohammed.

Feeding those mouths would start on the way to the airport and end when we left the airport grounds: laborers loading the goods onto the lorry at the store, drivers, men off-loading at the airport, etc., etc., and it would get really interesting when we got to the customs officials!

A few reflective moments later, he said, "We'll need these denomination afghani notes, totaling the equivalent of approximately $200 USD."

It was a sizable amount of US dollars back then. Also, a big wad of afghanis, as the official exchange rate was 71 afghanis to one dollar. In the money bazaar near Chicken Street, the currency substitution assessment was even higher. We thought it would be entertaining to watch Mohammed peel the correct amount off as we proceeded toward Kabul International Airport, passing money out along the way!

We noticed unusual activity now and then: Crowds of gathering in open places with banners waving and impromptu speeches on an overturned box. From time to time, we also noticed a caravan or two with occupants crowded into the back of a large lorry—accompanied by several buses loaded with people displaying banners with slogans. I was a veteran of the demonstrations against the Vietnam War a few years earlier and had joined a march on Washington, DC, in 1970. I was rewarded with a visit to the basement level of the DC jail for driving a makeshift ambulance to treat those wounded in scuffles with the police. Along with a hundred other people, I was pepper gassed. Civil disobedience, I recognized—these situations looked very familiar. Although the banners were illegible to me, they certainly looked like angry demonstrators expressing their dissatisfaction. Something was cooking with them, but missing were the police on horses with batons.

Time and distance revealed the threat to Afghanistan's peace and prosperity, but to us those events and observations were a diversion from our concerted efforts to get rid of the *Flying Wreck* and get carpets in the air. We didn't waste time with bird-dogging what was going on since it was nothing affecting us directly anyway. Famous last words.

Days ran into the next one, with little to distinguish them apart. It was imperative to make a decision to break the cycle. Summer was passing and fall was up next, after which was a long and harsh Afghanistan winter. We needed to get rolling. So, we smoked a chillum and kinda decided to do it right away.

Mohammed escorted us to the airport. The freight area was as we remembered. We even thought, as we entered the building, that the guy hunched down against the wall was still in the same place. The language barrier was prominent, but everyone seemed friendly and very curious about the odd-looking men with Mohammed. Upon reaching the customs office, the boss was introduced to us. We didn't get his name, but it was clear he was in charge. With coal-black hair and a dark complexion, his hair was stylishly long over the ears and he had a thick mustache. Totally attired in a Western suit coat and slacks; dark-blue, cuffed white shirt; a tie; but brown shoes. Clearly, he was not so fashion conscious and could be mistaken for an under assistant West Coast promotion man. He rose from his desk to greet us with a disinterested smile, making an attempt at formality and courtesy. But he blew that and got right to the point.

"Mohammed has informed me of your desire to export Afghan artistic goods to the United States." What he meant to say was, "This is going to cost you."

The tours with Mohammed provided an insider's view of the airport. That alone was a valuable experience and perhaps useful down the road. When we walked out of the main entrance of the airport into the sunny afternoon, the program was set. Flying carpets were soon to be launched toward the US. The die being cast, we went into high gear. The next day, they picked up the carpets and goodies and we were to meet Mohammed at the airport.

Back at our hotel headquarters, we took stock of the whole thing after smoking a chillum. The past months were a blur: a flurry of distances traveled, flirtation with danger, serious injury or death avoided, setups, escapes, and opportunities gained and lost. We'd had adventure, fun, and excitement, and met interesting, devious, creative, and generous people. And in moments of need, humans at their best, with our Guardian Angels' guiding hands. We were still young and full of ourselves, but we realized we had gained something valuable. It was a fleeting recognition, soon going up in smoke once again. I only fully acknowledged the immense contribution of the Dots years later. They had enabled our journey and potentially saved our lives.

That big wad of afghanis shrank slowly at first as the three of us and Mohammed arrived at Kabul International Airport the next morning. We were introduced to the top dog in the airport customs facility, whom

Mohammed had previously referred to as the "Big Guy." The depletion of afghanis sped up as we progressed closer to the carpets that were ready for loading onto the Pan Am jet at the terminal. The Big Guy and a handful of assistants met us deep in the bowels of the customs area, which now conjures up present day images of Kim Jong Un of North Korea and the lapdog military officers with pen and pad ready to capture every utterance. Every one of those minions got their due, according to Mohammed's rules. The Big Guy took a sizable chunk out of the remaining wad of bills. It was a signal that we must be getting close to the end.

We walked out on the runway into the sunshine. It was surreal. It was like we had passed through another world and were now observers watching the movements of beings in a parallel reality. Our carpets were being loaded on the Pan Am aircraft, along with the passengers' luggage. The choreography of movement enthralled us, but that's not meant to invoke a vision of a ballet. We were close enough to see the colors of the bundled carpets and the familiar cartons of related goods. You could almost get a whiff of the deep musty, earthy smell of the wool and see the beauty of the craftsmanship in the weaving. It was very cool. The passengers on board at the windows must have marveled at the three hippies and one Afghan standing on the tarmac. That was before the days of frequent hijackings.

After we were certain the cargo was loaded and the hatch closed, we retreated a safe distance and watched the pre-taxi activity around the aircraft. It was a quiet few moments of reflection after being fatigued by all the effort. We were glad to see the shipment off, but a little sorry to have the experience about to end.

Mohammed watched closely as the aircraft started up and moved across the apron. We felt antsy, assuming the show had concluded, but it was obvious Mohammed was aware of another act to come. Not wanting to give a sign we were without a clue, we made some joking small talk and watched Mohammed watch the aircraft—excitement extraordinaire. We'd often been inside such a jet, not paying much heed to the same stop-and-go movements, accelerating engine noises, and then calm. It wasn't much different from outside, only noisier.

With the aircraft in position on the runway, the engines ramped up as the plane shuddered and lurched forward. It gathered speed, the nose lifted, and the plane seemed to struggle free of the runway. Show over, curtains fall, and we go home. As the three of us started off, Mohammed didn't move. He was still watching the damn thing! Had he never seen a plane take off before? We made a slightly snarky comment, but without looking away, he said "*Na*," meaning *No, wait* or *Stop*. He watched until the plane was out of sight. Then he turned and we walked back into the terminal. He had imparted a final Afghan business lesson, having uttered only that one word. And good advice: "Don't trust AND verify."

The shade of our comfortable hotel garden was welcome, as it was a hot mid-July day in Kabul. Just as hot as it would be cold in a few months. After a couple days of adjusting to a new routine without carpet buying, we turned our attention to the *Flying Wreck*. The brutal fact was, we had not come up with a viable way to sell, give away, or abandon the car that would remove the stamp from my passport. It felt like a leech draining our enthusiasm.

That evening was a music night at our hotel, and we were happy to see Brian and Mark. It'd been a while since we'd seen them, and we brought both up-to-date on the shipping of our goods to the US and our plan for Scott and me to head that way soon. Mohammed had arranged for customs storage in Cleveland, so we had some wiggle room on timing.

Some banter, and then the bit about the car stamp hit home with Brian, and he let on that he'd seen the problem before.

Brian stated abruptly, "You need to drive it to the border at Torkham and give it to one of the border officials. You'll get nowhere trying to unload it in Kabul."

Torkham is the Afghan-Pakistan crossing just before the Khyber Pass. Brian's words rang true and resonated loudly. A sense of relief spread through the atmosphere, and we thoroughly enjoyed the rest of the evening.

In the light of morning, the Torkham solution still held water. It had risk, but we were next to desperate, so we agreed. Dave, Scott, and I would all pile in the *Flying Wreck*, drive to the border, get rid of the stamp, proceed to Pakistan, and do some exploring before we returned to Afghanistan. With a bit of preparation after returning to Kabul, Scott and I would set off for the US and Dave would hang in Kabul at our little hotel.

Recognizing the risk involved leaving Kabul and putting all our effort into weaving one rug—persuading a border guard to take the car and remove the stamp—was worrisome. *What if that fails? What can possibly go wrong? Right. That carpet has too many loose threads!* So, there was one last attempt in Kabul. An epiphany of sorts.

My passport pages were nearly full of entry/exit stamps from travels. I thought that might be used as a way to get a new passport, therefore eliminating the car stamp. I went to the US embassy in Kabul and said my upcoming travel plans posed a problem—no space for visas or stamps. They were very helpful when I asked for a new passport and said they could solve the problem quickly. They added foldout blanks to one of the existing pages in my passport. The very official-looking attachment had an embossed stamp of the Seal of The Kingdom of Afghanistan, which stuck out like a sore thumb.

I was worse off than before I arrived, now with a well-used, thick passport that looked more like a thin airport novel. It was loaded with a who's who of edgy and notorious countries—a list that always prompted customs agents to ask, "Why were you there and how long did you stay?" No suitable answer existed for those types of questions. It was impossible for any duty agent—honest or not—to overlook the continually increasing stamps from illustrious groups of drug-related countries...AND the Afghan car stamp!

That sealed it. Brian was right—we were wasting time in Kabul. Out of options, we had to make Torkham work.

The *Flying Wreck* would definitely be missed, but it had served us well and provided reliable transportation across a large part of two continents. As we were picking up some travel supplies, we encountered something unusual.

Our trusty steed had no windows, and driving slowly in Kabul allowed a surround-sound effect, in that we could hear everything. We were near the royal palace and heard a loud explosion a few streets away, which was unusual, even by Kabul standards. More car horns and shouting than was customary followed.

We later learned it was a coup by the king's brethren, General Daoud Khan, and the explosion may have been a shot fired at the royal palace by a Soviet-era tank. It missed! However, getting accurate news in Afghanistan was a slow process. There were few TV sets, no internet, and Afghans were a little prone to exaggeration. It took several days to get a copy of the *International Herald Tribune*, published by the *New York Times* and *Washington Post*, which was printed in Paris, to discover something reliable.

The king was not there—he was recuperating in Italy from too much fun, or some other valid reason. The news termed it a "bloodless" coup, although the driver of the only operable tank drowned in the Kabul River when he swerved to avoid a bus.

Incompetent tank driver, or very chivalrous? Perhaps some of both.

So, our observations and instincts about something brewing were spot on. *Big deal*, we thought, even though it was obvious now that our suspicions were confirmed. Our instincts also told us it was definitely time to get moving.

The stage was set for drastic societal upheaval in Afghanistan. The winds of change would blow in a sequence of events that would culminate with the Russian invasion in 1979. The Russian faction that had supported Daoud Khan in the 1974 coup were on the ascent and, over the next couple of years, tightened the screws on Westerners in the country. In 1975, there was a mass exodus of Westerners out of Kabul, with many headed for Amsterdam. It was the end of a golden decade of travel and adventure along the Hippie Trail.

As for us, the next couple of days were unremarkable, and little seemed to change. We still planned our return to Kabul after dumping the car, and had done a bit of sightseeing in and around Peshawar.

The *Flying Wreck* would take off the next day. Destination: Pakistan... Where tea was proper English served at a civilized time in the afternoon, cars drove in the left lane, drivers in the right seat, and some of the best hashish in the world came from Chitral, right up the road from Peshawar.

Peshawar via the Khyber Pass. Map data ©2024 Google

It was only about 250 km (155 mi) of driving on a narrow, two-lane, mostly-paved road traversing a gap between mountain ranges of the Hindu Kush. The road was prone to rockslides and somewhat frequent avalanches. Inadequate rock diverters were in place to reduce the danger and the number of delays while they cleared the road manually.

The road was the lead-up to the notorious Khyber Pass, an ancient trade route of military importance. Genghis Khan led his Mongol army through the pass in the early thirteenth century, chasing the Muslim army of Jalal al-Din to the banks of the Indus River. Khan's victory had a dramatic effect on the future of the subcontinent.

We hadn't been to that border crossing before, but we were comfortable we could deal with it. We had seen the likes of others previously and hoped we could leave Afghanistan legally. But we had the car entry stamp in my passport to deal with.

It would prove a challenge.

The creation of antique carpets

Getting ready to sell

Dave behind chair, watching the bundling of carpets

Scott inspecting carpets before bundling

Kabul International Airport - 1970s

Kabul Customs - Staff, Boss, Mohammed

Interlude Five

Take A Breath

The Moody Blues: *Question* > *Lyrics*

Time for a recap.

While sorting through hundreds of travel photos for this book, in these Interludes I've reflected on and analyzed key events and influential people I encountered during my travels fifty years ago.

Through examination of those incidents, events were identified that were unexpected, amusing, and even lifesaving. I recognized a pattern of cause and effect in those situations, but puzzled over the apparent repetition of luck and chance. I wondered how Guardian Angels could be so readily available to save the day. I couldn't dismiss the connections between frequent providential events and the mysterious arrival of a pivotal person as luck or coincidence.

Taken as a whole, the photos told a story of an unwitting guy who benefited from a series of remarkable events over a lot of years, protected from himself and others by busy Guardian Angels. From that viewpoint, I concluded that there must be a profound explanation that involves a correlation between one's feelings and significant individuals or locations. Those feelings include intuition, instinctive behavior, gut feelings—you know, the ones that you usually dismiss out of hand, often to your detriment. I surmised an unidentified force that operates over time and distance conveyed those feelings. Frankly, it was a stab in the dark, with no evidence to back it up. Pretty thin hunch to go on, but what the hell? I had a story to tell, and that was a big part of it.

I needed an identifier, a catchword, or phrase to focus my thoughts as my mind wandered over the places and events depicted in those photos. Explicitly, I needed a single word that would instantaneously and effortlessly embody the essence of my fledgling theory. I was looking for the unifier, the aspect in my life, and perhaps yours, that facilitated my serendipitous travel and connected it to events and people I encountered.

The word that conveyed the importance, if not miraculous quality, of those occurrences was *Dots*. I was *Connecting the Dots*.

Dots are important characters in this book. At critical times and places, they appeared as strange, convenient, fortuitous, redeeming, and protective embodiments. In Chapter 2, "spooky" James comes and goes. It's a strange event on its own, but it also sets the stage for Jack to materialize, launching my introduction to Europe—one of the defining events in my life. At the base of the Matterhorn Mountain in Switzerland, I met Scott, fomenting our trip to North Africa and back to Europe. As I reflected, the Dots continued to manifest and the connections between them were evident. This leads to the obvious question of, "How does that work? What triggers the connection, and how is it conveyed?"

Everyone is aware of intuition, instinctual behavior, Guardian Angels, gut feelings, and the familiar aphorisms that mention these circumstances. I posit they are the causality initiators we bundle together in a repository labeled *Dot Matrix*. In spite of the recognized value of intuition and instincts, they are often dismissed as frivolous and unworthy of attention. It's commonly accepted that dismissal does not eliminate them from existence, or obstruct their impact on human behavior. The Dot Matrix also includes karma. I posit that karma is the heretofore unidentified force that conveys the behavioral feelings and emotions that connect Dots at a precise time and place.

"Connecting the Dots" is a tagline for this book, and you can expect to hear more about it in future books. The Theory of Dots is presented as the explanation for how Dots are connected to each other. It also addresses the unexpected, and at times fortuitous, happenings that most of us have experienced. I believe the rationale for seeking such a theory is readily apparent, but establishing its veracity is challenging. In fact, many scientists, including the late Stephen Hawking, say that a theory never becomes a fact.

The Interludes pose interesting and controversial questions to explain my developing theory. I put potential avenues of explanation forward, and recognize philosophical implications and origins. The narrative uses statements and concepts as sticks that bang on the hornets' nest of oft-avoided subject matter in need of greater understanding, such as gut feelings, Guardian Angels, and good and bad vibes.

The story puts the spotlight on questions—the driving force in humanity. And I state my opinion that they are more important than answers.

I was a traveler in search of questions. Asking "How come?" would be the door opener to a wealth of experience and a fair share of near misses. But more to the point of this book, they put me in contact with a lot of Dots.

Which in turn generated questions about Dots...

- How come that gentleman stopped and helped us in the Kandahar desert?

- How come we were uninjured in such a nasty accident?

- How come Dots appeared often in our travels?

- How and where do I look for clues to explain these significant events and occurrences?

- Can I quantify them and extrapolate to include most other humans?

A Dot Matrix is a reservoir for venerated human emotions and sentiments often expressed in maxims such as:

- Guardian Angels appear at opportune times

- We can get good or bad vibes about a person or situation

- Coincidences don't just happen

- You have intuitions toward decision-making

- A person makes their own luck

- You rely on your instincts in unfamiliar situations

- And a biggie—in one form or another: Your karma conveys favorable or unfavorable results in your life, now and in the future

And two related observations:

- Karma seems to hang around and influence all the other members of a Dot Matrix, as if there's a network connecting everything

- The appearance of a Dot often coincides with the probability of a change in one's life

At the time of the events in this book, karma was a popular reference by my peers—some might say hippies, space cadets, and/or spiritualists. I doubt if most knew the origins or the defining features of karma in its traditional sense: "In its essence, karma refers to both the actions and the consequences of the actions. Karma is an action, not a result. It does not set the future in stone. You can change the course of your life right now by changing your volitional (intentional) acts and self-destructive patterns."[32]

I believe karma plays an important part in understanding the workings of Dots. The Theory of Dots relies on science to help us understand how Dot Matrix elements are linked and explore networks in relation to the theory. A bit of history, philosophy, and metaphysics will also contribute.

The theory explores networks, which provide a fast and effective solution for distributing nutrients, information, essential processes, and emergency aid. Late to the game, humans replicated natural networks when they and society developed enough to require them. The Interludes consider networks at the macro, or even micro, level, and then scale up to galactic proportions where they cozy up to dark matter. Despite being unable to detect dark matter directly, researchers speculate that it constitutes a huge amount of the matter in the universe. It's called *dark matter*, and/or *dark energy*, because its composition is still unknown. However, scientists believe a network structure exists in dark matter. The scale is so immense that it's hard to wrap your mind, or at least mine, around the distances involved. The connection of karma and Dots also requires the exploration of the smallest dimensions in science through the lens of quantum physics.

I compare a Dot to a particle in a quantum theory waveform. Waveforms function within the fabric of spacetime, and I posit that a reference made by Albert Einstein about strange activity over vast distances applies to our considerations. The unexplained existence and composition of dark matter in the network's spacetime gives my theory license to suggest a substitution of the definition and function of *karma* for the term *dark matter*.

The *Flying Wreck* comfortably hosted Scott, Dave and I. Fortunately, it was also spacious in metaphorical terms. We had the full Dot Matrix complement on board led by karma. Intuition was the quiet type, but not hesitant to speak up when appropriate. Instinctual Behavior had an attitude, shoving to the front without warning. Gut Feelings always had something to say but had enough life experiences to not be pushy. "I told you so," was a favorite phrase of the twins, good & bad vibes. Lady Luck and coincidence would show off their multilingual skills by speaking in the local language.

Soon after departure adventure and danger jumped on board with destiny tagging along.

Destiny had an authoritative air about itself, was quick to express opinions, and had an uncanny ability to predict the road ahead. Without any human input the passenger consensus was destiny rides shotgun, but karma is behind the wheel.

It was a little crowded inside the car, so our Guardian Angels flew outside, guarding us in front, behind, and along our flanks.

We would need their intervention frequently...and soon!

Back to the story.

Chapter Thirteen

Flying Wreck, Flying Bullets

Rolling Stones: *Gimme Shelter > Lyrics*

"Holy shit! Look at this! You won't believe it!" Scott was pulling himself out of the passenger side of the *Flying Wreck*, holding something in his hand. We were preparing what was left of the car for the drive from Kabul to Torkham to hopefully eliminate the passport stamp problem. He was shaking his head with a strange look on his face. Dave and I walked over to him to look at whatever had him wound up.

A German car came with a green registration booklet. It stayed in the glove box and was required to be included in a sale. It and the license plates, title, and registration papers all went with the automobile when sold. In our case, we were not German, and the car had international plates, but the ownership lineage was in the green book. Scott was looking at a page showing the prior owner. It jumped out like a barking dog. And the bark was THIS IS YOUR KARMA. It took a moment for the info on the page to sink in, then it hit. We all recognized the previous owner's name: Autovermietung Schultz GmbH. It brought a strained bit of chuckling from each of us.

That was Schultz, the car rental agency in Frankfurt that we rented the VW Bug from and preceded to abuse in so many ways. The laughter became muted and nervous now. It was the automobile we rented to find a suitable car to purchase for the drive East. We drove it hard on the road and then in a careless act, off the road. We plowed through a muddy field, damaged the front bumper, trashed the inside, left it filthy dirty and the fuel tank empty. A shameful act that we were being repaid for. Karma writ large! We deserved the payback.

The odds were off the chart against us buying a VW sedan in Frankfurt from a random used-car lot and have the previous owner be Schultz of VW Bug fame. There was poetic justice in us crashing our Schultz VW sedan in the Afghan desert. But there was a deeper connection found in the beneficial knock-on effect of the car accident. The crash in the Kandahar desert and the arrival of the Afghan merchant to rescue us from the hostile nomadic tribe was a powerful experience. It was a wake-up call and a reminder that there is no free lunch. Unacceptable behavior creates a negative space that will be filled with the same that you created, fitting within the Theory of Dots interpretation of karma. The crash had a sobering effect, and we interpreted it as a cautionary message. We duly noted it, and our mood reflected it.

Additionally, the chaos that was the serious accident in the remote desert was the catalyst for positive knock-on effects in Kabul. The desert accident ended any further travel aspirations by automobile. Our carpet program was born from that reality. That cascaded into a string of fortunate connections between people and events, resulting in incredible experiences.

Our pending departure from Kabul would have implications for our future, and we needed to go with eyes wide open. We'd been really—really lucky!—so far, and didn't want to screw that up. We were a little ashamed of our prior behavior, but we were also young, so we gave little thought to that. The discovery of the green book in the glove box and the events before and after the accident was drama enough. We needed no rehashing of those events to get the point.

It was time to hit the road again, a little more respectful with some added worldliness. We appreciated those last few chillums, as we had to leave it and the rest of our hash with Boy, a self-named "employee," at the hotel. Leaving Afghanistan with hash was far less tolerated than when entering. A thought for those Swiss guys at the border in Herat came to mind.

We would also leave our Sony portable cassette player at the hotel due to the *Flying Wreck*'s open-air cockpit, causing wind noise and buffeting that made it unusable. A scarf and goggles would have been appropriate, but sunglasses were all we had.

The flight plan for the *Flying Wreck* called for a drive out of Kabul through Jalalabad and landing at the Torkham border crossing with Pakistan. The twisty, narrow road did its best to mirror the Kabul River as it flowed east of its Hindu Kush origins into the Indus River in Pakistan. Water had been only one of several irritations between the geographical neighbors for ages. Tribal affiliation, political conflicts, and relations with India were a constant source of bickering. There was no love lost between the governments of Afghanistan and Pakistan, and we weren't sure how it might affect us and the car stamp situation.

The departure from Kabul was abrupt, as very little preparation was required. We got an early start, filled the tank in Kabul, but didn't wash the windshield, as it had long ago been abandoned. There wasn't much in the way of stuff. We lost or left behind large chunks of it along the way to Afghanistan. We smoothly adapted to traveling with less.

Once again, we blasted out on to the highway and adventure headed our way, but with no music. Improvise! Scott drummed the steering wheel. The first words of the Steppenwolf classic *Born to Be Wild* lurched out of his mouth, and Dave and I joined in. We sang the song and heard it in our head, just like Steppenwolf played it. It felt free, fun, and fantastic. It was a perfect match for our state of mind and helped us momentarily forget about the border. We sounded absolutely terrible, if truth be told. The sound of the wind was perfect for those moments, then it dissolved into a droning background noise.

As sudden stopping was frequent, all the roads required the full attention of the driver. Rockslides were not uncommon and seemed to happen right after a tight curve where the road narrowed further. The Afghan government constructed partial landslide diversions, like an eave over a window, attached tenuously to the side of the mountain. If lucky, it would divert the rocks to just over the outside edge of the road and, with further luck, into the river. It didn't look like luck smiled on that road with any frequency. As a bonus, it kept our speed low, which was a blessing; the wind buffeting at speeds over 100 kph (62 mph) was intolerable for anything but short lengths of time.

From Kabul to Jalalabad, we traversed the hilly expanse of the gap between the Hindu Kush mountains, the adjacent range to the Himalayas. These were serious mountains in rugged lands that have done in countless travelers and invaders for centuries. Intrigue, tribal conflicts, and conquering despots all rolled through Afghanistan, and more often than not, got their asses kicked and moved on. They had employed various conveyances, including horses, elephants, camels, and donkeys—we had the *Flying Wreck*. We were chewing up kilometers until we didn't, being forced to halt at a landslide, and a doozy. We got out and gawked like the other motorists. There was nothing to do but wait for the poor bastards who had to manually shove the boulders over the edge into the river. Then they cleared the remaining rubble rather quickly.

When we arrived in Jalalabad, it was still early in the day. The town was a transition in the geography and in the people. It was the last substantial town in Afghanistan before the border with Pakistan. The hills turned into mountains, and it had the feel of a place where the rules changed. A place where the law was less defined, where ruthless power held sway in long-standing ways. And tribal affiliations were above all else, which was a stark difference to Kabul and the cohesive and tolerant city way of life.

In Jalalabad, the smell of charcoal, animal sweat, and feces permeated the air. The familiar human clamor—vehicle horns honking, unmuffled engines, and diesel smoke—enveloped us. The underlying cacophony of human endeavors was prominent and undeniable. It was Afghanistan, indelibly etching its memory into the departing visitors' psyche.

We had settled into life in Afghanistan during the preceding months and become comfortable in what was a stark reality compared to Amsterdam. It was a superficial comfort; our appearance, not speaking the language(s), and not Muslim were all a filter preventing a deep understanding of the people and culture. We reached a personal comfort level largely based on a sincere desire to learn, and therefore felt a kinship with the Afghanis. Our arrival in Jalalabad was a reminder of what we were leaving and elevated our impending confrontation at the border to alert status. We were getting close to leaving the familiar and entering the unknown of Pakistan. A chillum was in order, but that would have to wait.

After Jalalabad, the road was much the same—a narrow two-lane road with no shoulder. Stone fortresses invoking images of the Great

Game, the Silk Road, and passing invaders loomed in the distance. The mountains of the Hindu Kush edged closer to the road, and the river moved faster as it narrowed. We had been wind-beaten for most of the drive and welcomed our arrival at Torkham about midday. No, that's not wholly correct. We were indeed tired of the constant wind in the cockpit of the *Flying Wreck,* but did not look forward to what awaited us at the border.

It was show time! We had done this before at border crossings—playing the part of enthusiastic travelers eager and pumped to enter the country (or leave it). Innocent, and to the casual observer, naïve—what harm or danger could we conceivably be? And we had the unique and intriguing prop of the *Flying Wreck*! All we had to do was act naturally and start taking photographs. Photos were our go-to diversion—nearly everyone enjoys having their picture taken, even border guards, soldiers, or authority figures. Music always added to the overall effect, and the absence of our Sony player was lamented. But the show must go on, and we improvised where needed.

In our favor was the recent coup d'état overthrowing the king in Afghanistan. The level of distrust and outright animosity between Afghanistan and Pakistan governments had ratcheted up. Not between the people—their tribal affiliations took precedent. In theory, the border personnel were supposed to be on higher alert, but that was via government edicts and held little sway here. The *Flying Wreck* and crew acted out a scene on the ground in our little theatre. We were a hit, or at least we eased our way into the sphere of nonthreatening tourists. The customs staff culled automobile traffic from the trucks and buses and directed us to a less chaotic zone. The lower rung workers frequented the usual outbuildings, leaving the officials sequestered in the not-so-much better "offices."

It was a bright sunny day in late summer, and people were in a favorable mood. There was nothing in the air to acknowledge the recent coup in Afghanistan; it was business as usual, as far as we could tell. Our theatrical activities were popular, and the interest was moving up the food chain. We kept moving toward the final border crossing, entertaining fellow travelers and customs people with our little show... Until someone with authority took notice.

Our first potential client appeared, walking out into the sunshine while putting his official cap on his head to shield his eyes. We watched him approach, observing his body language. He wore the makings of a uniform: his shirt was a bit too large, tucked into his pants with a too-long belt cinching the pants in place. The epaulettes on his shoulders were askew and worse for wear. He was tall and skinny (the higher-ups usually were more well fed), with a day or two of stubble beard. He asserted his authority by addressing us in English. We had him pegged as a long-suffering public servant who had been stuck in this position and would be until they used him in some other capacity. So we had to humor him and work our way up to his boss.

"You have a need for my services?"

Not knowing what he had heard from his spies everywhere, we responded, "We ran into a minor problem back in Kandahar, and our car took a beating. What's your name?"

He introduced himself as Officer Ali of the Customs Service. "You may call me Abdul." Abdul stood as straight as a ramrod, projecting a formality that was the direct opposite of our performance routine. We scaled it back a bit but hung on to the informality that he would have been familiar with from Westerners.

"Our car obviously has some damage, but it runs as well as before the accident. We drove from Kandahar to here with no problems." We knew the real value of our car was multifaceted, with international license plates, the German green book registrations, and the vehicle chassis and engine. With those ingredients, an experienced car importer could make good money. We were certain Abdul recognized that, and absolutely, his boss. And that's who we needed to get to.

"We'll make a very good price for you, but we need to remove the stamp on my passport as part of any deal," Scott added. Abdul replied, "Your car has many damages and the value is small. To remove the stamp requires special things that only Immigration Services can provide. For these things to happen will be difficult."

With a bit more posturing and 1,000 afghanis later, we finessed the introduction to Immigration Services. Our car was now parked within sight of the weighted crossbar that separated Afghanistan customs from the "no-man's-land" near Pakistan's border—the same type of crossbar we had blasted through after leaving the Afghan border in Herat. The three of us were standing about 50 m (164 ft) from the guard operating the crossbar for pedestrians, and considered the open distance from it to Pakistan. It wasn't far. We judged the no-man's-land to be about 200 m (656 ft) wide, but it would be a vast distance if armed customs agents were in pursuit. We grabbed our few belongings, including the green book from the glovebox, and a uniformed agent directed us to a nearby building.

Mr. Immigration Man received us in his office, holding court in a tattered chair behind a metal desk in a dimly lit space. An offer of a seat in one of the several upturned wooden boxes lingered, but we weren't going to just stand there, so we seated ourselves. A breach of etiquette on both sides.

"Gentlemen, I understand you have a serious problem. My name is Ahmad, Immigration Commissioner for the Republic of Afghanistan. Perhaps I can be of service."

Show over, we were at the curtain call. Stating we had a serious problem needed no interpretation. He clearly understood that we had zero bargaining power.

"You know it is illegal to sell or dispose of your car, no? Then you must understand for me to assist you, I have a big problem myself."

We correctly assumed he would confide his solution to us.

"However, if you were to offer your automobile to the republic with me as the agent, I may be able to solve your passport stamp problem. But, there are several penalties and fees involved to our esteemed republic in even such a generous offer."

We were hours into this drama and ready to move on. Since it was my passport involved, I offered, "If we were to agree to accept your help, how would we proceed, and what is the approximate cost of the fees and penalties?"

Mr. Immigration Man leaned back in his chair and laced his fingers together over his bulging stomach. With only a moment or two of exaggerated thought and a sigh, he replied, "I'm not the only one that must agree. My superior will need to agree as well. I believe the required amount, in addition to a properly granted release for the automobile, will be 7,500 afghanis."

We were relieved that the republic was still accepting the previous kingdom's currency for government activities. The Republic of Afghanistan's services amounted to a little over US$100.

All three of us shifted around, looking as uncomfortable as we thought was useful, and some of what we actually felt.

"That's a lot of money for us to pay, as you must understand." We'd done a lot of bargaining while in Afghanistan and knew when we'd reached the end. And we couldn't bluff and walk away, waiting for the shopkeeper to call us back. "You have a deal."

We were soon to find out that we didn't.

"Very well, gentlemen. Bring the automobile papers and your belongings and follow me."

With a glance between us, we let out a silent collective sigh of relief, which retained an element of suspicion, and prepared to walk out of the office back into the sunlight and semi-chaos of the Afghan border crossing in Torkham, only meters from our freedom and release from the bloody car stamp. Looking around as we neared the door, the smells, sounds, and flow of humans seemed a bit like a dream. Maybe the release of the built-up tension created a collage of déjà vu and a compression of experiences that were expressed at the moment. We shook it off and we were back in the moment, presumably being escorted to Mr. Big's office to relieve ourselves of the car papers, afghanis, and hopefully the *Flying Wreck*. Ahmad, Immigration Commissioner for the Republic of Afghanistan, rose from his desk and then paused, as if he forgot something. "I will need your passports, key, and of course, the correct amount of afghanis. You may put the afghanis inside the car papers and leave the car where it is."

Accompanied by Ahmad, aka Mr. Immigration Man (MIM), we proceeded to the crowded little office, where hordes of pedestrians awaited the attention of customs officials. We had apparently circumvented Mr. Big Immigration Man. Strange, we thought, but the sooner we got past this point and on our way to Pakistan, the better.

As we entered with MIM, it was apparent that we were worthy of a private appointment in the small processing shack. Only one immigration officer was behind the counter, and he immediately moved aside for MIM, who requested our passports, car papers, and car key. He laid our passports on the counter, picked up the exit stamp, turned to the page in each of our passports that contained the Afghanistan entry visa (mine had the car entry version) and went *whomp!* (on the ink pad), *whomp!* (on the page with the exit stamp). He did the same for my passport. I thought the car stamp would require something additional, but it was what it was.

"Gentlemen, have a pleasant journey."

The primordial human instinct of flight kicked in: Our feet started moving before the rest of our brain processed the information. We indeed wanted that pleasant journey, and for it to start now! We collected ourselves and our stuff and walked out into the sunshine once again.

An appreciative glance at the *Flying Wreck* had to suffice as we headed toward the frontier. A guard with his rifle slung over his shoulder hefted the handle on the weighted crossbar and lifted it into the air as a final salute as we approached. We walked past and into the no-man's-land that separated the two countries.

So much had transpired in recent months. The map of Europe and Asia spread out on the floor in Amsterdam revealed that the distance from Frankfurt to Kabul was approximately 7,500 km (4,660 mi). Coincidentally, the fee for us to leave Afghanistan was 7,500 afghanis—one for each kilometer to get there. The drive through Europe held the anticipation of a journey and associated adventure. It had been fun and a valuable experience. We couldn't forget the stark contrast between Western European countries, with social and political freedom, and Eastern European countries, without it.

· · · · ● ●· ● · ● · · ·

The walk in no-man's-land provided a few moments of reflection. Our automobile, which we had selected at random and bought from a used-car lot near the Frankfurt Airport so many months ago, became the *Flying Wreck* after our karma returned to us in the desert between Kandahar and Kabul. In the middle of the Desert of Death,[33] a Guardian Angel materialized that may have saved our lives, and certainly saved us from a very dangerous situation. Only later did I identify the merchant as a Dot. "What were the odds?" of the Afghan and two servants arriving at the scene of our accident in the remote stretches of a desert at precisely the time needed to save the necks of three passing Westerners?

And five decades later, I considered another aspect of the accidents. Scott, Dave, and I were participants in both events: abusing the Schultz rental car in Frankfurt and the car accident in the Desert of Death. Karma was involved in both scenarios. Was the intervention of the Dot causality equally shared by the three of us, or primarily one or the other? Was a previous Dot in my life, or was Scott or Dave an element? Can a Dot's influence in a specific time period embrace others who are involved?

• • • ● • ● • ● • • •

A sudden change in the atmosphere interrupted our brief moments of reflection. Other pedestrians became anxious with commotion, and we heard the shout of "STOP!" We weren't sure who or what was supposed to stop, but odds were high it involved us.

We turned and saw a flurry of activity from the guard who had lifted the crossbar. As we were no longer in the mood for further negotiations or discussion, we bolted. We ran as fast as we could toward Pakistan. We heard one shot, followed by two more. If you think about those old cartoons I mentioned before, you'll be familiar with the Roadrunner and the flash and ball of smoke where he had been. In that ball of smoke, you could see the Roadrunner's legs in an insanely revolving circle of running. That's how I perceived the jolt of speed as we lowered our heads and ran like hell. We chewed up the distance in no-man's-land like a flash and the crossbar on the Pakistani side lifted in greeting as we approached. That was reassuring, but still pumped with adrenaline, it was an effort to scale back and prepare mentally for what kind of reception we were about to receive. To our great relief and surprise, the Pakistani guards met us with laughter.

We slowed down to a walking pace and realized we were still alive, which made us feel grateful. It was clear we had provided some entertainment along the way. We hadn't humored ourselves, however. Did they shoot at us and miss? It wasn't likely, because the Pakistani border guards were directly in the line of fire, and it would have ignited an international incident between two countries that were itching for a fight. The obvious answer was they shot over our heads. OK, if that was correct, what did the Pakistanis intend to do? Send us back?

Nope, they watched the scene unfold and were happy to receive us. Anybody that got one over on the Afghans was all right with them. We had to explain what transpired to one of the Pakistani border officials, and he got a chuckle out of it. Out came our passports and *whomp!* on the ink pad and *whomp!* on the passport page. It's always the same at frontiers.

As the adrenaline waned, we laughed too. Our exit from Afghanistan was on much the same terms as we had entered it. Our book wasn't closed on Afghanistan, though; we only finished a chapter. We'd return soon to continue the story. The appreciation and attachment to the country, its history, and the people stirred our determination. In fact, we already missed it in a lot of ways. We were fortunate to have formed an attachment to a region of the world that was fascinating and deeply complex.

Scarcely having crossed into Pakistan, it had a unique feeling and different appearance. But scratch the veneer and the differences were superficial. We were still in the tribal area of the Pashtun, which encompassed a large swath of the Hindu Kush that knows no political borders. The British Empire had left a lasting mark on daily life, language, and government. The comparatively well-dressed border officials, the English accent, and traffic—foot and vehicle on the left side of the road—made it apparent! We knew from experience that driving was easier than walking, as you must pay closer attention behind the wheel. A pedestrian must be alert—a vehicle horn will blare when you try to cross the street without looking in the correct direction! It's also well understood that using your horn frequently while driving is prudent and expected in Pakistan. I doubt a Pakistani car will start if the horn doesn't function correctly. It is an essential element of driving.

In August 1947, Britain granted India independence and then divided the territory it had ruled over into India and the new state of Pakistan (with East Pakistan later becoming Bangladesh). This created a massive upsurge of violence, in which 15 million people were displaced and an estimated one million died. India and Pakistan have remained rivals ever since.[34]

The legendary Khyber Pass awaited us, only a few kilometers outside of Torkham. It had played a crucial role in developing trade between the East and West for thousands of years. The Hindu Kush mountains are the "shoulders" of the Himalayas. Rugged and treacherous, they have stood in the way of travelers, traders, and invaders for eons. In our time, hippies frequented it. The Khyber Pass developed from a footpath and animal trail to a twisting and narrow vehicular road. Travelers used it to avoid danger, traders to trade, invaders to pillage, and hippies to seek nirvana in India or Nepal.

Landi Kotal was a tribal-controlled area located at the halfway point of the Khyber Pass, known for its illicit trading and weapons.

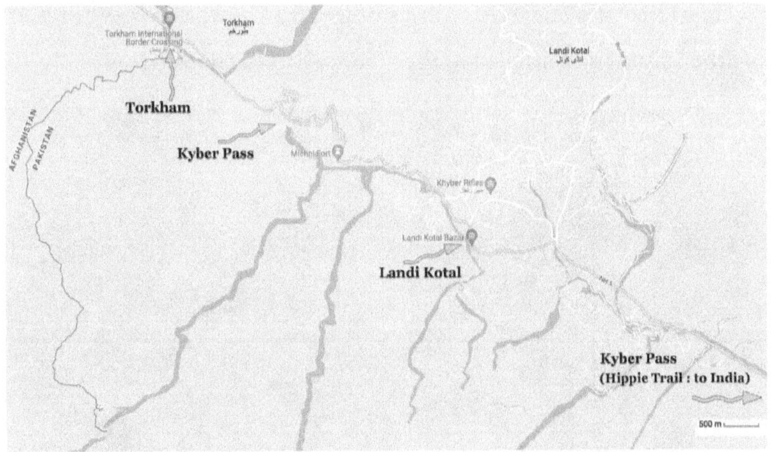

Part of Hippie Trail to India. Map data ©2024 Google

And, of course, Landi Kotal was our immediate destination.

To get there, we had to arrange transportation. The immediate zone after clearing customs was a chaotic area of commerce and cultural diversity. Afghan over-the-road trucks, commonly called *lorries*, were nose to tail in a long, winding queue waiting to traverse the pass. Most had traditionally colorful paintings on the sides, and bright and flashy chrome accents. The Pakistanis had similar lorries with equally proud drivers coming through from the opposite direction. Although different vehicle manufacturers, the same belching diesel smoke was choking the air. Dust, noise, blaring horns, charcoal smoke, and the chatter of bargaining for everything was quite familiar.

Although the Pashto tribe predominated, a variety of other tribes were present—not to overlook the international tribal affiliation of travelers.

Taxis had their own area. I use "taxi" to describe moving objects that were once easily identifiable as a particular model and brand of an automobile. In their current condition, one had to inspect the alleged vehicle to find the origins of it. In the beginning, such a vehicle had a standard feature known as a *seat*—a specific place for humans to sit.

Most also came standard with a storage area known as a *trunk* or *boot*. Neither distinction applied to the taxis we had to choose from.

Waiting for a few more fares to fill up the taxi

Those taxis departing from Torkham for Peshawar held (inside and outside) too many people to count. However, I got a photo of a taxi during the loading process. How many fares can you count in the photo above?

Uh, no thanks. We started rooting around for a somewhat more comfortable form of conveyance. Wandering through the busy area and taking in the scene was interesting and bordered on fun. However, we wanted to get to Landi Kotal with enough time to check it out, move on, and clear the Khyber Pass before sunset. Our luck held when a decent-condition Vauxhall sedan with a driver—on the right side—came into view. It appeared to be a Pakistani car looking for a fare to go back home. We flagged him down and confirmed our suspicion. He would take us to Peshawar for a fee that we found agreeable. We told him we wanted to check out Landi Kotal, and he was good with that. In fact, he was familiar with the area. The only caveat was that we needed to get to Peshawar before dark. We agreed and off we went.

We hurtled through the Khyber Pass, passing two cars at a time and coming dangerously close to infinity, which was just over the edge of the road. The sound of his horn blaring off the mountainside to the left of the car rose and fell as we narrowly missed the oncoming cars by jinking to the right—toward infinity. Ahmed took it all in stride, comforting us with a translated Pashto phrase into his Pakistani English: "It's in God's hands." His horn blaring prevented a response from us. We made it to Landi Kotal—alive and without having unintentionally relieved ourselves in his car.

There was a hint of menace in the air, stirred by a raft of people who could be mistaken for a den of thieves having a deadly weapons convention in the middle of a desert. The local saying, "*Topak zaman qanoon dae*" (My weapon is my law), ruled. Landi Kotal was very cool, as long as we stuck together. Ahmed warned us not to wander too far, but we thought it was probably overkill. Or maybe not. The guns appeared to be authentic—at least those the local citizenry carried, although the area had a reputation for manufacturing knock-off weaponry. Need a sniper rifle? British Lee-Enfield rifles were in abundance. Automatic weapons? Russian, Eastern European, or Western? Handguns, ammunition, and most likely more advanced and dangerous weapons were available—we didn't ask.

Ahmed sensed our hunger—for food, not guns—and rustled up some fruit, a rice dish, and water that he assured us was safe to eat and drink. We didn't realize how much we needed that—maybe because we had been too close to death on the drive there to notice.

There were other attractions in Landi Kotal besides the military sort. The bazaars sold most anything—the things you could get in Kabul, only cheaper. We quickly lost interest and headed for the car. Ahmed was delighted and probably relieved. We were back on the fast track for Peshawar.

Landi Kotal was the halfway point and the summit of the pass, so it was all downhill from here. That there were fewer switchbacks, blind corners, and death trap passes only meant Ahmed could drive faster. And he did so with relish.

He was a damn skillful driver. It was the mechanical condition of his car that was an unknown. Based on watching him wrestle the steering wheel and matching it to the car's movement and the adequate braking response, we assumed it must be in excellent condition and well maintained—opposed to the poor condition of most Afghan cars.

We had soon descended onto the plains of Peshawar on a comparatively straight stretch of road. Ahmed took that as an invitation to relax. He crossed his left leg over his right leg and incessantly jiggled his left foot. His right hand held prayer beads, which he fingered in a repetitive movement, continually caressing them. That comfortable situation allowed him to pass three or more cars at a shot. There wasn't a car, lorry, or curve that was beyond his perceived ability to reach Peshawar without further delay. It was a near religious experience to witness the frequent close calls with oncoming traffic. Situations like that are best endured by having previously smoked a chillum. It was fascinating to see how close he came to the edge of the road without putting a wheel over—time after time. There were lots of "Holy shit!" and fingers pointing that out.

Dave showed his appreciation by his shit-eating grin and a grunt here and there.

Our arrival in Peshawar, alive and in one piece, was a miracle. It was also an opening for Ahmed to offer further service by suggesting a hotel to us. There isn't a taxi driver worth his salt in any country that doesn't have a brother, cousin, uncle, or friend who is a local expert with insider knowledge of anything related to a visitor's needs, and at a much cheaper price. Hotels are at the top of that list.

We cut him short. "Take us to the InterContinental Hotel."

Ahmed responded, "That would be the Khyber InterContinental, one of our finest."

"That will do just fine," from me, which ended the matter.

We arrived at the entrance in a more appropriate style than at the previous InterContinental in Kabul, but a collective smile gave homage to the *Flying Wreck*.

We'd grown quite fond of Ahmed. He'd proven his mettle on the drive and handled himself well at Landi Kotal. He wasn't obtrusive or overbearing, and seemed to have good common sense. Let's agree that Dots have personalities. Ahmed's Dot would be a wise, benevolent, and experienced rascal. It's meant as a compliment. As we were giving our thanks and appreciation, we paid the fare and gave him a generous tip. We also informed him we wanted to travel north to Chitral. Chitral was a long day's drive, as we figured.

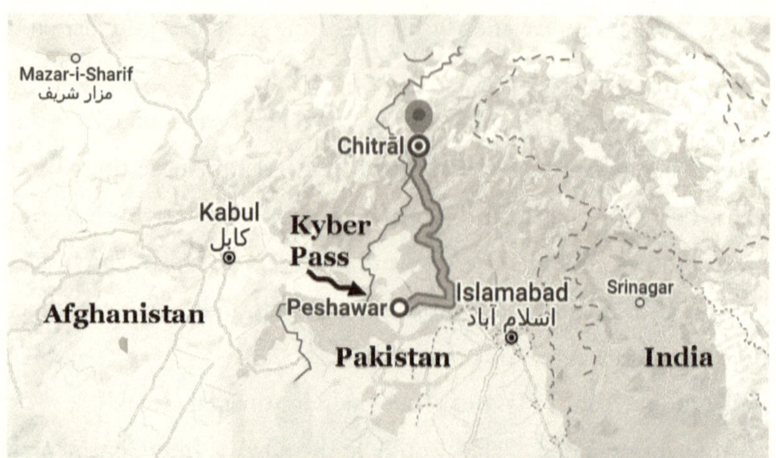

Chitral, north of Peshawar. Map data ©2024 Google

"That is a very long drive, and it is in a troubled area at the moment," he replied with a concerned look on his face. "It is beautiful, and is also a destination for hashish. What is the purpose of your visit?"

"Only as tourists" was our mostly sincere reply.

Ahmed smiled. "For tourism, there are closer places to visit, as there are for those interested in hashish."

We too smiled. "We want to rest here for a couple of days. Then we want to visit both destinations with you."

Ahmed spoke to the bellman, shook our hands, and said, "When you are ready for me, this gentleman will let me know."

Rock slide blocks road near Jalalabad

Khyber Pass after Landi Kotal

Flying Wreck at Torkham border crossing

Through Khyber Pass, Hindu Kush in background

Interlude Six

High Fidelity

Led Zeppelin: *Kashmir* > *Lyrics*

It's often said that the universe makes things happen, wills it, or puts one in the right place at the right time. Not exactly fatalism or destiny, but an external force that initiates or directs events and timing to a desirable outcome. Some people would also say they have a sense of relief by sharing responsibility with something that is beyond their control. A similar allowance for intuitive or instinctive behavior playing a part in decision-making is generally understood. However, people also have a habit of ignoring their intuitions. Seeking a connection between decisions one makes, and the result, is baseline human.

The previous Interludes reached the conclusion that nature's most efficient way to exchange most anything is by a network. For human conscious mental reactions, the neural network of our brains exchanges that information. The Theory of Dots posits that those instinctive human feelings, often dismissed in everyday life, have deeper meaning and a networked connection to the physical world.

The events of this book would not have transpired as they did without the many circumstances occurring in the precisely described timing and sequence. But more than that, it was the extent of the interactions and the depth of the connection between me (us) and the Dot(s) that was extraordinary—the *fidelity* of the connection. To quantify, I use the Afghan desert car accident as a benchmark. If the connection has low fidelity, a motorist who happens upon the accident scene will pull over to the side of the road to ask if any help is needed. Noting the tense situation—debris strewn about, shouting, and children crying—after a quick look around, they quickly decide that no one is severely injured. They return to their car and drive off. A low fidelity connection is purely on the level of luck or coincidence.

High fidelity is a higher level and type of connection achieved by a karmic resolution involving at least two Dots. Said Afghan merchant arrives at the scene moments after the accident. He has two capable persons who leap out of his car and start sorting out the car and collecting the salvageable debris. The merchant diverts the angry crowd away from Scott, Dave, and me, addresses their grievances, and takes money out of his pocket and pays a woman holding a crying child. His men have hobbled our car together enough for departure and the merchant hustles us back into the car, informing us we are in grave danger and must leave without delay. We do, and never see him again. A high fidelity connection is much deeper than luck or coincidence.

But fidelity also has a place within the description of luck and coincidence. For example, there's a distinction between luck and a Guardian Angel in everyday vernacular: "You were lucky your Guardian Angel was there." Luck played a secondary role in the favorable outcome resulting from the Guardian Angels' intervention. Luck is a result brought only by chance. That leaves out intuition, or instinctive decision-making. Unquestionably low fidelity. However, coincidence has a bit more influence—it's something that's not planned or arranged but appears that way. A coincidence is often two things concurrently; therefore, there could be exterior forces involved. There's more room in the Theory of Dots for coincidence than luck, BUT not enough for coincidence to rate high fidelity.

High fidelity is a term familiar to Baby Boomers. In the early days of 33⅓ LP music records—"albums" in the common vernacular—were only available in "mono" sound format (uses just one channel out of both speakers). The big deal was when "stereo" became available (uses two channels: a left and a right). In the interim period was high fidelity, which replayed at an advanced level of recording accuracy. Therefore, it sounded significantly better.

High fidelity hits all the high notes and nuances of intuition, instinctive behavior, intentionality, gut feelings—the whole Dot Matrix pond. Karma is the groove in the record that transmits the essence of the music with high fidelity. There's a symmetry between music and fidelity that will be identified when quantum mechanics is considered in the next Interlude.

Scott, Dave, and I had driven over 5,000 km (3,106 mi) from Frankfurt to the desolate spot in the desert just past Kandahar. For us, high fidelity from chillums was our usual state of mind. The few days leading up to our dreadful case of dysentery before the car wreck had curtailed our intake of hash, so that was not a cause of our accident. The Afghan merchant was driving in the opposite direction, presumably from Kabul, about 500 km (311 mi) behind him. He appeared moments after our accident—the wheels of our overturned car were still slowly rotating. The timing of his arrival couldn't have been more perfect. I vigorously refuse to accept that luck or coincidence will suffice as an explanation. Nor would they adequately explain the other fortuitous occurrences along our journey.

My consideration of more satisfying explanations, albeit more complicated, forces these Interludes into physics and the theories of quantum mechanics.

Several current interpretations exist to explain the behavior of sub-atomic matter. Go to this Endnote for a layperson's rundown.[35] The many-worlds interpretation (MWI) of quantum mechanics would allow the version of events that I experienced as one of many, but it's the one I lived; therefore, I posit the connection between me as a Dot and the other Dots existing at those moments—at least once.

So, what was it that ignited or prompted the Dot named James to enter my life abruptly and vanish just as swiftly? Or the Afghan merchant Dot to arrive on the scene of our car crash at a critical moment in the desolate stretch of desert between Kandahar and Kabul? They were Dots that connected us and merged with perfect timing at the exact location.

What started the connection and how did it span the distance? Could you also correctly say it's an attraction? Questions, always questions.

Chapter Fourteen

Pakistan

Rolling Stones: *Out Of Control* > *Lyrics*

Abdul, the bellman at the Khyber InterContinental Hotel, was good at many things. He really understood Westerners who looked like us. We dispensed with his first attempt at providing goods and services by declining his offer of a girl. In a Muslim culture, in that part of Pakistan in the early seventies, was something we really didn't want to visit. We could take care of that desire in another country on our own. It had been a while and seemed longer, but nope... Not going there.

He was successful on his second try when he offered us superb hashish. He might have overheard us tell Ahmed that we wished to go to Chitral, because he smiled when we complimented him on the quality and said it was from Chitral. It wasn't, but close enough.

Being back at an InterContinental was a delightful experience of luxury. A shower with hot water if you wanted it! A flushing toilet where you couldn't see where the flush went. And a bed with sheets, clean even. We figured it was all good, but we knew better than to even think about getting used to it. Our tips had spread enough good cheer among the hotel staff that they treated us kindly, despite our appearance. After a shower, we smelled a lot better, too.

We abstained from alcohol, as we had had none for months. Ha, ha, had you there! We did the obvious thing for men of our age and stature. We went to the bar and drank beer that was refreshingly cold. And got a reasonable buzz. And then took a nap, after which we had a snack and then laughed and shot the shit, rehashing, literally and figuratively, the events of the recent months. There was a lot to laugh at, much to give thanks for, and things to miss, like the *Flying Wreck*. If it hadn't been wrecked, it still would have been useful. However, we didn't dwell on things that were beyond our control. Our exhaustion and probable drunkenness led us to fall asleep early on the first night.

In our rush to grab our stuff out of the *Flying Wreck* in Torkham, Dave had grabbed the map of Afghanistan and Pakistan from the glove box. The precious document was appreciated in our hotel room as one of the few remaining souvenirs of a lost friend. We noted our estimate of a day's drive to Chitral from Peshawar was close—about 350 km (217 mi) on a road we hadn't traveled. It could be a lot longer than we thought. Peshawar was in the valley, and Chitral was in the Hindu Kush mountains. It also looked like we would drive out of the valley and start climbing about halfway there. We couldn't stay long enough during this trip to check it off our list.

We noted that our other prime targets on our to-do list, Kashmir in India and Pokhara in Nepal, were both fairly close by. They too were beyond our reach, but lent encouragement to the big picture. Adding to the calculation, we could see that both would be even closer if we were to travel farther east to Rawalpindi, still in Pakistan. Coincidentally, there was another InterContinental Hotel there.

Pakistan and India were connected by just one border crossing at that time. It was farther south, near Lahore, at a legendary place along the Hippie Trail named Waghan. We knew about it from Hawk, who, with PK, were frequent visitors to that border crossing. You may recall from an earlier chapter that they operated the bus from Amsterdam to India. There was an Indian female immigration officer who was allegedly a psychic. Hawk and PK swore it was true, firmly establishing their belief when PK came face-to-face with her. Their eyes met. She gave a nod and a hint of a smile and motioned him to pass. When they had cleared customs, Hawk asked PK what he had done with it. PK had forgotten he had a sizable chunk of hash in his bag. There's no shortage of wondrous things in the East. And karma and Guardian Angels are on duty there as well.

Our sense of proportion and limits didn't survive our stay in Afghanistan, meaning that our tolerance for smoking hash was off the scale, and the amount we normally smoked was rather extreme. Smoking several grams at a time in a chillum was no big deal—in Afghanistan. In a Khyber InterContinental Hotel room, they considered it to be a bit much.

We hadn't lost touch with reality. We knew we weren't in Amsterdam, where you could smoke a hash joint on a bridge enjoying the view in the Red Light District. Or in Kabul, in the comfortable garden of the hotel, where chillums ruled. And not overlooking the chest-high hubbly-bubbly that we pressed into service when visitors came calling. No, we were aware we were in a five-star hotel in Pakistan. We'd just forgotten our manners, so to say. We nearly got the boot for it.

The knock on the door was unexpected. We hadn't ordered room service. We weren't expecting visitors. Dave looked out the door peephole but said he couldn't see who it was because the glass must be dirty.

We shrugged our shoulders, and he opened the door. When the smoke cleared, we could see it was Abdul, the bellman, but we could not see either direction down the hall. We cracked up. Ahmed was concerned.

"Guests are complaining of smoke in the hall. You are fortunate the front desk sent me to investigate." We had obviously miscalculated from where the hash smoke was venting. We thought the window was open wide enough to take care of it. It would have been if we'd put a towel at the base of the room door...or maybe had smoked less hash, or even not smoked it in a chillum.

"If the wrong guests are complaining or there is fear of a fire, you will have trouble."

We didn't have to consider that for long and placed the equivalent of about US$10 in rupees in his hand.

"I'll see to the problem out here."

We chuckled as we closed the door, but we put a towel at the bottom of the hotel room door and opened the window wide. We backed off a little and got a grip on the fact we were not in Afghanistan anymore. The trouble Abdul spoke of was real in Pakistan. We got some looks in the lobby the next morning that supported our concern that the events of last night had not gone unnoticed by the hotel staff and guests. Abdul was a little less friendly than before, but didn't give us any sign he was in trouble. Or us. We asked him to contact Ahmed on our behalf to tell him we were ready for some sightseeing.

"Good day, gentlemen," was the cheerful greeting from Ahmed as he entered the lobby at precisely the appointed time. The confirmation came from a glance at the half dozen clocks in the lobby, each engraved with the name of another InterContinental Hotel from around the world.

We felt certain that Abdul had apprised Ahmed of our escapade before he arrived. Assuming that was correct, we were legitimately concerned about how Ahmed would react, or even if he would show up at the hotel. It wasn't a stretch for us to imagine Ahmed receiving the briefing as a totally stupid thing to do, or maybe humorous, or even both. Whatever his opinion, he had come.

We asked if Ahmed was amicable to do a combo package: drive us to Rawalpindi and take us to visit a hash factory. A stretch, yes, but we thought it was an opportune time to move on, and we had a feeling that Ahmed had excellent connections. We had already decided that he was dependable, and we were not intending to buy any hash. We wanted a first impression of a source, its accessibility, and organization.

He listened attentively to our request. "It is a considerable drive of approximately 200 km (124 mi). We would need to leave early in the morning to achieve both of your desires."

His fee was pricey—our request was unusual. A plan emerged—our departure was set at 0730 hrs the next morning. We didn't realize how relieved we would feel to have a plan and to be leaving the hotel without further incident. We were ready to take the show on the road for its Pakistani finale at the Rawalpindi InterContinental.

The Khyber InterContinental Hotel, along with the city of Peshawar, was fading rapidly behind us. There were evidently traffic laws in Peshawar, particularly at the roundabouts, where traffic cops in smart white uniforms with brass buttons and white Pith helmets ruled with a fierce whistle. Their white-gloved hands sliced through the air with precision, in near perfect sync with the whistle, providing guidance to motorists who consistently ignored them.

Ahmed was a prime offender. He seemed unbothered by the intrusion of a whistle, and less so of pedestrians, beasts of burden, or automobiles.

He paid attention to the large and heavily ladened lorries that were top heavy and leaned over; they were dangerous obstacles, or so it seemed as we only got a glimpse as they flashed past.

There was a significant difference in the geography. The Khyber Pass was a dangerous mountain road full of blind curves, switchbacks, and rockslides, with infinity beckoning on the passenger side. Rawalpindi's highway was located in a valley. The road was wider, providing a bit more breathing space when passing. Pedestrians, donkeys, and carts dragged by animals with up to four legs used the level shoulder as another traffic lane, along with motorized and nonmotorized vehicles of endless descriptions. Which also meant catastrophe was on both sides instead of only one side, with equal opportunity to wreak havoc.

As the noise, clamor, and congestion of Peshawar fell behind us, we got our first glimpse of the country that Ahmed had alluded to. We were happy to breathe fresh air, even at the velocity it came through the open windows of the car. Ahmed was muted, giving us the chance to ponder and make our own judgments.

In short order, Ahmed continued where he had left off just after we departed the hotel. "Our drive is easy, and without stopping, we should be in Rawalpindi in about two hours."

It didn't escape us that the description of the drive went from "considerable" to "easy" after the negotiation. We also noticed the smile when he said it.

"However, to satisfy your request, we will make an excursion into the hills to visit a small factory I know of."

That put a smile on our faces.

We soon crossed the Indus River. Ahmed's claim that the Indus Valley civilization was one of the oldest known stirred memories of my high school geography lessons. That helped to explain the condition of some roads we traveled. Alexander the Great, like many, had a difficult time in Afghanistan. He eventually subdued many of the tribes and then moved on to the Indian subcontinent. Ahmed's dialogue placed Alexander crossing the Indus River at about the same place we did. We continued, but Alexander's army had called a halt, undefeated but worn out. We were sympathetic.

We took an exit off the main highway onto a less traveled, but still paved alternative that continued east. The geography changed as hills and distant mountains became visible. Ahmed slowed, which got our attention, and came to a stop at a military checkpoint. The uniformed young man affably greeted him, and we were soon on our way after the briefest delay.

"These checks are normal. We will encounter another before we return to the highway. It will be more thorough."

Our map was useful to follow our progress until Ahmed turned off the road at some indistinguishable landmark only known to him.

He explained, "Had we taken a road more traveled, we would have gained elevation quickly and entered a beautiful mountain area that includes snow skiing and mountain lakes." He continued, "Our destination is not far, and at a lower elevation."

The road degraded swiftly into a trail, with clear signs of prior vehicular usage. We continued climbing, rounded a corner, and an armed guard stopped us. He was not alarmed and didn't unshoulder his rifle. He exchanged a few words with Ahmed, and we proceeded.

We pulled into a compound that did not look like a hash factory, although we had no experience for comparison. A mud brick hut stood alongside several lean-tos with slanted roofs made of rusted corrugated metal. Smoke drifted out, suggesting human inhabitance.

A 1955 four-door Chevrolet, or what remained of it, was parked off to the side. The raised hood exposed overstuffed goatskin bags stacked on the sides of the small straight-six engine. Someone had removed the front fenders, revealing the wheel wells with were packed with bulging bags. We'd seen something similar back in Torkham. The flattened roof appeared to be intentional, maybe to keep people and freight less prone to fall or shake off. Some doors were roped shut, and some were agape. Needless to say, there were no windows. Overall, it had a similar appearance to the *Flying Wreck*. The wheels were steel, but not original equipment. What caught our eye was that the tires were in excellent condition. They also weren't original, suggesting that dependable transportation was essential, and implying that the car's running gear was well maintained.

We were in a naturally protected area on the side of a hill, away from the elements and unwanted attention. So perhaps it was a decent layout after all.

Ahmed parked well away, and a man in a clean white *shalwar kameez*, which usually indicated a leader or an official, approached. He nodded to us as we were exiting the car and greeted Ahmed in a fashion that showed familiarity.

He signaled to walk to the small building and, upon entering, it appeared much bigger than the exterior would suggest. Smoke filled the room, some coming from the open firepit and faulty chimney. The rest from a well-used hubbly-bubbly getting a workout from two workers squatting on the floor in semiorganized squalor. It was reminiscent of several places we had frequented in Afghanistan. They and a half dozen others glanced our way and went back to what they were doing, which seemed to be nothing. No introductions were made, or expected.

It was a fascinating collection of antiquated contraptions that represented time-honored solutions for fabrication of one kilo slabs of hashish from pollen. Heavy steel molds of kilo slab size were scattered here and there. Handheld balance scales, recognizable from any bazaar merchant selling goods in third world countries, lay on a stuffed goatskin sack. Several handheld rollers were visible, which first compacted the pollen into the metal mold base. Similar to a common wooden kitchen roller, only they were solid steel. Along the wall were stacks of cloth sacks stuffed full of pollen, and when hefted seemed about 50 kilos (110 lbs) each. Stacks of kilo hashish slabs lined the wall, approximately a hundred in sight. Crudely cut open tin cans containing ghee, also known as *clarified butter*, were waiting for action. It's used in lesser-quality pollen to aid in consistency and make it more pliable, and it helps bond the pollen together under heat and pressure during the processing of hashish.

There were several workstations for compressing hashish with a lever system. Square, hand-hewn logs from a very hard local wood measured about 3 m (10 ft) long and 30 cm (12 in) wide on each side. They suspended these at well past the middle, between two upright posts of similar hand-hewn logs about 1.5 m (5 ft) tall. They used those posts as a pivot to bring the heated steel molds with the pollen/ghee mixture under pressure for a specific amount of time. From the looks of the staff and facilities, I doubted the process was always consistent.

The energy in the space was chill, with no tension or wariness. The operators seemed safe and content. Ahmed translated the discussion that had earlier ensued while we took it all in.

"I explained to our host that you are not seeking business today, merely interested in becoming acquainted with him for future consideration. He is comfortable with that and welcomes you."

"Please thank him for his hospitality and generosity. We have a few questions if we may."

Ahmed nodded and spoke to the Guy in White.

Based on our brief observations, this operation did not produce top quality hashish. The operation had been in place for some time and likely had a loyal customer base that was satisfied with the quality, assuming it had a reasonable price. In principle, the quality depended on the starting resin/pollen—the same as did our bat-pressed hash back in Kabul. This pollen needed ghee to press properly. It was locally grown in Pakistan and was not the quality of Chitral Pakistan.

Certainly, both Ahmed and the Guy in White were sensing our assessment. We did not want to offend the host; we recognized the hash to be of decent quality and it would be considered excellent in a place like the US. Not so much in Amsterdam. We weren't intending to buy anything, and the quality was well below our expectations. Something needed to be said.

Scott offered, "How many kilos can you produce in a day?"

Ahmed translated, paused, and said, "Approximately 50."

"Can you produce Chitral quality?"

Ahmed's reply, "Yes, of course, with sufficient time...and at a considerably higher price."

We left price considerations for later, as we knew what a reasonable price was from Hawk and PK.

The boys on the hubbly-bubbly were lighting it up again, and the aroma was much more appealing than when we entered. They had been paying attention to the discussion and invited us to indulge. A test, maybe? We were up to a challenge. These guys were no rookies, but neither were we. Scott, Dave, and I relished the chance to sit with hashish makers in their space and smoke their pipe and hash at the source. It's what this trip was all about and why we had driven across Europe, through Asia, endured what it threw at us, and survived. We relished those moments and the five of us filled that hut with a thick and rich aromatic smoke. No need to be sorry we couldn't communicate with words. The smiles all around through the wall of hash smoke were enough.

Scott picked up the thread with Ahmed. "Please give our thanks to our friend once again. We have unfinished business in Kabul, but intend to return here."

Ahmed acknowledged the Guy in White, and he nodded and smiled. At that, our host produced a nice chunk of hash and handed it to Scott. We had no choice but to accept, and we viewed it as a sign of his agreement with our statement. We flashed on the last time this happened at the Afghan border in Herat...and the checkpoint we went through on the way to this factory. Ahmed had said there would be another one before we got back to the main highway. Like before, we couldn't say no to the offer, nor to a nice chunk of hash. *Here we go again.*

We departed and thanked Ahmed for his choice of destination and for his help. What his cut would be for any deal in the future was a mystery to us, of course, but it was good to have this option if the opportunity arose down the road. We had a lot of ground to cover between now and then.

Scott hid the chunk in his personal hiding spot. We enjoyed our pleasant buzz as we drove past the factory guard, down the path, and rejoined the road.

It wasn't long before we were once again on the paved road running east, and sure enough, the expected checkpoint was just ahead. Ahmed was not alarmed, nor acted concerned. As we slowed to a stop, several soldiers were approaching with the checkpoint guard. Showtime. I grabbed my camera and the three of us opened the doors and got out, smiling and waving. I pointed at the camera, making motions for the soldiers to come over. After a brief hesitation and us in our tourist mode, they walked over, and I took photos of the smiling army guys and us goofing around with them. It worked as it always had. We shook hands with them as Ahmed was finishing any formalities with the checkpoint man. We piled in and Ahmed started off.

"That was a risky tactic, but successful." He smiled. "We will be at the hotel in Rawalpindi in about an hour." We were indeed there in the allotted time, and with plenty of sunlight remaining in the day.

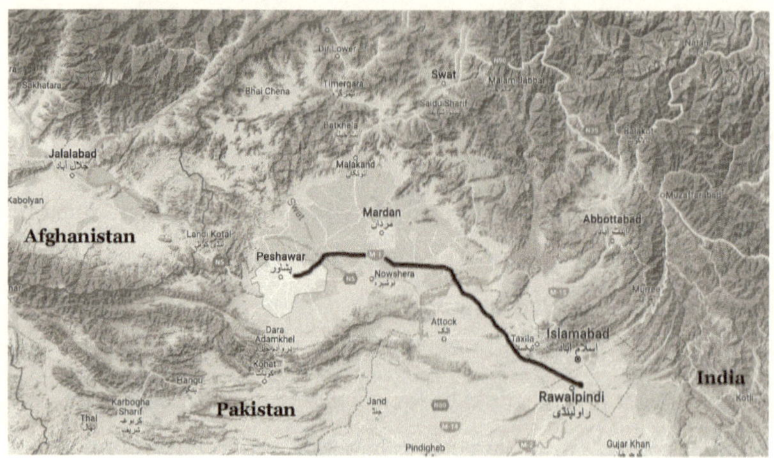

Peshawar to Rawalpindi. Map data ©2024 Google

Ahmed ensured that our reception at the Rawalpindi InterContinental Hotel was smooth. He was a proper gentleman in those situations, a savvy and sharp guide and an excellent interpreter. We were fortunate to have made his acquaintance. At this hotel too he had a preferred contact to whom he introduced us. With those formalities in place, we gave a warm and appreciative adieu to Ahmed, feeling gratified and comfortable with him as a future contact. He appeared to feel the same. We were under no illusions, however, and kept our consul to ourselves, sharing candidly but circumspectly. We settled in, recognizing that this hotel was considerably more organized and conservative than Peshawar. There were loads of diplomatic types and government bureaucrats hanging about, as it was close to the Pakistani capital in Islamabad. We hadn't planned on staying long anyway and took advantage of the modern facilities.

After traveling 8,000 km (4,971 mi), we were lounging in a pleasant hotel, a stone's throw from India, within spitting distance of Chitral, Kashmir, and Nepal. Our carpets were en route to the US, and we were free of the *Flying Wreck*—mixed feelings on that one. A sense of accomplishment was in order. OK, we briefly acknowledged it.

But youth and adventure were there as well, and the itch for continuing into India was strong. But that would have bitten off more than we could chew, and we needed to get back to Kabul to see through our current program. There was a lot to do. Scott and I needed to leave Kabul expeditiously to avoid our carpets becoming an issue with the forwarding company.

We made reservations with Pakistan International Airlines in the hotel lobby for a flight to Kabul in two days' time.

Hash Factory staff

Can of ghee on hash press

Sacks of pollen

Compression rollers and slab molds

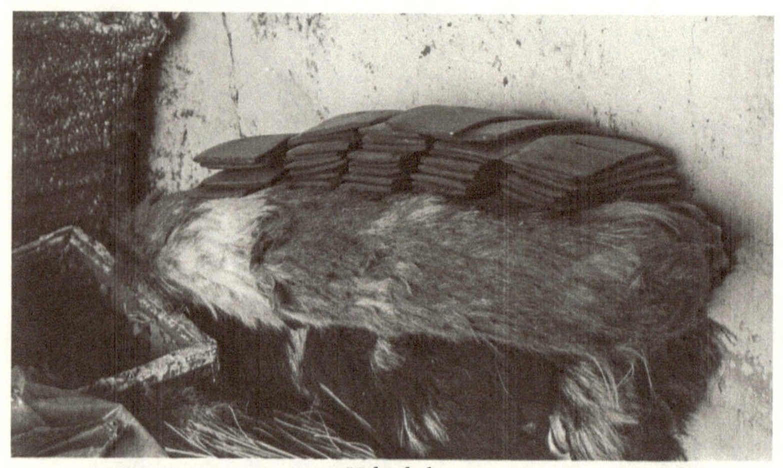

Kilo slabs

Cross section of a kilo slab

Break time!

Answering the challenge

Interlude Seven

It's A Physics Kind of Thing

Jimi Hendrix: *Stone Free* > *Lyrics*

Previous Interludes have included karma in the context of Dots—what they are, how they function, and the potential impact Dots can have on one's life. Karma has different meanings and applications to a vast array of individuals. It's understandable, given its religious roots, with their conflicting beliefs and rules. My interest in karma has no relation to religion, per se. I don't disallow a relationship—it's just not my focus.

You may recall that the word *karma* derives from Sanskrit, meaning action, work, or deed. "For the believers in spirituality, the term also refers to the spiritual principle of cause and effect, often descriptively called *the principle of karma*, wherein intent and actions of an individual (cause) influence the future of that individual (effect)."[36]

I disregard the numerous secondary meanings or beliefs for karma that have arisen from centuries of exploitation for selfish or opportunistic purposes. I wholeheartedly lean toward a philosophical understanding of karma, notably its metaphysical aspect. A metaphysical hypothesis is, according to David J. Chalmers, "Where physics is concerned with the microscopic processes that underlie macroscopic reality, metaphysics is concerned with the fundamental nature of reality. A metaphysical hypothesis might make a claim about the reality that underlies physics itself. Alternatively, it might say something about the nature of our minds, or the creation of our world."[37]

Metaphysics is now in on the action, and you might think, "Here we go, things are getting deep." Let's take a step back from physics and recall common sense. My nascent theory has been road tested and keeps on proving itself over the last five decades. You, dear reader, could also contribute to the circumstantial evidence. Have you identified any Dots in your life? A remarkable individual who had a significant impact on your life? I think you can. But a Dot is one who appeared in your life out of the blue and had an outsized impact. I bet you can say yes to that too.

Not a spoiler: The next Interlude will consider Dots as the knots in an imagined woven cosmic carpet, and the loom for weaving the carpet is rather large—spacetime. Some context for that is in order. Science agrees that spacetime contains the structure of the universe, including our sun, Earth, solar system, Milky Way galaxy, and billions of other galaxies. This is where our lives take place. Where everything we, and all the humans who have ever existed, lived out their lives. Where all known matter exists and everything in the future will exist. The universe and spacetime is where it all goes down...unless science has overlooked something. A simulated reality, for example. Simulated realities are also argued, by some researchers and scientists, to be contained within the structure of spacetime.

Scientists believe a network structure exists in the mysterious dark matter that occupies spacetime. The Theory of Dots posits karma resides in that realm. Such a network could have many uses, but we'll focus on its potential for Dots.

Our brains have trouble processing scientific concepts that entail more than the four dimensions that we can experience. Perhaps I'm overreaching in that statement—it's my brain, with its many restraints, that is challenged to grasp them. The scope and size of the observable universe defies my imagination as well. The diameter is estimated to be 93 billion light-years. Light travels 9.46 trillion km (31 trillion mi) in a year. Ninety-three billion x 9.46 trillion km—19,000,000,000,000,000,000,000 km!

The Theory of Dots posits to operate without limitations of distance. However, for the foreseeable future, humans only have to be concerned in earth terms. That's still a lot of space and it's hard to fathom the chances of connecting with any particular Dot. It happens, though, so there must be an explanation, right?

Dots have a physicality in various forms—often a person, a place, an event, or in an artistic endeavor, such as music or art. The concept of a Dot encompasses more than the physical aspect. It's the connection to your life, the resulting effect it has, and the timing of when the encounter takes place. How does that happen? Why does it happen at that place, time, and with that particular Dot? Where lies the explanation?

A clue may be found in a quip from Albert Einstein when he said, "Spooky behavior at a distance,"[38] referring to quantum entanglement. His comment refers to a theory of how particles can instantaneously interact with each other, even if separated by a great distance. Quantum entanglement may put us on the trail of how karma brings Dots together.

The next Interlude will delve deeper into the subject.

Chapter Fifteen

Mission Accomplished

We had only been gone from Afghanistan for less than two weeks when the PIA flight from Rawalpindi landed in Kabul. From the air, nothing had changed. Deplaning was still down the rickety portable stairs with a walk to the terminal building. The disorganization within had worsened since the coup. The new regime had, of course, replaced most of the poorly trained customs staff with their supporters, who had even less training and little knowledge of the new government procedures, if such procedures actually existed. We thought the coup might have caused flight suspensions, which could explain the unfamiliarity with immigration procedures. That might work in our favor.

We were some of the first to enter the republic, greeted by an enthusiastic, if not clueless, passport control official. In English, but with some menace, he said, "Welcome to the *Republic* of Afghanistan," as he flipped through the pages of our passports, looking for the previous Afghani visa issued by the Kingdom of Afghanistan. When he found it, he made a big X across it and stamped the new Republic of Afghanistan visa with relish and satisfaction. That was an enormous relief, as an experienced agent would have noticed the vehicle entry stamp in my passport and looked for the exit visa of the same. Which I, of course, did not have because of our eventful border departure. Another stroke of luck—we were back "home" in Kabul. Time to check out what the new republic was like.

The overthrow of an Afghan king was not a major concern to the travelers along the Hippie Trail. But it would soon come to pass that the easygoing, Westerner-friendly Kabul would determinedly, then more firmly, begin driving foreigners to leave the country. General Daoud had disposed of his cousin the king, aided by Russian-influenced political parties in Afghanistan. That support was something he came to regret, but the writing was on the wall for Western observers. The inevitable came to pass. General Daoud was assassinated in 1978, followed by the Russian invasion in 1979.

The overthrow of the king did concern the extended royal family and the hangers-on who relied on the established pecking order. The deposed King Zahir Shah was the last of a continuous line dating back to 1929. He was an educated, worldly man who spoke several languages. Many Afghans respected, and even revered him. His policies allowed life in the capital, Kabul, to enjoy many liberties not accessible in neighboring countries.

We were hearing rumors about Russian influence after we had been back for a while. We knew of some people who weren't waiting for the pressure—they were winding down their programs and preparing for a departure in the fall of 1974. In mid-1975, a flood of Westerners left the country. A reverse Hippie Trail was created—a string of refugees reversing course and landing in Amsterdam or moving on to the UK.

The situation in Afghanistan had a knock-on effect on those in India and Nepal, as the most direct overland route was through Afghanistan.

Being back in Kabul felt good. Boy greeted us at our hotel with a smile and feigned disapproval, wagging his finger about some unknown infraction. Our same room was unoccupied. In fact, our stuff was in the same places, even the twin speakers of our essential traveling partner, the Sony cassette player. He took excellent care of us and was a good kid. Dave hit the Play button on the Sony and Van Morrison belted out "These Dreams of You." Perfect!

For the travelers passing through Kabul and coming and going along the Hippie Trail, there was little to discern there had been a coup ousting the king. Gone were the large portraits of King Zahir Shah in the markets, shops, and offices, all replaced with General Daoud. The new republic's flag looked a little different, but neither the portrait nor flag change would jump out at a visitor. Foreigners living or having headquarters in Kabul had more to take note of. You had to look for evidence, and some of it was intuitive. Walk down Chicken Street and the merchants were still hustling, the street beggars working, and the Westerners bargaining. But an undercurrent of concern and doubt was present. Talk to longtime residents—concern about the prospect of greater stifling Russian influence was there. Life and business had been very good for Kabul city dwellers, if less so for the rural residents. People felt free of many religious constraints. Women had a choice to decide if they wished to conform to the strict Islam dress codes or not. Some women still wore the full burqa, or a version. But many didn't, particularly the young. You would see student-aged women in Western skirts and sweaters and no face coverings at all. Some walked freely on the streets without a male escort. For a Westerner it sounds ridiculous to make those distinctions, but in a Muslim country—then, and even now—they're important issues with real ramifications. Education was available to all, with no restrictions for women. This basic human expectation would end, along with many freedoms in Afghanistan, when the Russians invaded in 1979.

We felt a sense of foreboding, but not impending doom. We were looking for signs of change, and we weren't aware of any obvious signals that pointed to a specific concern. Life in Kabul was the same in the social strata we engaged with regularly. But still...

We checked in with Noor, who welcomed us back graciously and with genuine warmth. He informed us that the carpet shipment had arrived in the US and was undergoing import formalities. No concerns had surfaced. However, due to the change in Afghan government, there would probably be postponements in releasing the goods to the freight forwarder. Paperwork now needed to be verified. It could be as long as a 30-day delay. Or longer. That was an unwelcome bit of news.

We had expected to catch a flight to Frankfurt within a week of our return. Scott and I, truth be told, thought that was not enough time, but Dave was eager for us to get to work so we could get back before he got bored or otherwise uncomfortable in Afghanistan. Our recent assessments of the atmosphere in the capital reinforced his opinion, and ours. Now it looked like we would need to hang out longer than expected in Kabul anyway. Mohammed of Pan Am walked in while we were drinking chai and talking with Noor. Mohammed was warm and friendly also, so we asked both their opinion of the coup.

Mohammed may have been speaking for both when he commented he thought they could do business as usual with the new government in place. They saw there hadn't been sufficient preparation for the change of administrative people, which showed that maybe the coup hadn't had sufficient planning. More telling from our point of view was the comment by Noor that everyone had put up a picture of the king (both

Mohammed and Noor were Pashtun, as was the king) because they wanted to, now some exchanged the king's picture for General Daoud because they felt pressure to do so.

We didn't expect outright expressions of sympathy for the king, and certainly not statements of opposition to the good general. We took the comments at face value, finished our chai, and excused ourselves, saying we'd return later in the week.

Brian had a long-term relationship with Afghanistan from an intimate understanding of Kabul, and had traveled extensively within Afghanistan. Now and then, it became apparent that he had some Farsi and Pashtun language capabilities. His take on the coup and what might be on the horizon would be interesting and worthy of consideration. We were glad to see him shortly after our return to the hotel. He and Mark arrived on the first music night, and we all had stories to tell and events to catch up on. They were in Kabul during the coup and, along with everyone else they knew, agreed it was a hasty and unorganized overthrow of the king. But like us, they had genuine concerns about the repercussions of the event. There was a shared feeling that the boot was going to come down, and the good old days of Kabul were under threat.

Brian had already begun defensive maneuvers to prepare for a quick departure if need be. He had deeper connections and many dependents who had accumulated during his time in the country. We were a lot more mobile, but needed to take stock to avoid being caught out if the pace of the Russian threat picked up, or if Westerners became targets.

We checked regularly with Mohammed and Noor, pushing to the extent we could to get the green light from the freight forwarders that our goods had cleared in the US. We couldn't make flight reservations until that happened. Based on our more limited experience, we didn't think it likely that matters would deteriorate that quickly. Brian agreed, and we fell back into our daily routines.

There were many mythic characters and musicians connected with drugs in the mid '60s to late '70s. Northern California is the home of the Grateful Dead, Ken Kesey, Merry Pranksters, Owsley Stanley, and Timothy Leary. The Brotherhood of Eternal Love shifted the focus in Southern California from surfing to LSD's Orange Sunshine and then hashish in Afghanistan. The Brotherhood was legendary and nearly every hippie had heard of them, but few really understood the extent of their influence. I was one of those. In Kabul, you heard references to them from time to time, but to us, there was no interest in digging deeper.

We identified an occasional blip on our radar screen as *hash oil*. As we were killing time waiting to leave for the US, the blip showed up more often. Word on the street was that it was being manufactured locally by The Brotherhood. *Hmm, interesting.* We stirred from our routine and investigated the "new" hash kid in town.

Hash oil was an intriguing substance. With the consistency of honey, the best quality was a little darker but clear, with no impurities. Ambient temperature changed the viscosity. The warmer the better. Dip a stick into it and watch it stream back into the jar. It burned cleanly, but the smoke was harsher and sharper than high-grade hashish. It had some interesting applications—it took little to get a buzz. You could smear it on a cigarette, spread it on anything edible, or smoke it in a joint or a pipe. We figured the most interesting aspect to The Brotherhood was how many more options existed for ways to transport it back to the US.

For Dave, Scott, and me, it just didn't have the appeal of hash. We preferred the wholeness of smoking hash in a chillum, or rolling a joint. Time, effort, and attention to detail were necessary to prepare the hashish to enjoy its aroma, taste, and effect. The process was intentional, a ceremony with defined procedures that were time-tested and passed down. It was a ritual of sorts, and we felt it showed proper respect to traditions dating back hundreds, if not a thousand, years. We bought a small jar of the best hash oil we could find and ended up mostly just playing with it.

Summer was fading, and hints of fall were stirring. Dave was comfortable; Boy would look after him when Scott and I left. Rumors of alleged Russian pressure passed through the expat community like a wave, then subsided until the next wave arrived. Mostly it was calm, but an undertone of anticipation was there. We finally got word that we were clear to leave, so we made our air reservations to Frankfurt and a connecting flight to Amsterdam.

We spent several days checking in with friends, but did not mention that we were taking a leave of absence. Dave seemed chill, so we grabbed a taxi to the airport and bid adieu to Kabul for a couple of months.

Our flight to Frankfurt was uneventful, mostly. It was on Ariana Afghan Airways, operated by Lufthansa, the German carrier. The pilot was a youngish Afghan, and the copilot was German. Scott and I ate a little chunk of hash to take the edge off. It was a good chill mood, and we were dozing off and on when the aircraft started a hard turn to starboard. The pilot announced we would circle Mount Ararat in Turkey. *The place where Noah had landed his Ark? Uh, OK, that's cool…* But he was banking hard, the right-side window view right down on the summit. We were on the left side, almost spilling out of our seats. We didn't hear another word from him until we landed back in Frankfurt. Too bad he didn't circle the Matterhorn in honor of Scott and me.

The US Rhein-Main Air Base that adjoined the Frankfurt Airport was as busy as ever, shuttling American soldiers and supplies back and forth to Vietnam. We stayed in transit, remembering that there was a nightclub in the basement level of the airport, but we had to clear customs if we were to go there. We headed to the transit bar instead.

We caught our connection to Amsterdam and had no issues with immigration or customs. We found Schiphol Airport to be efficient and familiar, having discreetly explored almost all of its facilities during our previous times there. It felt good to be back at home, and we took a taxi to the Centrum. We hung with Hawk and PK, as well as our associates at the coffee shops and bars we used to frequent. We had decided not to bring any hash from Kabul, as the local supply was plentiful and our sources were excellent.

Scott and I deliberately left our chillums with Dave in Kabul. It made sense to buy several unused chillums in Amsterdam, just to be on the safe side when we entered the US. We could use a proven method of transport for a handful of hash for personal consumption. Amsterdam seemed like a good place to start our reentry to the Western world and get some rest. Our friends thought differently. The Rolling Stones were in concert at the Ahoy in Rotterdam in less than two weeks' time! Tickets materialized. We ended up staying longer than expected, but the idea of not going to the Stones' concert never entered our minds.

We were eight stoned hippies leaving Amsterdam in PK's VW microbus. You had to have one of those in the early '70s to get your official hippie certification. We consumed a whole lotta Mother Nature in the two-hour drive, and we were ready for the Stones when we arrived. They didn't disappoint. The ride back was a little less rowdy, and PK stayed awake long enough to deposit us safely back into Amsterdam.

We indulged in delicious food, saw some early arrivals that had defected from Kabul, and got caught up on things that mattered. There were a ton of shops selling Afghan goods and carpets. We shopped and took notes, not knowing if there would be any relevancy to the US market. It seemed like all things Afghan were popular here, so it was useful for that standpoint, if nothing else.

The KLM (Dutch national airline) flight to NYC went by fast. I thought I'd face some questioning at US Immigration and Passport Control due to my full passport pages with interesting country stamps, but the accordion extra pages attached in Kabul were even more worrying—like waving a red flag at a bull. Standard procedure was that Scott and I did not clear customs together. We allowed people to deplane and put distance between us. We added a few more passengers between us, just to be extra cautious.

Good thing, too. A throng of people gathered as the arrivals from Europe were due. We were standing in distinct lines. Scott was ahead of me and had no issues. My agent had a crew cut and a military posture. *Great.* One look at the hippie approaching (me) and he saw red meat. Computers had not yet taken over the entry process, so they had a book to look up passports and any notes from previous entries. I handed him my double thick passport.

He smiled. "How long have you been out of the country?"

Easy. "Eighteen months."

"Business or pleasure?" Smiley asked.

"I'm a budget traveler," said I to answer that and what he would probably ask next.

Smiley pushed back from his kiosk a bit, held my passport by the edge of the accordion pages, and lifted it into the air, and it unfolded to the full extent. He got a snort of acknowledgement from the agent across from us.

"Kabul, huh? Did you bring any drugs with you?"

Fully prepared, I responded, "No, sir, I did not."

He started flipping through his book, probably thinking he'd find something incriminating or a tidbit to enquire about to trip me up. He found nothing.

"Where are you going?" He had access to my flight info.

"First to Cleveland, then to Kansas City, to visit my family."

Apparently satisfied, he said, "Have a nice trip."

Whomp! on the ink pad, *whomp!* went the stamp in my passport. I was very glad our plan worked.

Scott had passed passport and immigration, collected his luggage, and cleared customs ahead of me. We met up at the gate for the flight to Cleveland.

Scott chuckled and said, "My guy missed his chance for a promotion."

We both lifted our yellow "See Buy Fly" duty-free bags we purchased in Amsterdam's Schiphol Airport in acknowledgement. It was rare to see a traveler arriving from Amsterdam who didn't have one or more of those yellow bags in hand. They were so prevalent, they almost became invisible to travelers...and to immigration officials. More pertinent to us, customs agents around the world perceived them to be innocuous and secure. The Dutch had achieved that status with their diligent and innovative procedures for travelers to purchase duty-free goods. If a traveler had any Dutch guilders left in their pocket, Schiphol Airport Duty-Free Shopping made it easy and enticing to spend them before boarding the airplane.

But Schiphol also concentrated on security. They made it easy to buy and securely packaged the goods with special materials, secure tags, and unique closures. Then they placed the goods in those highly noticeable yellow bags and sealed them shut. The rule was you could not break the seal on the See Buy Fly yellow bag until you cleared customs at your destination airport.

The flight to Cleveland passed quickly and without incident.

Our immediate destination was Cleveland, which complied with the rules—and we certainly were ones who followed rules. We broke the seal on one of our bags, pulled out and tore open one of the securely sealed packages, in which we had replaced the original contents, and extracted some Dutch treats.

On the grounds of the Cleveland-Hopkins International Airport, we rented a commercial type of van, thinking we would go straight to the freight forwarder. We eyeballed the empty interior and figured everything would fit, just. We had an extensive file of paperwork from Pan Am in Kabul, including the custom clearances and export papers. Our file also included a copy of the telex message from the Pan Am office to the freight forwarder. There was a lot to digest that we really had given little attention to until that moment. We realized we should call the freight office to get directions and make contact.

We walked back to the rental counter and asked where the freight terminal was located. She reached under the counter and pulled out one of those pads of local maps, tore one off the pad, turned it over, grabbed a pen, and quickly circled an area near to where we were. "Better hurry. They'll close soon."

Skipping the call to save time, we hustled to the van. Thankfully we immediately saw a sign with an arrow pointing to the right for International Freight. We parked and walked in.

The receptionist was nice and when she said, "Can I help you?" she added, "The freight area is closed until Monday. Do you have your waybill?"

By then we had figured out that must've meant today was Friday. Welcome back to business hours.

We had the file and presented the document. She shuffled some files, found one that she pulled out, licked her finger, and sorted through a bunch of paper.

"Looks like it hasn't cleared yet."

We showed her the telex to the Pan Am office in Kabul. "Yes, this is a notice of preclearance acceptance," she said with confidence. "Final clearance usually takes about a week to ten days."

That rattled and upset us, but it wasn't her fault that they misinterpreted the document in Kabul.

"Can we at least look at our carpets?"

She was apologetic. "Your shipment is in the restricted area. Even if our guys were still here, they wouldn't have access. I'm really sorry."

It was an hour and a half drive to Scott's parents from the airport. We both agreed I might as well get my visit to Kansas City out of the way and return to Cleveland when Scott confirmed the goods had cleared customs. We had been honest with Noor and Mohammed. Since only the items we declared were in the shipment, there was no reason for customs to be playing games.

"Let's go back to the ticket counter and see if I can get on a flight tonight to Kansas City." I could and I did.

Travel in third world countries is full of frustration and delays to a Westerner used to efficiency and familiar standards. However, it slowly beats one into a submission called *patience*. We were well practiced by now, but practicing it in a first world country pushed us back into the realm of frustration.

I would poke around in Kansas City and Scott would have the time with his family. When he called with the green light for customs, I'd hop on a plane and we'd hopefully sell a bunch of Afghan goods for cash. The fragility of our plan? It was based on a whim and a lot of good faith. It was very clear to us, but it didn't dampen our enthusiasm or cause us any regrets.

Rawalpindi flight arriving in Kabul

Welcome back! Fire up the Chillum!

Interlude Eight

The Dot Net

Jethro Tull: *Reasons For Waiting > Lyrics*

According to my theory, the connectors (e.g. intuition, gut feelings, instinctive behavior) are entities in a person's Dot Matrix. Those connectors are fundamental to the process that facilitates karmic connection between Dots. Some inanimate objects, such as an event, or even a place, can be influenced by a Dot Matrix. The Theory of Dots acknowledges that a person's Dot Matrix can leave "fingerprints" on certain inanimate objects, creating a connection comparable to that between two human Dots. Those lingering fingerprints are left by the Dot Matrix in the time and location, when and where the Dot and event or place came into contact. My theory can then refer to an important event or thing as a Dot as long as a person's Dot Matrix is involved. I posit the Dot Matrix for each person is guided and carried by karma to a precise time and place in order to connect the Dots. You may recall that the theory includes the terminology dark matter, which was rebranded as karma.

The concept of quantum entanglement referenced by Einstein in his "spooky behavior" quip is intriguing for us to consider within the karmic network. Entanglement of the quantum-type has two point-like particles reacting in sync no matter the distance between them. That relationship suggests a connection that is not fully understood in physics. Karmic entanglement could describe a synced relationship, but not necessarily an instantaneous connection between two Dots. A quantum-type connection between Dots could allow Dot Matrix entities, like intuition and gut feelings, to experience a direct and unobstructed path to connect with each other. My theory posits that Dots materialize in one's life at a certain place and time because of karmic determination that the timing is correct.

String theory is a framework in physics in which the point-like particles are replaced by one-dimensional objects called *strings*. There is only one kind of string in the shape of a loop, but it can vibrate in different ways. The nature of the string is determined by its vibrational state.[39] Perhaps human intuition or gut feelings, each at their fundamental level, have the same vibration regardless of the person? It's not too far a leap to suggest that two such vibrations could attract each other. The Theory of Dots posits that karma, aka dark matter, is the medium that brings Dots together using the Dot Matrix entities as connectors.

My theory is in its early stage; however, I'm prepared to provide a couple of analogies to illustrate conceivable scenarios of Dots in action.

Think of an Oriental carpet as a Magic Carpet, if you will. I'll use the structure of real carpets to describe the Dot-filled Magic Carpet. The structure of the Magic Carpet is a network of threads in a loom, with the north to south threads representing time (warp) and the perpendicular threads representing location (weft). This loom is on the scale of space-time, much bigger than one used to weave an average Oriental carpet, but bear with me.

Knots create an Oriental carpet, hand-tied one at a time to each warp thread across the width of the loom. Once the row of knots is complete, the weaver pushes the weft threads evenly across the width of the loom, jamming them together with the previous row of knots below. Done time after time, a pattern forms.

The Magic Carpet version employs karma to tie the knots (Dots) on the warp (time) threads as the weft (location) threads and deploy Dots in contact with each other. The two Dots, now in contact with each other, merge into the moment, reacting to the situation at hand.

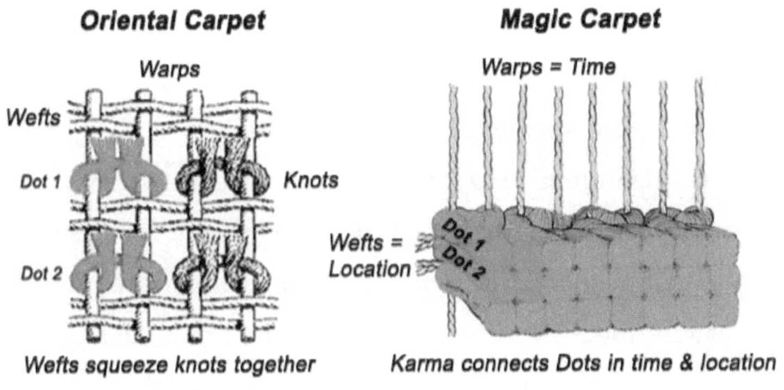

Magic Carpet Illustration of Karma Connecting Dots

The hand-tied knots contribute to a larger, emerging pattern as each row is pressed down onto the row below. Eventually, the pattern becomes noticeable, achieving the desired design.

The imagined Magic Carpet doesn't have a predetermined pattern. Dots, including the two in this scenario, and all other carpets, create a pattern that evolves from the collective karma. The weaving of the Magic Carpet has been going on for eons and will continue into the future. It brings to mind an often-quoted phrase by Arthur C. Clarke: "Any sufficiently advanced technology is indistinguishable from magic" .[40] Karma is responsible for uniting the connectors of each Dot—such as instinct, Guardian Angels, intuition, and gut feelings—at precisely the right time. In my theory research, I've anointed karma as the dealmaker and illustrated its handiwork in the Magic Carpet example above. Here's another analogy to imagine how karma might accomplish its magic.

Google the word "fish" you will get about 3.75 billion results. Google "saltwater fish" you receive about 446 million results. Search "best tasting saltwater fish" you receive about 105 million results. Search "largest saltwater fish" you receive about 79 million results. The sequence is obvious. An increase in specific parameters produces fewer results. The winnowing process focuses on similarities that are suggested in the search criteria and included in the results. The search criteria to link two Dots would grow exponentially.

Internet algorithms manage most search results. Each searcher determines what descriptions best meet their specific requirements for that result in that moment. The algorithm determines what results are the best match. Applied to Theory of Dots, I posit that the Dot Matrix replaces the algorithms in a Google search and the intentionality[41] of the Dot takes the role of the searcher.

The Theory of Dots posits that networks are the most effective solution for handling transactions involving Dots.

Let me introduce you to the Dot Net: the internet on steroids.

Karma is the carrier of the Dot Matrix elements and permeates space-time. With access to all locations and all time, it seeks and locates similar fidelity and intentionality. The algorithm of a network seeks all matches with and limited to the search criteria. Karma also has a multitude of matches based on its available criteria. Dots are at least as plentiful as Google matches.

The internet is a network that provides the medium in which a Google search can function and produce the desired results of a search. The Dot network accomplishes a similar outcome of connecting two entities, but the method used is fundamentally distinct. Unlike the internet, where the process is driven by the intent of the searcher, the Dot Net uses the intentionality and connections of the Dot Matrix.

A man-made system of machines and cables allows the internet to function. The Dot Net relies on a natural network in existence since just after the Big Bang. This medium, karma, aka dark matter, permeates space, connecting all matter.

To do a Google search, you don't need to know how the internet works. You just need to enter data into a translator (browser), which converts it into machine language using software. You receive the results after the system processes it into a format that is understandable and us-able. In its early years, the internet was enthralling, but slow. Now, with a fast internet connection, it is virtually instantaneous. *Instantaneous* is a relative term, of course.

The Dot Net would require a more sophisticated form of user access than the original internet. Securing personal information remains a pri-ority. Personal data needed to use the Dot Net will increase, with a much more sophisticated two-step authorization process required to protect privacy. I propose that humans and nonhumans will have access—here we'll focus on a human user. Both a *dcode* and a *crypcode* would be necessary for access to the full capability of the Dot Net. The *dcode*[42] is like a combo driver license, business card, and cellular number. It would be a digital identifier, but with a galactic reference. A 9–12 digit code represents your basic, nonencrypted info, including your star, planet, moon, habitation, and location. The *crypcode*[43] has an encrypted pass-word function of 9–12 digits, which could be memorized like a phone number. The *crypcode* contains an excessive number of digits, making it difficult for humans to remember. Using the *dcode* with the *crypcode* is necessary to allow access to the Dot Net to perform targeted searches for other Dots, or to use search terms to find new Dots. Your personal Dot Matrix would serve as search parameters to navigate toward other Dots with similar inclinations. The possibilities for the use of Dot Net's search feature go beyond connecting with Dots.

The theoretical Dot Net is faster than the internet's best performance, and input isn't required via voice or keyboard. It's a long-established and reliable network system that covers not only Earth, but our entire galaxy. Connecting Dots is a key function of the Dot Net, but we'll explore the far greater potential in the next Interlude.

Chapter Sixteen

Stranger Than A Strange Land

Blind Faith: *Can't Find My Way Home* > *Lyrics*

Darkness blanketed everything. Ok, the flight to Kansas City arrived after sunset, but it still seemed like something was missing—lighted billboards, streetlights, and… Shit, everything! It was a blackout. That recognition triggered a recollection of what I had read in the *International Herald Tribune* newspaper. The country faced an oil crisis in the wake of a *supposed* supply and demand issue. More demand than supply, and the countries with the supply were making a demand for a higher price. That's what capitalism is based on, right? Sometimes you must make a point, and darkness was the exclamation mark. Who's scamming who?

The airport taxi driver was, of course, an expert on not only local matters but also politics, the petroleum industry, and domestic (USA) policy. Taxi driver said, "The f***ing A-rabs turned off the tap."

It looked like they also turned off the lights. I was curious. "Did someone not pay the electrical bill?"

"I pay my bills; the bastards [OPEC countries] are saying they're running out of oil!"

Around the same time I had also read in the *Tribune* that the OPEC countries had placed an embargo on the US as punishment for supporting Israel in the Yom Kippur War.

Capitalism, at least regarding the petroleum industry, was functioning at a handicap—the process got rigged. Who was the rigger? The "A-rabs," the oil company consortiums, or the "free market system?" My guess, all of the above. Possibly unplanned, but pros can spot an opportunity when they see one. It was apparent to me that an informed analysis of the OPEC oil embargo was far more complicated than the taxi driver expressed. The strings were likely being pulled by murky alliances and, of course, MONEY.

I didn't plan on hanging around the US for long enough to gain an informed opinion. My concerns were more immediate: Selling our Afghan goods.

America had a reputation around the world as a melting pot of cultures and a showcase of diametrically opposed opinions which, at that point, had not boiled over. Many Americans, especially travelers, took that as a compliment and a point of pride.

But the fallout from the Vietnam War was stirring up long-festering issues about racial inequality, amplified by a cultural upheaval that started in the 1960s. American society was engulfed by a generation gap between those who heroically fought and won World War Two, and their Baby Boomer children. American society was now at war with itself.

My arrival in Kansas City brought the realization that I had been gone for only 18 months into sharp focus. The strange lands that me and my traveling companions encountered had melted into a new norm for us.

Now the United States of America was the strange culture. What had happened? To the locals, it was the same, same. To me, it was a country gone haywire. The Vietnam War was still grinding on, with body counts announced on the evening news by Walter Cronkite. An oil embargo was producing expensive gas at the petrol stations. Protesters were being killed by police and the military.

All of that social upheaval must have been a catalyst, as rock 'n' roll music was flourishing. Good things happened in the music scene despite distractions from politicians and people over 30 years old. The stopover in Amsterdam on the way to the US allowed Scott and me to marvel at all the fabulous albums that had launched while we were in the East. In Amsterdam, several record stores permitted customers to choose an album, proceed to a booth, and don headphones to listen to it. WOW! The stereo sound was incredible! Scott and I were so reluctant to leave that the store personnel had to practically drag us out. We listened to albums from the Rolling Stones, Led Zeppelin, ZZ Top, Lou Reed, Pink Floyd, Lynyrd Skynyrd, and The Who. Absolutely stunning to hear fresh music after the repetition of the few cassettes we played in the *Flying Wreck*.

My emergence in the US triggered a flood of recollections of experiences and emotions harvested from the recent flurry of travel. I imagined the *Flying Wreck* as a time machine that transported Dave, Scott, and me from the Old World (Europe) to the ancient civilizations of the East. We traveled through countries and distances, briefly encountering recent events: Cold War divides, Communist governments, dictatorships, ancient and modern religious conflicts, and the overthrow of a king.

We took all of that in stride, enjoying and appreciating it. It shocked us when we returned to the first world country thought to be preeminent in the world, now cast into darkness by countries thought to be third world. That was strange in the extreme, and worrisome.

I was expecting some culture shock when dropping in on the Midwest of America. I already went through reentry in Cleveland, even meeting Scott's parents and siblings. I wasn't sure if Cleveland also qualified as Midwest, as there seemed little difference from what I recalled. No culture shock with my family either. They were happy to see me, as I was to see them. My sisters Deré, Melissa, Leigh, Maureen, and my brother Jeb had grown up! They were wonderful to hang with and asked insightful questions that reflected their advancing intellect and societal observations such as:

"Is the hash really that good?"

"Have you heard the new Stones album?"

After all, they were intrigued by the travels of their oldest brother. I was happy to share.

Near to my thoughts was their generosity and love in sending money to me in Munich when I needed it.

My mother was relieved to see me alive. There was no distance between us. Despite the falling out between her husband and me, she remained supportive and encouraging. I didn't even mention his name to her.

How long was it since I'd given thought to the mutual disowning of a father and son? Years, certainly. And more distance, literally, than time. My thoughts drifted to incidents that materialized like the transitions to a dream in a movie, like my parents' visit to Woodstock Trailer Court in Columbia, Missouri. It wasn't much of an apartment for serious study, more like a psychedelic-decorated hangout. Black lights illuminated the rock 'n' roll posters crowding the walls and ceiling, with huge speakers that often made the trailer throb. The look on my parents' face when they entered was priceless. A slight smile from my mom, disgust from my father. I hadn't given thought to the prominent poster glowing in the black light opposite the entry door that read, "Fornicate for Peace."

That image dissolved into a visit to my parents' home shortly thereafter. I had a "peace sign" decal, the round circle with the lines inside reminiscent of a bird's foot, on the driver's side wing window of my car. Perhaps you wonder what a wing window is. In the past, when car windows were raised and lowered with a handle, a smaller triangular window was located in front of the larger door window. It allowed air to circulate while driving—great for airing out cigarette smoke, or other types of smoke, and discarding ashes out the window. Getting into my car, I noticed someone had smashed the wing out. It looked like someone had taken a hammer to it. It was confirmed by my siblings that our father did precisely that. A silly but resentful act that led to an escalation of grievances, culminating in the schism between us. My focus returned to the here and now, with no interest in reliving past events any further.

At a moment my mother felt appropriate, she sincerely said, "Your father would like to see you."

I hadn't considered that possibility. I wasn't motivated to start contact because I didn't think it was coming from him—most likely a loving attempt to nudge two hardheaded men into reconciliation. I wasn't in the mood for that, and I doubted he was. It was clear that this would make her happy, and I had been causing a lot of worry and not much else for her in the recent years. I said, "OK, I'll be back tomorrow evening."

After the passport performance in New York by the immigration officer, one of the first things on my to-do list was get a new passport. It was a quick and easy process, but critical. It needed to be done straight away, with plenty of time to spare before it was required again. However, you needed a reason to apply for a new passport prior to the allotted expiration of the old passport, and you had to send your old passport along with the application. Sending the old one with all of its revealing stamps, and additional pages added in Kabul, was not an appealing idea. I pondered this as I loaded the washer with my new jeans. As I was checking my pockets, I forgot about my old passport in the back pocket because I didn't keep a wallet. I wanted to give the jeans some character, so I poured in a lot of bleach and detergent and put the machine on the long cycle. When I returned and opened the lid, I saw bits of paper on the outside of the jeans. Oops. Although the passport was mostly there, the bleach rendered anything written or stamped on the pages illegible. Best to follow instructions, so I included it with my new application and ticked the box "Return expired passport." I paid a little extra for expedited service and used my parents' address. About ten days later, both old and new passports showed up in the mail. Usually they issued the standard green-covered passport with about ten blank pages for visas and entry/exit stamps. My new passport had about 30 pages—more like a small book. It made me think. *Did someone at the State Department choose which passport to issue, or is new technology used to decide?* Probably a little of both, but it was a bit unsettling to consider.

In Kansas City, I stayed with friends that I hoped could connect me with potential rug buyers. We needed a young and hip demographic, with lots of disposable income. They would have their ears tuned to music, the rock 'n' roll scene, and its clothing and fashion trends, or intentionally go for the simplicity of Eastern appearances—the John Lennon look or Grateful Dead vibe. Above it all, would be a desire to gain authentic Eastern originals direct from an importer: A status symbol that they could show off, trade, or use. Our stuff was handpicked with that in mind. We also could back it up with personal stories and gear from the source.

Without forethought or a plan, the upper echelon of the demographics we identified as buyers of our goods deemed me as "cool" in Kansas City. The same accordance was given to Scott and me in Ann Arbor—very convenient simply because we wanted some adventure, we were in the right place at the right time, and no one told us we couldn't go to Afghanistan if we so desired. We looked the part, and all we had to do was act naturally. We brought the Afghan bazaar to the Midwest and made cool stuff easily accessible. What wasn't to be liked?

Word of our stature preceded us, and we were welcome among the elite. Along with the rugs, carpets, camel collars, donkey bags, jewelry, and other items that represented places and deeds they hadn't experienced, we became a trinket symbolizing their coolness. It was a surprise to Scott and me, but it served our purpose. It was entertaining and brought advantages with the opposite sex. Not to overlook the fact that it also sold rugs.

My stay in Kansas City was brief, but I had a lot on my to-do list. Talking to my father required perspective. Our differences in politics and social values were difficult to overcome, but I decided to confront them. I hadn't lost track of the fact he had been a fabulous father to me before our split, and he was equally generous to my siblings. We did not hold the fact he was gone frequently for business against him—he had six kids!

I arrived at my parent's home. He and my mother were sitting, having coffee. Our eyes met and a recognition of mutual mistrust passed and dissolved into an attempt by both of us to be civil as a courtesy to my mother. Mom was prepared for the situation and, with great love and sincerity, she segued into a reiteration of the travel stories that I shared with her the day before. They were short on detail and content, but all were true. I gave my father the short version of our travels, carpet purchase, and US shipment without being enthusiastic or engaging.

Then I said, "Hence, being in Kansas City and sitting in your home."

His body language changed. His facial expression relaxed, as if removing a burden, and he became animated. "Hot damn, I knew that family blood was in you."

Coming from him, it was an unexpected concession. I took it with lingering doubt, but the hopeful look on my mother's face was enough for me.

He was a self-made man from a modest background. Small in stature but with an enormous ego, he demanded respect and usually received it. He had been a World War Two fighter pilot in the US Army Air Force, flying the fastest aircraft, a P38 Lightning single-seater, twin-engine attack fighter. The plane was the top of the heap for pilot achievement. He had the drive and ambition that came from surviving that war, as did many of his peers. He was clever and a quick thinker on his feet. It was a long moment, with many thoughts quickly passing through my mind. *Accept his words without further consideration* would have been the thought bubble above my head in a cartoon.

My mother was visibly relieved upon hearing those words from my father, which were the beginning of a long truce between us and the pause to our father-son Greek tragedy saga. I had pressing matters to attend to and left, thinking that there was a lot to digest. I pushed it to the side for consideration in the probable, yet distant future.

My market research was brief. I consulted the yellow pages (remember those?) and found an Oriental carpet store located in Westport, a popular nightclub and hangout area in Kansas City. Stacks of Oriental carpets filled a storefront window on the street, and the building didn't even have a sign. I guessed they did not need it, as it was obvious what they sold. I entered the dimly lit store and had to look around for someone to talk to. The Americanized Iranian proprietor lounged on a stack of carpets, reminding me of Noor.

We made our introductions and I got to the point. "We have Oriental carpets in US customs we want to sell, direct from Afghanistan. Are you interested?"

He was slick and had forgotten nothing from the old country bazaar. "We are well provisioned, as you can see, and we have extensive contacts that allow us to import and sell direct to our retail clients."

His inventory ran the gamut—large Iranian silk room carpets to small prayer rugs from Afghanistan and other "-stan" countries. What I could see were predominantly large room carpets and were likely expensive at retail prices. What I didn't see were the other Afghani accoutrements that we had imported.

Named Bijan, he said many Americans had trouble with the name, so he was OK with "Sam." I showed him some photos of our carpets and a page from our inventory with retail prices we had set arbitrarily. He pondered the info as I looked for hints of his response from body language and facial expressions. Unsurprisingly, no clues there.

His considered response was telling and useful: "I would accept these items on consignment."

My understanding was "You've got some rugs that fill gaps in my inventory. I can easily double your retail prices and I will not have any money invested." Following some pleasantries, I closed with, "We will consider your generous offer and discuss it over chai when I return."

Fortunately, his "generous" offer wasn't required.

My best hope lay with two friends who were active in the local marijuana distribution network. I wanted to access the higher echelons and hoped they would agree. It wasn't an attempt to skip over them in the distribution channel for pot; I was peddling merchandise out of that stream of commerce. Both friends were cool about it and agreed. The resulting name provided was very useful and led to a further jump up the ranks to a person in Ann Arbor, Michigan. Home of the University of Michigan, a renowned hotbed of Vietnam War resistance, a mega center for pot distribution—and our target demographic. I would soon rendezvous with Scott in Cleveland, which was conveniently close by.

I had followed my nose or, to put it into the context of this book, had connected the Dots. With 20/20 hindsight, Dots take on many forms: good, questionable, undecided, and best discarded. I had experienced some of the best and my good fortune extended to Ann Arbor, where Scott and I met Bonnie and Thomas.

The Kansas City introductions scaled up quickly to some good people who enjoyed my hash, but the amount and frequency of imbibing was a bit too much for them. I was still functioning in travel mode and needed to adjust to local customs and amounts.

My tolerance to smoking hash was off the Richter scale in the US. Although I didn't voice it, my reference point was that cannabis leaves and flowers were the source of resin to make hash, then that waste part of the plant was discarded. An elitist point of view to some, but accurate. I had brought one of the Amsterdam chillums with me to Kansas City. I put it away until I thought it wouldn't freak out the potential clients.

Socially, I was a curiosity, passed around as "the guy from Afghanistan." I kind of got into the act: tell some stories, smoke some hash, move on.

I accepted an invitation to the Cowtown Ballroom, a popular music venue, and wound up backstage. I don't recall the band that night, but the marquee outside had the Ozark Mountain Daredevils showcased in the coming week. It was a rather small space for performers and preshow activities. I loaded up the chillum twice, to noticeable effect. The smoke filled the room and probably more of the building. As was not unusual, the start of the show was delayed. Maybe it was the smoke. In any event, they suggested I leave before the local men in blue got wind of the festivities. I needed to be more circumspect. We had pulled the same mistake going from Afghanistan to Pakistan, when our chillum smoke filled the hallway at the InterContinental Hotel. Guess I'm a slow learner.

I perceived the US was stranger to me than the "strange" lands of the East were in the beginning. Among other observations, I was flabbergasted that the US was caught unprepared when OPEC stopped the oil supply. My perception was that the US didn't see it coming, from a blind spot or ignoring signs, perhaps. It reflected my perceptions of the strangeness of the US to me—I too was indeed stranger than a strange land.

The guy that would connect me to the Ann Arbor group was coming to Kansas City. I could see it was a big deal, so I prepared to be the "guy from Afghanistan," which didn't take any preparation at all. I brought my chillum and a nice chunk of hash. They escorted me to the president's suite (no kidding) of an upscale hotel and introduced me to "JW." I liked him right away. Worldly and well-traveled in Europe, but no Asian experience. He seemed genuinely interested in what we imported, and we engaged in conversation as he led me into a room. There were many people. The tag "beautiful people" came to mind, a term used in the counterculture of the '60s and '70s to describe attractive individuals who were sometimes rich hypocrites trying to be cool. I realized I was quick to judgment, so I flowed with it. Lots of gold chains and expensive watches on the guys and lots of bare skin and jewelry on the girls. Beautiful people indeed...at least the girls!

It certainly wasn't hard to spot me, the Afghan guy. "He's the long-haired guy with the beard wearing a long-sleeved T-shirt and an embroidered vest, probably from Afghanistan," as opposed to the designer clothing that everyone else was wearing. I wore what I brought, which wasn't much, and I didn't really care. It had become a game to see how people would react. I drew a small crowd of the curious, including some girls. A few of the guys, except JW, were throwing bad vibes. One of them, and I swear it's true, was wearing a velvet smoking jacket like you would see Hugh Hefner wear, the owner of *Playboy* magazine. In the breast pocket was a fan of $100 bills. I shit you not. A real hotdog. I could go on, but you get the picture.

I talked to several other guys who eventually warmed up as their curiosity got the better of them. As you would expect, there was a mix of people—the more over-the-top types looked shady and set off alarm bells in my head. They didn't have the laid-back attitude of a pot dealer of the era. I also doubted that the money for the designer costumes came from just pot. Perhaps I was witnessing the beginning of the transition in the business to big money, dangerous drugs, and unsavory people who would subsequently change everything, although I didn't specifically classify anyone there in that category.

Scott's call came to my parent's house and Mom got the message to me via my brother. I learned from Scott that our shipment had cleared and we could pick it up after making an appointment with the forwarder. I got a flight reservation to Cleveland for the following day and called Scott to give him the itinerary. He called the forwarder. Finally, we could get our hands on the goods.

With the engine running, Scott parked curbside at the baggage claim. I jumped in and he drove the van to the freight terminal. As we entered and walked in deeper, we could smell our stuff before we caught sight of it! The musty, earthy aroma was delightful. It got our blood rushing. There were the right number of bundles and the three boxes of goodies. We did a quick estimate of the carpets in each of the bundles; it seemed about right. We wanted to load up and get out, so we took it on partial good faith that everything was there. We completed the paperwork, got some help to load the stuff, and it fit nicely in the van. Now, we had a van full of valuable (we hoped) goods to be concerned about.

There weren't any issues with customs, which we didn't expect, but it was a shipment from Afghanistan and it didn't tax our imagination to think of plausible scenarios for trouble. Now we were clear of customs and free to become marketers of Afghan goods that were the rage of coolness in hippiedom.

We found a pay phone, and I called the number for Bonnie that JW had given to me. She answered right away, very nice and full of enthusiasm. I explained we had received the carpets and assorted trinkets from Afghanistan and were at the airport in Cleveland. She had expected this and asked if we could come to Ann Arbor right away. Her friends were very interested and she was really excited for herself and her partner, Thomas. We would make the two-and-a-half-hour drive and call her when we arrived.

That was the most encouraging news we could have received. We were eager to go directly there and hopefully move some of the stuff right away. We didn't like the idea of having a lot of valuable goods in the van and nowhere enclosed to park it.

Bonnie had given us directions to a restaurant, where she and her friends wanted to host our dinner and she would make arrangements for our lodging. Sounded good to us. Neither Scott nor I had ever met Bonnie or her friends. She was a lead from JW, who was a friend of my friends. What could possibly go wrong? Nothing, as it turned out. Bonnie and

Thomas were special Dots and don't fit an off-the-shelf description. Smart and honest, for sure; above reproach in business dealings and fun to be around; worldly and well-traveled, but firmly grounded. We found them trustworthy, and once friends, you can count on them. It didn't take long to forge a bond that still endures.

We still had an hour or more of daylight. The restaurant was in a trendy part of a university town with parking in the back. Later, we found out that Bonnie and Thomas operated a catering company, were connected to the rock 'n' roll music scene, and were renowned in the community. Bonnie, Thomas, and several friends were eager to see what we had. When we slid the door back, the aroma was delicious. They had huge smiles; Scott and I set about producing carpets to admire, and then we opened the boxes to reveal the other Afghan delights. They were gobsmacked at the quantity and diversity. They wanted it all! NO, really, they wanted to buy everything, and we hadn't even given them the prices or the inventory. It was an exciting prospect, but we were taking it one step at a time. We would have our meal and talk to them further. They would want some stories about the origins and how we came about the goods. With some luck and enticing stories, we would hopefully sell a good quantity to them, even if it wasn't everything.

Ann Arbor had a vibrancy and enthusiastic feel to it. The university student body was in the thick of the Vietnam War–protest movement and had been for years. This defined the pulse of the under-thirty crowd, including tens of thousands of students, faculty, and much of the business community. Counterculture, the "establishment," capitalism, and almost any type of protester were seemingly accepted by the town. Not to be overlooked, there was a lot of pot being smoked. Tons of pot also moved nationally from Ann Arbor, a major distribution center in the US.

We tidied up the Afghan loot and moved the van to the front of the restaurant in a more visible location. Everyone sat down at the reserved table—in a prominent position, but with privacy. Bonnie had anticipated and skillfully organized our personal meeting and the preview of Afghan goods. Bonnie and Thomas were seasoned professionals and projected sincere personalities.

We had a thoroughly enjoyable time with the delicious meal and friendly conversation. Overall, it was a great evening. We stirred their imagination about Afghanistan, and they found our stories humorous and enlightening. We all observed the unspoken rules of those skirting the law, but we learned a lot along the way. For them, too. There was sufficient reconfirmation of their previous desire to buy it all. We agreed to meet again the next afternoon to sort out the details.

We explained we weren't really prepared to jump immediately into a sale and needed some time to ourselves to get organized. With everyone in agreement, we ended the evening in good spirits, with a sense of goodwill and a spirit of adventure.

We thought Bonnie had reserved a motel for us, but she surprised us by offering her guest house for our stay. There was plenty of space, privacy, and it was nearby. Believing that made sense, we agreed. We also were glad to have a secure location, not only for the overnight stay, but privacy to sort through the paperwork and items we hoped to sell. We had already figured out that there were a few outliers that they probably wouldn't want, and we wanted to keep some stuff for ourselves and Dave.

The guest house was all we expected, and comfortable. We could settle down after the evening's festivities, pull out our files, and digest the shipping paperwork to be sure it looked right. We also discussed the inventory sheets and the prices to see if we still thought they were in line with local market realities.

I relayed to Scott what Bijan had said in Kansas City. My opinion was that our prices were low. It took a brief discussion for us to agree that our original pricing strategy amounted to little more than a guess, and we had more than that to go on now. Our instincts would need to guide us when it came time to negotiate a large quantity deal.

We arose early to a beautiful fall day with sunshine and a light breeze. There was one of those hotel-type coffee machines in our kitchen, and fruit and milk in the fridge. Quite hospitable of them! Coffee would have to do, as there wasn't any chai to be found.

That reassuring and welcoming aroma rushed into our faces when we slid open the door of the van and inventoried our goods. We still had film to develop, with photos of the shipment (another thing we needed to get done right away), so we only had our written description of the goods. It was barely legible and not insightful. We relied on our collective memory of our purchases as a reference guide.

We had plenty of space on a nice paved-stone apron along the driveway where we had parked. It was quick work to pull the rugs out and stack them in groups. Our consideration began with the bundle from the night before, and we were laughing as we rediscovered one fabulous rug after another. There were also some that we shouldn't have bought but did in a moment of nostalgia, or a forgotten impulse. Like an excellent quality Bokhara rug in bold yellow and black—not colors that any self-respecting rug weaver would choose. It had the Dunlop Tire company logo splashed across the center, but they misspelled it: Dunlap. The idea was since Ohio was a tire manufacturing center, someone in the industry would pay big bucks for such a cool rug. We set that one aside.

As we sorted through them, we remembered why we bought a particular rug, and why we priced them as we did. But we needed to make some adjustments. Initially we set the selling price on prayer rugs based solely on size—the bigger, the more expensive. We realized that the better quality but smaller Bokhara rugs were cheaper than the lesser quality but larger Baluch rugs. We made the necessary adjustments to reflect our opinion of the carpet quality, which covered a range of prices and sizes. Scott and I both thought that our selection of carpets chosen back in Kabul was sound, and it satisfied us both that we performed well as rookies. As long as people bought them!

We thrilled ourselves when we dug into the boxes. We had forgotten what we bought, as our focus was on rugs. Wow! Cool stuff. We marveled at the cork carvings from China. They were delicate and intricate, resembling beautiful landscapes. All of them arrived in perfect condition, which really boggled our minds. The lapis lazuli jewelry was beautiful. Rings, necklaces, earrings, and pocketknives were stunning. We had camel collars, some table runners, and several things we didn't know what they were. Some fragmented donkey bags were there too. They usually hung over the donkey's rear quarter like a saddle, but they cut a few in half. We puzzled over that, then we remembered Brian's shoes. The half bags could make shoes, or even pillows. New product category! We kept those for ourselves. There were a few smallish pillows that were cool, and some silver pillboxes, prayer capsules, and jewelry boxes. I had included several additional Afghan vests, like the one I wore daily, and a really cool black velvet "dress" vest for myself. I still have both. Rummaging through those boxes was like a treasure hunt; it brought back memories of the fun we had discovering all that stuff.

We put aside some prayer rugs and a carpet or three, plus a few goodies for each of us. That left the items we wanted to sell. We staged everything in areas so we wouldn't get them mixed up. Scott and I decided that if Bonnie and friends bought at least 75 percent of the goods in cash, we would offer a 10 percent discount. We were eager to cash out and head back to Kabul, so we would likely have done the same even if they only bought more than half. We hadn't beaten the bushes yet for alternative buyers. Though we thought there was a decent chance of finding them, it would take time. We could also put what remained on consignment with Bijan, but we'd have to ship or drive them to Kansas City. More time and money.

The best option was to work this deal to success. Our sorting process was painstaking and took a long time. When we finished, we were famished. We called Bonnie, and she gave us directions to a restaurant to meet for a late lunch. It was close, and obviously a happening place. Bonnie and Thomas were with a guy we hadn't met. It was her brother, Jimmy. Cool guy—smart and clever, by our reckoning. He was quick to turn the conversation to business.

"Bonnie is sold on your Afghan stuff. She loves it. She's got a good sense of what will sell. Do you have an inventory list and price breakdown?"

Scott said, "We do, but only one copy."

I threw in, "Can we get a copy made nearby?"

"We can do that at our office. Bonnie can ride with you and look at it as we drive there."

Bonnie absorbed herself in the papers during the ten-minute drive, occasionally making noises. We arrived at a strip mall where the catering business' office and warehouse were situated. The warehouse held essential equipment like tables, chairs, cooking utensils, white goods, etc. We walked inside and Bonnie barely looked up from the inventory.

"Can we take a quick look at it again?"

We were glad we had separated out what was for sale and put it in the van's rear, and our stuff in the front. We could slide the side door open, as well as open the rear door for easy access to the for-sale goods. Bonnie and Jimmy dug in and chatted while they perused the merchandise. They appeared to be having fun, but were also quite observant.

"We'll go make a copy for you. We'll be right back." They were and had an offer. "It's cool stuff. We want to buy it on the condition we can negotiate the price, but we also have to get all of it."

Cornering the market was a bold move, and we hadn't thought about that angle. They were proving savvier than we gave them credit for. We liked that. I told them the story about Bijan in Kansas City, using it to illustrate our take that our prices were already low. But if they bought everything for sale, we would concede an additional 10 percent. They agreed.

"We'll meet you at the guest house at about 6:30 P.M. with the cash. We can off-load everything into the house, then celebrate," enthused Bonnie. "There's a guest safe with instructions in the bedroom closet."

"We'll pay in large bills," added Jimmy.

We retired to our accommodations, courtesy of Bonnie and Thomas, and took stock of the last couple of days.

"She's buying everything, just like she said." I spoke my thoughts aloud.

"We don't have the money yet," replied Scott.

That was a fact. We'd know in a few hours if this whole thing was a setup. Neither of us had that feeling, but it was a possibility that would soon be decided. We'd only made a rough guess about the sale amount for "everything," and we were delighted with the number we eventually got. We did the math again, and it was the same number. Dave would be pleased.

"Hey, have you sent a letter to Dave?"

"No. We need to do that."

It had been several weeks, and we told him we would send updates to him. There wasn't an AmEx office in Kabul, so we arranged for the letter to go to Mohammed at the Pan Am office, who agreed to get it to Noor. Dave would check there every so often.

We really didn't have any news until now, so we agreed to send Dave a letter the next day if we got the deal done.

Scott and I gave a copy of our inventory and price calculations to Bonnie and Thomas. They stationed themselves in the house, and we carried in armfuls of carpets at a time as they checked them off and stacked them. We used the same process for the other goods. It took about an hour and a half. We consumed some alcohol and smoke along the way. They were good for their word, and we settled in cash with no complications.

An air of celebration, success, and relief chuffed us and injected a sense of camaraderie that proved to be long-lived in the coming decades. We needed to organize ourselves, the money, and the remaining Afghani stuff. The plan was already formulated. We merged our Afghan goodies into one bundle of carpets and one box of other stuff and split the money up into separate locations: the safe, the van, Scott, and me.

"We've got reservations at a Thai restaurant close to here," said Bonnie. "Let's celebrate! Here's the location. We look forward to seeing you there."

A bottle of chilled champagne sat at the table. Unusual for a Thai restaurant, but Bonnie corrected, "It's a Thai fusion restaurant." It was a new term and idea to a couple of guys fresh out of the East. The food was delicious, and so were both bottles of the champagne.

Deep into the delightful evening, Thomas said, "We are catering for the Allman Brothers concert at Cobo Arena next week. We've got a couple of extra tickets. Wanna go?"

They were rock 'n' roll royalty and at the top of their game. An opportunity not to miss. "Hell yes!" shouted Scott and me, nearly in unison.

We had about five days to fill before the concert, so we drove the 2.5 hours to Scott's parents' house to store the Afghan stuff until we returned to North America with Dave. We could also stash the bulk of the money there after the Allman Brothers. Our plan was to leave from Cleveland for Kabul a couple of days later.

We regrouped at the guest house early in the afternoon on the day of the show and hung out with Bonnie and Thomas. We were totally comfortable with them, got high and laughed a lot. They had to leave soon enough to get ready for the show, so we would drive separately. They adroitly slipped into the conversation that chillums in Cobo Arena would be highly visible. We had already reached the same conclusion, so Scott and I leisurely rolled up two big handfuls of hash reefers to take with us.

The seats were excellent. We had friends of Bonnie and Thomas on both sides, and the row in front and back. It was a strategically helpful way to mask the origin of the steady stream of reefer smoke that would flow in all directions from our central location.

We were in the US and did not want to extend our stay as a guest of the government, so we took stock of what the locals were doing. They were smoking pot and didn't seem too concerned. We didn't smell any hash, though. They would certainly notice good Afghani. We waited until the Allman Brothers were into the second song, and then Scott lit 'em up and passed to his left. I did the same to my right. The cloud of hash smoke was catching the attention of more and more people, and the joints kept expanding the range as we encouraged socializing. We adopted a strategy of blasting the reefers out in an ever increasing area to avoid being identified as the source. Worked like a charm...it always did. We looked around with satisfaction. The smoke was pretty dense, and many people were happy.

We paused the reefer circulation to let the smoke diffuse a bit. Not everyone could handle the hash reefers, as the hash needs to be mixed with tobacco to burn properly. But they would at least pass it on to keep the joints moving.

We hadn't heard a lot of live rock 'n' roll music the past year, so the Rolling Stones in Holland and the Allman Brothers in the US were a treat. Both concerts seemed to be over too quickly, though. We made our escape during the enthusiastic clapping and noise that followed the encore before the house lights turned on and the crowd detained us. Safety first was an idiom we often ignored but heeded when appropriate.

Bonnie and Thomas would work late, so Scott and I made the short drive back to Ann Arbor and retired to the comfortable accommodations provided by our friends' guest house.

We had some last-minute packing to do. We had retrieved the film that we brought back with us from the lab and briefly looked at the slides. The lab had also loaded the processed B&W film negatives into plastic sheets for later scrutiny. We left both at Scott's parents' house, along with our Afghan goods, before our return trip.

We also had bought more bulk unexposed B&W Tri-X film and 150 (15 cartons) Kodak Snap-Cap 135 film magazines. Bulk loading film saved a lot of money.

The Kodak film cartridges came in a carton of ten, each within a little white box with "Kodak Snap-Cap Magazine" printed on each end of the box in bold letters. If an inspector were to get curious and open the carton, they were presented with ten sealed boxes of unexposed film clearly identified. So we filled up five of the fifteen cartons with 36 shots in each magazine, neatly sealed each film canister in the little white boxes, and placed ten boxes in each carton. That left ten cartons of empty film magazines for for future use.

We met up with Bonnie and Thomas the next day to say our goodbyes and confirm that we would be back, giving them the first right of refusal for whatever Afghani goods we brought. We were sad to leave. They had become fast friends and good company. They were each a special Dot that would populate our shared world for a very long time.

ARIANA AFGHAN AIRLINES

AIRLINES GENERAL SCHEDULE
ALL DEPARTURE FLIGHTS FROM KABUL

TO	DAYS	TIME	FLIGHT NO
KANDAHAR_DAMASCUS ISTANBUL_FRANKFURT LONDON PESHAWAR	SUN	0700 1200	FG 701 PK 607
TASHKENT TEHERAN PESHAWAR LAHORE_NEW DELHI	MON	1100 0845 1200 1030	FG 604 IR 713 PK 607 FG 302
TEHERAN_BAGHDAD_ BEIRUT LAHORE_AMRITSAR	TUE	0900 1030	FG 703 FG 304
(TEHERAN)_ISTANBUL_ ROME_PARIS_ FRANKFURT	WED	0700	FG 705
NEW EDLHI TEHERAN TASHKENT_MOSCOW PESHAWAR LAHORE_AMRITSAR	THU	1130 0845 1100 1200 1030	FG 306 IR 713 SU 532 PK 607 FG 308
(TEHERAN)_ISTANBUL PARIS_FRANKFURT	FRI	0900	FG 707
NEW DELHI PESHAWAR TEHERAN _ BEIRUT	SAT	1030 1200 0900	FG 310 PK 607 FG 709

FG: ARIANA AFGHAN AIRLINES
IR : IRAN NATIONAL AIRLINES

(TEHERAN) TECHNICAL STOP _ NO TRAFFIC ACCEPTED

AIRLINES GENERAL SCHEDULE
ALL ARRIVAL FLIGHTS TO KABUL

FROM	DAYS	TIME	FLIGHT NO
BEIRUT_TEHERAN PESHAWAR	SUN	1315 1120	FG 710 PK 606
TEHERAN LONDON_FRANKFURT ISTANBUL_DAMASCUS PESHAWAR NEW DELHI LAHORE TASHKENT	MON	0745 0915 1120 1745 1520	IR 712 FG 702 PK 606 FG 303 FG 605
AMRITSAR_LAHORE	TUE	1700	FG 305
MOSCOW _TASHKENT BEIRUT BAGHDAD TEHERAN	WED	0945 1315	SU 531 FG 704
TEHERAN PARIS_FRANKFURT ROME_ISTANBUL (TEHERAN) PESHAWAR AMRITSAR_LAHORE	THU	0745 0930 1120 1700	IR 712 FG 706 PK 606 FG 309
PARIS_FRANKFURT_ ISTANBUL_(TEHERAN) PESHAWAR NEW DELHI	SAT	0800 1120 1745	FG 708 PK 606 FG 311

PK : PAKISTAN INTERNATIONAL AIRLINES
SU : AEROFLOT

1973 Ariana Afghan Airlines Timetable

Rolling Stones Concert In Rotterdam

Back in Amsterdam. Check money in shoes

Empty film magazines

Interlude Nine

Embracing Small Is Thinking Big

Traffic: *Light Up Or Leave Me Alone > Lyrics*

You made it! I appreciate you sticking with me on this Theory of Dots journey. The events in this book loomed large in the doing but small on the world stage. Unraveling the mystery of Dots was truly daunting for my small brain. Large, small, big, and little—I enjoyed sharing the journey with you. Coming up are some thoughts on potential applications for offshoots of the Theory of Dots and the untapped potential of them to engage the small realms of our existence.

So, let's not be small-minded and concentrate solely on the Dot Net as a network to connect Dots, even though that is the thrust of this book and a concept dear to my heart. I view the Dot Net having far more potential. *Connecting* is the operative word. Connecting humans foremost, but also connecting nonhuman life-forms, sentient or not, with humans represents an enormous opportunity. In this Interlude, I'll explore some examples.

Living organisms communicate in various ways. There's the familiar touch, sight, hearing, smell, and taste of humans and animals. Beyond the human ability to perceive are the chemical, sound, and electrical techniques of communication of animals, plants, and microorganisms. Regardless of the method of communication, all involve networks to send and receive information, the human brain included. Our brain has a multitude of complex systems in two categories: structural and functional. Other mammals have similar neural networks, and almost all other animals have functional similarities. But nature doesn't stop there. Plants, trees, and fungi communicate and share nutrients through a network of roots, or a mycorrhizal nexus. Some span great distances. I classify all the previous networks under a "hardwired" description. They have a physical connection—some are micro small, but there's a "wire" of sorts involved.

The Dot Net is not hardwired. It's more like Wi-Fi writ large. I posit it will eventually connect human instincts, intuition, and emotions over vast distances—in high fidelity. In order to network humans to other living organisms via the Dot Net, a "router" would be required for interfacing. Karma would be the ultimate high-speed network, using quantum entanglement to scale up to galactic proportions. A brief description of an imagined method to access the Dot Net with your personal dcode is in the last paragraph of Interlude Eight. For greater detail, please visit the Interlude Endnotes.

Let's begin by looking at some applications for the Dot Net and then end by discussing how the Theory of Dots' interconnectedness principle applies to climate change.

• • • • • • • • •

Medical

I use the mobile phone network as a model for a BioSignal[44] medical diagnostic and treatment tool. The proposed use for a BioSig is to direct a prescribed medical action or procedure written by BioWare authors to medicate the malady at its source. The Dot Net would deliver the BioSig in a prescribed language for the patient's cell(s), or to the offending bacteria or virus. Finding the chemical, electrical, or other language for the recipient is a challenge, but research has shown progress.[45]

For temporary medical issues, the patient could use a wearable device like an Apple Watch. It would be possible to connect with the body in far more intimate ways than what's currently workable. For more permanent health issues, an implant may be more suitable. The person's device would receive the BioSig through Dot Net, instead of using cellular or satellite.

BioSignals could replace prescriptions, disrupting the drug industry and creating entrepreneurial opportunities. A more effective cancer treatment would be communicating precise remedial actions to microorganisms rather than using radiation or toxins. Imagine the ability to communicate instructions to bacteria, microorganisms, or enzymes to behave in a certain way. Or fungi to take a certain action, responding with expediency, perhaps saving a life.

Communication between humans and organisms could replace harsh drugs and invasive surgery in medicine. For example, a recent BBC *Future* article by Roberta Angheleanu states "...bacteria and fungi to take up residence within cancer cells and even some immune cells. The bacteria and fungi excrete chemicals or otherwise interact with the cancer cells. That can either compromise or support the cancer's growth."[46]

A specific BioSig with instructions for the bacteria and fungi to attack the cancer cells or support the immune cells would be a phenomenal achievement.

Taking it up a notch, is communicating with the disease-focused genes in the human genome feasible? We enter an arena of science with a Pandora's box of risk. One could argue that a person's genome is the most private information possible. A complete reading may not be on the horizon yet, but one that is accurate, if not complete, is.[47] Protecting such information is critical. Science will have already gained relevant experience in securing and fencing in artificial intelligence, both the current basic versions and their future progeny. Scientific progress requires taking risks. But those risks can pay off handsomely. Sending BioSig instructions for specific genes directly to an individual using their dcode address via Dot Net would have significant implications for medical science.

Another example comes from a connection between microbiota in the gut and the human brain, which has a significant influence on mental health. A research paper in Researchgate.net by Natasha Irum, et al, states "The gut-brain axis is a communication pathway that allows a two-way exchange of information between the microbiota of the gastrointestinal tract and the nervous system of humans."[48] The resulting metabolic processes can be beneficial or detrimental to a person's state of mind. Further research holds promise, as described in a July 8, 2023, NPR article by Joanne Silberner: "It's clear there's a physiological connection between brain and gut," says Dr. Glenn Treisman, a professor of medicine and psychiatry at Johns Hopkins. "Gut microbes make chemicals that affect your brain," he says. "They can be carried by blood directly to your brain, or they can be carried through nerves that connect to your brain. And your brain can speed up your gut and change what your microbes are."[49]

Communication

Humans have been slow to recognize and respect the interconnection between all things living. In the Interludes I have posited that connectedness is a prevalent theme throughout the living world. It may also be an attribute of the universe. My consideration of karma, aka dark matter, allows for the possibility that all constituents in the universe are part of a network. Research has shown that communication between known life-forms is not limited to human capabilities.

It will be challenging for humanity to recognize nonsentient life as worthy of our respect. As a species, humans don't have a stellar reputation for treating other beings, even sentient ones, with due respect and consideration. The Dot Net, functioning as described, could open the door to eventual communication with the entire diaspora of life inside and out of the human body. We can't WhatsApp them, but signaling between living organisms already exists. Researchers are just beginning to bridge the communication gap with humans.[50] People have a history of resisting change, especially if it threatens long-standing social norms, beliefs, religious doctrine, or way of life. Exchanging information with microorganisms, bacteria, and fungi might trigger unreasonable fears of change. But the smaller the creature is, the less threatening and more palatable the concept of interaction becomes to the faint of heart. There are nearly limitless applications for Dot Net information exchanges between humans and microorganisms.

The idea of humans communicating with living organisms is an exciting concept that could change our relationships with nonsentient creatures. Could humanity cross that threshold with a benevolent and respectful outcome? I choose to be optimistic, but it will take a shift, a collective reckoning by humanity, to lay the groundwork for such a dramatic change in human nature. That's not to overlook or underestimate the laws of nature that prevail on this planet. Perhaps it can only happen after humanity has moved beyond planet Earth.

Small

Of course, the term *small* is relative, but in the *small* category, most people would include bacteria and microbiota. The Theory of Dots finds opportunity in very small things. Where does the small end? Or begin? For that consideration, quantum mechanics is needed. My theory finds help there to advance further discovery of its karma concept. Quantum mechanics has several prominent theories as its underpinnings. The one most interesting to me is superstring theory, which originated in the late 1960s. Now we're getting *small!* In that theory, the smallest particle is not a point—it's a one-dimensional object that vibrates. The utterly limitless array of frequencies determines what a string represents. The notion that the smallest unit of everything vibrates akin to music is something that I find beautiful. Rock 'n' roll finds its vindication! It's embedded in the fabric of spacetime. OK, that's from me, not science. Anyway, it's comforting to note that the Rolling Stones existed before superstring theory.

Big

It takes a whole lotta small to make something big. Take the third rock from our star, Earth. It's a vast area of diverse environments when viewed as a human on the planet. Viewed from the edge of our solar system, it's a Pale Blue Dot.[51] As with many things, it's a matter of perspective. NASA says our sun is one of at least 100 billion stars in the Milky Way galaxy that we call home. To put that in perspective, the Milky Way is one of billions of galaxies in the universe. That's an unfathomable number of one-dimensional vibrating objects. What appears enormous from one perspective may seem small from another. The Theory of Dots suggests that billions of people and countless Dots can be connected over vast distances. When viewed in the grand scheme of the universe in its vastness, it's not so remarkable.

With apology to Arthur C. Clarke, et al, I skew his famous quote to read, "Any sufficiently advanced natural process that is not thoroughly understood is easily mistaken for magic." A perception of magic can lead to a mistaken belief that further investigation is not worth the effort. My considerations in these Interludes have only scratched the surface of potential applications that have their origins in the Theory of Dots.

The possibilities of Connecting the Dots with other living organisms and exacting results that will prove to be beneficial and breathtaking. The realm of the very small remains enigmatic, giving rise to seemingly magical possibilities. Seeking understanding is the bridge to discovery. Humanity is on the threshold of very big discoveries.

From my vantage point, the Theory of Dots supports the distinct possibility that a "do-over" in life, a rejigging of a Dot encounter within a virtual simulation, is on the horizon. The ability to redefine the path toward or away from a connection to a Dot, identifying a different Dot, and encouraging people to explore different life trajectories resulting from a connection of Dots could give birth to a new category of entrepreneurship in the gaming, life coaching, and the entertainment industries. However, I find the opportunity to improve the lives of individuals even more enticing. This falls within the realm of possibility for the metaverse's use. Lots of uncertainty there, but that's life, isn't it?

Climate Change

Those two words now carry a burden of meaning. If taken word for word, they suggest a sustained process in the earth's atmosphere over time. But *time* is another relative term. Earth's climate, its ecology, and the life-forms that inhabit it are vastly different in our era than 100,000 years ago. That's but a blink of an eye in the earth's context of time. However, it's far too long a period for humans to put into perspective and into the context of their lives.

When people talk about climate change today, they are referring to significant changes within the last century because of human causes, impacting the atmosphere and ecology to a level that has a detrimental effect on humans. The Anthropocene Epoch[52] is the unofficial name for this period. Further muddying of the waters comes from catastrophic events like tornadoes, hurricanes, drought, heatwaves, and floods—events that have been with us throughout history. The frequency and intensity in familiar locations, as well as the events happening in areas not affected before, are concerning. We see evidence of this from news sources every day. Many consider these sudden changes an early warning system from nature. Others prefer to scoff at the "warnings," preferring to consider it business as usual for Mother Nature. Business as usual for her is successful regardless of the outcomes. Humans have a very different perspective. Climatic changes can produce outcomes that are life-threatening.

The term *climate change* has become politicized throughout the world, especially in the United States, as a tool for political parties, environmentalists, and industries. A tool that serves to advance two vastly different stances. One urges immediate and comprehensive action to minimize and postpone the impacts of climate change that are perceived to pose existential threats to human life. Others argue that the use of Earth's finite resources should continue unabated because they believe that climate change proponents are exaggerating or creating misleading threats to humanity.

Both sides have credible sources that support their beliefs. There's no doubt that the climate of the earth will change even without human intervention. Will those changes within the human time frame of reference be detrimental or beneficial to humans and their preferred way of life on this planet? I'm an optimist, a glass-half-full kind of guy, but the water itself is getting dirty. The term *climate change* cannot encapsulate the complete impact of ACORN (Arrogant Consumption of Resources Now). Arrogant as in "a claiming for oneself of more consideration or importance than is warranted."[53] We correctly cite finite resources in discussions about sustainability, which is a kissing cousin to climate change. I can't think of any finite resource more important than a habitable human environment—one that maintains the diversity and beauty of our planet. I'm not against consuming some of the finite resources available to sustain a comfortable life now, and it's not up to me to define for anyone else what that definition is. However, I'm not comfortable with an arrogant disregard for future generations not to have alternative resources to substitute for those we deplete. Ignoring or disregarding nature's warning signals is not wise.

The current malaise in the United States, and to a lesser extent much of the Western world, is that of a hardening of one's position in politics, religion, education, and climate change. There's little allowance for differing opinions, or even discussion. Our species' survival may depend on recognizing the interdependence of all life-forms, understanding those relationships, and taking responsible action now to prevent further irrevocable short- and long-term harm. Cooperative dialogue now between the polarized factions must reach a working consensus for immediate action before the level of climate change reaches a tipping point of no return.

Few expect that existing multinational entities will volunteer to relinquish their stranglehold on key industries or control of finite resources for manufacturing. Incentives and societal pressure are required. I begrudgingly allow that certain governmental regulations are necessary as well. Some of those entities are in a favorable position to cash in on the transition from finite to sustainable resources. The smart and focused ones will only grow stronger—another issue to be concerned about. There shouldn't be a right or wrong approach, only that which is most relevant with proven results.

By not reaching a consensus on the threat of climate change and taking adequate steps to mitigate it, we are declaring ourselves enemies of a healthy and sustainable environment. That won't end well.

A realignment of the human perspective of where we fit in the big picture of small to big may be the key to our survival. Rather than seeing ourselves at the top of the food chain, it won't dethrone us to perceive ourselves as interconnected to all life—a chain, but not a pecking order of importance. Human interdependence on the very small, including fungi and bacteria, was considered in Interlude Four. That discussion further recognized that life on Earth would not exist without the mycelium networks. Humans are a small part of the big picture, and not an essential link in nature's chain. The existence of humans is not necessary for life on Earth to continue. Not so if, for example, we eliminated mycelium networks.

Interdependence extends beyond living organisms. Climate change affects Earth's habitable zones, from the atmosphere to the sea floor, mountains to beaches, and rivers to oceans. Earth—Mother Nature, if you will—has a much different perspective than humans. Horrendous flooding shows the immediate damage to life and property caused by torrential rains. That catches the attention of humans. Long-term damage is the slower process of erosion caused by the warming of the atmosphere and water temperature of the oceans, resulting in melting ice caps and rising sea levels, both of which lead to significant changes in geology and geography, with far more knock-on effects damaging the climate. Human populations can overlook or dismiss this slow transformation until it's too late to reverse.

Many argue that for way too long, we've been using up finite resources with an inadequate Plan B—kicking the can down the road, so to speak. In 1950, Earth's human population was 2.55 billion. According to the United Nations, the population reached 8 billion in late 2022. That's an enormous increase in hungry mouths to feed. And those additional people consume a lot more stuff made from nonrenewable resources. There's a breaking point of no return somewhere, so either this or the following generation is on the verge of being stuck with the check and no credit card to use for payment. That's a shitty deal to leave behind for someone else to clean up. I don't think humans alone have the discipline to pull back from the brink before it's too late. But there's hope, and it's called *science*.

The current climate crisis has emphasized the interconnection between all living things, including those that are not visible. Giving adequate priority to the small things is a wise decision. Without the micro world of fungi and bacteria, our big human world would cease to exist.

Understanding photosynthesis and microbial processing is crucial to safeguarding the Earth's life-supporting network.

Establishing priorities for climate action in the big picture is, well, an enormous task. The work needed to address the existing and future ill effects of climate change is staggering. Climate experts have established clear priorities despite having been flogged heavily in every corner of responsible reporting and investigation for decades, with no shortage of biased opinions in both questionable and reliable news sources. It's easy to reach the conclusion that the posturing and bickering needs to stop.

For me, water is a huge climate change priority. There's not much that happens on this planet that doesn't involve water. I'm very thankful to live near the sea. It's a big part of my life that I don't take for granted. Some sobering facts: "...about 71 percent of the Earth's surface is water-covered, and the oceans hold about 96.5 percent of all Earth's water. Water also exists in the air as water vapor, in rivers and lakes, in ice caps and glaciers, in the ground as soil moisture and in aquifers, and even in you and your dog."[54] Our bodies are up to 60 percent water.

Earth's oceans have to be one of the top priorities for immediate and sustained alleviation of harmful climate change. From NASA: "Covering more than 70% of Earth's surface, our global ocean has a very high heat capacity. It has absorbed 90% of the warming that has occurred in recent decades due to increasing greenhouse gases, and the top few meters of the ocean store as much heat as Earth's entire atmosphere. The effects of ocean warming include sea level rise due to thermal expansion, coral bleaching, accelerated melting of Earth's major ice sheets, intensified hurricanes, and changes in ocean health and biochemistry."[55]

A good example of an ocean-related climate threat is sargassum, a type of floating algae. At sea, the plant rafts can be many kilometers wide and stretch for great distances. It's a beneficial habitat providing food, safety, and breeding areas for a variety of animals like fish, crabs, shrimp, sea turtles, and marine birds. However, when the currents and wind push it ashore, the story changes.

This floating macroalgae is an example of the potential to use living networks to solve a combined climate/human-exacerbated problem. Until 2015, it was a benign floating ecosystem in the central Atlantic. Changes happened because of deforestation and the use of nitrogen fertilizer in the Amazon. The runoff water carried the nitrogen to the mouth of the Amazon River, where it acted as rocket fuel for the growth of sargassum. Climate change and the resulting warming of sea surface temperatures triggered a sargassum bloom unlike any other.

It has created a crisis in the Caribbean Sea, the Caribbean coast of Mexico, Gulf of Mexico, and along parts of the coastline of Florida. When it remains at sea, as mentioned previously, it provides a habitat for a variety of sea life, absorbs carbon from the atmosphere, and contributes to the balance of nature. But when it washes up on the shore, it decomposes and creates risks for nesting turtles, smells like rotten eggs, and discourages beach visitors. It has been a disaster for countries that rely on tourism, so there is a pressing need for an immediate solution to a big problem. A potential natural solution could involve fungi, which use carbon to sustain its life, and sargassum, which is a carbon sink (it stores carbon). A system of mycelia channels from on shore would terminate in a seaside harbor, where the fungi consume the accumulated sargassum and channel it via the hyphae (that make up the) inland for sustenance and carbon sequestration. The consumption of sargassum by fungi is one potential solution to a problem caused by climate change. It's also one example of the interconnection between living organisms that results in a symbiotic relationship with a bonus—it includes humans in the bargain.

· · ● ● ● · ● ● · · ·

There is light at the end of the tunnel, and reasons for optimism. Despite the ill-fated bouts of war and ongoing risky behavior of governments and leaders that could lead to an existential threat to humanity, we are still here. A sustained effort in critical environmental areas to mitigate the climate damage already inflicted is underway. It will take time to determine the most effective solutions. Technical innovation, capital investment, and entrepreneurs are essential contributors. Science, used for the good of humanity, is key to a better world for all living organisms.

I encourage you to visit my website and weigh in with your thoughts and opinions. Please visit ctdbook.com.

Chapter Seventeen

Flip Side

Van Morrison: *Glad Tidings* > *Lyrics*

Schiphol Airport in Amsterdam is like going home for me. The airport is large and chaotic, but the moment you step off the plane, you feel the Dutch atmosphere. There's a vibe and an energy that the Dutch project—it's called efficiency, enthusiasm, and rules! Lots of rules, but it doesn't dull the sense of their can-do attitude.

The Dutch passport and immigration authorities have heard and seen it all. They don't suffer fools gladly; they want straight answers, and they expect to be looked in the eye. The passport control agent noticed the thickness of my new passport, flipped through all the empty pages, and looked at me. I could hear the wheels turning in his head—new passport, extra pages, first usage? The trick is to utter a few Dutch words with a smile. He acknowledged me and I got the *whomp! whomp!* of an entrance stamp in my passport.

The first stamp in my shiny new passport felt appropriate. That's the compromise I will take in getting a new passport. A clean start with no stamps from notorious countries also meant that the new stamps would be highly visible for a while. The deal satisfied me.

Scott and I each boarded the flight in Cleveland with a large camera bag loaded with our camera bodies, lenses, and lots of film. We split the loot up in two special money belts, our shoes, and the hidden gap at the bottom of the camera bag. We had checked in our new superlight tube-frame backpacks and stashed a handful of rolled bills in those handy-dandy light aluminum tubes. Back then, hand baggage wasn't X-ray screened, but word was out that some flights were doing scans of checked baggage. We thought we'd run a test on that assumption. We boarded our connection to Amsterdam in JFK with no issues. The scanning of checked luggage in New York remained inconclusive. Maybe they only scanned for explosives or weapons.

We arrived at Schiphol early in the morning; there was a chill in the air when we exited the airport. We took the airport bus into Centrum and checked into a little hotel on Spuistraat. The Amsterdam sun spirits smiled on us and granted a brilliant, sunny day, if not toasty warm. The Amsterdamers cherished each day of fall like this, as did we. Our hunger led us to a restaurant on the Singel Canal where we ordered two uitsmijters, a simple but delicious meal. Two pieces of white toast, thinly sliced ham, fresh Dutch cheese, and two fried eggs on top, side by side, are what you'll get, regardless of where you order it. Jet lag insisted that it was time to grab a pils—a glass of Pilsner beer. So we had a couple. Just the thing for jet lag. We kicked back and watched the boat activity on the *gracht*. Being sunny, the ladies were exposing lots of skin and we google-eyed them—that was before Google became a different activity decades later. We knew well that the best way to get adjusted to jet lag was to stay awake through the day and go to bed at a normal hour, if not a bit early, on local time. We'd done it the right way often enough. Our good intentions were derailed after three pils and a hash reefer, which was passed to us by the person at the next table. We went back to the hotel and crashed into the evening. Once we were rested, we got ourselves over to the Branderij to see who was around.

Hawk and PK were fresh back from India, having driven both ways. They too were not optimistic about the future in Afghanistan, as the Russian influence was growing. We were concerned about Dave, but they said Westerners were still OK there.

The Hippie Trail had been a thing for ten years. It started and grew with the rock 'n' roll era, and gained notoriety as soft drugs blended with the music. The allure of the road that people have traveled for centuries was strengthened by a fascination with India and Nepal. To think it might be in jeopardy now was hard to accept.

Upon our return to Amsterdam, we had to find a more convenient and secure place to call home, so we spread the word and found a small flat near the Nieuwmarkt. Secure, yes, but with four flights of stairs leading up to it—far from convenient. The top floor. That's where almost everyone our age had to accept. Youth could do four flights, but the narrow and steep stairs in Amsterdam made it a challenge anyway.

We'd sent the *Par Avion* letter to Dave from Ann Arbor the same day we closed the carpet deal for cash. We weren't explicit in our update, but Dave would have understood several things by our choice of words and reading between the lines:

- We sold everything except what we held back

- We got a higher price than we expected

- We were going to leave for Kabul in about a week

- A stopover in Amsterdam to stash some money

- News or request, send a letter to AmEx in Amsterdam

- We depart Amsterdam for Kabul three weeks from date of letter

We doubted Dave would have enough time to get our letter from the US and send one to the AmEx office in Amsterdam before we were there and gone. The AmEx office did not have a letter from Dave, as expected. We went to the post office on Spui and got in line to make the call to Kabul. They were 3.5 hours ahead of Amsterdam, so the call was made from the post office at midday to catch Noor having tea in the carpet store. We called him and he answered right away, surprised to hear from us. We minimized our chatter since the call was pricey. The upshot was Dave was fine. It was different in Kabul, but all was good. We asked Noor to tell Dave we would be there in less than a week. We were relieved, and that got us in gear to wrap things up in Amsterdam and make our return trip to Kabul.

Scott and I had flown on one-way tickets from Cleveland to Amsterdam. From Amsterdam we bought round-trip tickets to Frankfurt. And we bought round-trip tickets from Frankfurt to Kabul. Dave would buy his one-way ticket to Frankfurt from Kabul when we got there.

I previously mentioned the ubiquitous bright yellow Schiphol See Buy Fly duty-free bags that everyone—I mean everybody!—carried with them on board after shopping at the airport in Holland. Duty-free meant true savings, and Schiphol Airport was famous worldwide as the best place to buy, so customs authorities around the world saw them day in and day out on flights from Schiphol. It was like a wardrobe item for travelers.

We arrived at Schiphol with plenty of time to shop. Scott and I knew exactly which items we wanted. We loaded up on half a dozen kinds of Dutch chocolates, in boxes and canisters; cheese; stroopwafels; Dutch spiced cookies in a tin; tulip bulbs; and of course, Bols Genever gin in the crock jar, because, well, everyone did. We each had several duty-free bags when we boarded the flight to Frankfurt.

As we deplaned and entered Frankfurt Airport immigration and customs, it was clear which flight had arrived from Amsterdam. It was funny to see nearly every passenger had one or more Schiphol duty-free bags.

We cleared customs, exited the terminal, and took the train into the Hauptbahnhof in Frankfurt. Upon arrival, we off-loaded our duty-free bags into a private locker in the public storage locker area for retrieval on our return trip.

Once back at the Frankfurt Airport, we spent the night in the airport hotel to catch the early morning flight to Kabul. As we waited to board, we idly looked out the seating area window at the aircraft being serviced. We noticed the side window next to the pilot's seat flopped open. I didn't know those windows even opened, as I had never seen that on the many flights I had taken.

Then a young Afghan guy with fairly long hair in a pilot's uniform pulled himself out to waist level, reached for a rag, and cleaned the windshield of the aircraft! Ariana Afghan Airways was always a bit different from the norm in the Western world, but this was over the top.

We had a good laugh and looked through the cockpit as we boarded to make sure he got all the bug juice cleaned off and visibility was good. We gave the flight crew a thumbs-up and smiled, but didn't congratulate them on their attention to detail. We landed safely in Kabul, so the pilot must have been able to see OK, or the IFR procedures—the radio and the radar gear—were all working correctly.

We deplaned in the same manner as before. We kept an eye out for any changes to customs procedures by the Republic of Afghanistan after the king had been overthrown. None were in evidence. That was a good sign...maybe. The familiar indifference, or perhaps poor training of customs officials, was still in place; we passed through passport control and customs without incident.

It was late afternoon when Boy greeted us at the hotel. It was like we had just returned from a short local sojourn out and about. That finger was pointing, and Dave this and Dave that was flying about.

He was, of course, smiling all the while.

We feigned concern and walked into the garden, where Dave looked up with his shit-eating smile and said, "What took so long?"

We told him. He had visual evidence when we divided up the loot.

Dave gave us a more nuanced appraisal of the situation in Kabul—he hadn't ventured out of the city in our absence. It was still a hospitable place for a Westerner with money, but less tolerant of hippies passing through on the cheap. A little more circumspection was called for on Chicken Street, but a chillum in our garden was still quite acceptable. So we indulged. It was apparent from the coughing that our resistance had dropped in the weeks we'd been gone. Dave laughed like crazy at us and took deeper hits to show off. We would have done the same if the roles were reversed.

In short, we felt like the universe had aligned properly to nudge us toward the last stretch of our excellent Afghan adventure.

In the ebbing days of 1973, neither we nor any of our peers could have known that 1974 would be the beginning of the end for the "good 'ol days" of the Hippie Trail, and Afghanistan in particular. I don't think any locals who we knew were expecting that extent of change either. In 1975, there was a mass exodus out of Kabul by Westerners, followed by a reverse migration of hippies from India and Nepal westward, pulling the remaining foreigners out of Afghanistan. The Russians were on a path that would lead to their invasion of Afghanistan in 1979.

Without that knowledge of future events in our pocket, we continued to act normally and focus on the here and now.

We brought Boy a T-shirt from the Allman Brothers concert and American cigarettes for Noor and Mohammed. Both were doing fine and had no visible qualms about business prospects for the near future.

Dave agreed that a more focused and smaller shipment of Afghan stuff was a good idea, so we made a quick buying visit to Noor and bought only prayer rugs (none larger), camel collars, donkey bags, and carpet remnants, along with some lapis lazuli jewelry. We had it sent exactly as before. We entrusted Mohammed to see it off at the airport, hoping with good reason to see it again in Cleveland (we did).

Dave wasn't into photography and was happy to let Scott and I handle the documentation aspects of travel. He marveled at all the film we brought back and the contraption I had to load bulk film into film canisters in daylight conditions. I told him about the little boxes of film magazines that were not loaded with film. Ten of the cartons holding ten little white boxes each were empty film magazines.

Each can of bulk Tri-X black and white film I brought to load the empty film magazines held a little over 30 m (100 ft) of unexposed film. It would take six cans of unexposed film to load all the empty magazines I brought back. I only had two cans of unexposed film. He looked puzzled.

I then told him that a 36-exposure roll of unexposed Tri-X in a film magazine weighs about 27.5 grams (1 oz). If one removed most of the film, leaving only enough for a film leader to stick out of the film magazine, there was usable space for about 10 grams (2 tsp) of anything pliable enough to wrap around the film spool. Something like The Brotherhood was allegedly offering. A quick glance confirmed there were 100 of those empty film roll boxes. A moment of silence.

"Maybe we should take a quick trip to Peshawar and stay in the InterContinental Hotel and see if Amir is still around for a price check," Dave said with his signature smile.

The flight on PIA over the mountains to Pakistan was awe-inspiring. The aircraft was not. It was a worn out 19-passenger de Haviland twin prop plane with an interior more like a bus than a commercial aircraft. The overhead wings were great for sightseeing, with unobstructed views below with a large flat surface overhead formed by the wings and fuselage. I looked carefully as I boarded to see if there were any luggage or humans planning to strap onto that useful exterior of the plane. It was overbooked, of course, with every seat taken, and I saw one person standing up during the flight. I think two people were taking turns in one seat. The plane followed the Khyber Pass, giving us a bird's-eye view of the drive we had taken only a few months before. It was flying at a low attitude and banked left and right when it passed through a crevice of the mountains. Maybe the noise and vibration of those flights created those frequent rock avalanches, one of which we witnessed on our drive. The Hindu Kush had seen civilizations come and go. Lifetimes of history to humans, merely a blink of an eye to those mountains. More civilizations would come and go, including the one we are currently living in. Dots and questions are meaningful and important to humans, but irrelevant to these mountains and the planet that support them. Or so it appears to me.

The Amsterdam-to-Kabul experience, whether by land or air, was soon a thing of the past. The era of the Hippie Trail, youthful optimism, and a cultural naïvety were all finally put to rest by the Russian invasion of Afghanistan in 1979.

Scott, Dave, and I were on a roll; we had youth, enthusiasm, rock 'n' roll, time, and Afghan carpets to sustain us. Our story had many chapters left to write.

We weren't wasting any ink!

Our plane ready to board - Frankfurt to Kabul

Kabul hotel garden. Manager and Boy chatting

Dave had adopted more of the Afghan look while we were gone

The End of the Beginning

Epilogue

The Byrds: *Wasn't Born To Follow > Lyrics*

Standing in the open air of Earth without an Evo suit was wonderful. I was taking in the open sky above me, clouds passing, and Earth's sun giving life as it had done for eons of time before and after the Eco War. Our species evolved on this planet when there was nowhere else to go. No Plan B existed. I had vizzed that era, but for the most informing history, I had to read it with my eyes on old digital devices, or holding a book with paper pages. The connection with the past was deliciously emotive when smelling the ink and the aged paper of those books.

Wars or their aftermath were frequently associated with transitional periods in Earth's history. To me, it was a parochial method for humans to settle disputes, real or imagined. I'm aware of the many explanations for war; most falling into the category of "You have to fight fire with fire." I also think there were credible examples of that necessity. It's taken humanity far too long to begin to move past that ancient human genetic inclination. We aren't there yet as I relate my thoughts now.

Prior to the Eco War, the earth experienced World War One, succeeded by World War Two, and finally, the Cold War era. All within one century of time. There were also smaller wars leading up to the Eco War. All of those countries fighting each other. The post–Eco War period evolved to Mega Corps fighting each other, with countries as proxies. I assume at the time that many people thought it was necessary. Many of those that survived did too. The millions who died may have had a different opinion.

But the Eco War was different. There was a long lead-up, with numerous warnings and escalating risk. There wasn't a well-defined starting point—no assassination of a dignitary, no military invasion of a neighboring country. It was an insidious march toward a point of recognition with a crescendo of events that triggered a transition into a war for survival. It was humanity against the earth's environment.

Humans against the very environment that had allowed them to exist... From my viewpoint, that's the most difficult thing for me to understand. The only good thing I could find was that the wars after the earth recovered were diminished in their ferocity and frequency. You can't expect humans to learn a lesson without having to endure it repeatedly.

To be honest, all the ingredients of human nature are still with us, and sometimes the cooks in the kitchen create an ill-tasting soup called *war*. We have evermore tools to cause harm in evermore ways. The threat of self-destruction is greater now as well. We manage it with the lingering remembrance of the Eco War as a moderator. But it seems mankind has been through that before. So we circle the ring of death.

If I could say anything to Duane, my distant relative who prompted my visit to Earth, it would be, "Hang on, better days are coming."

As it is with a life partner, you take the good with the bad. So it is with humans. We are a conundrum of traits, and ignoring the obvious when convenient is one of the worst.

Another trait is the tendency to remember the best parts and forget the bad. It works both ways. Humans remember survival but play down the struggles. They move on and gloss over the reasons conflicts evolve into war. It seems that was part of the explanation for the two world wars and the subsequent Cold War. It's hard to believe that humans collectively everywhere on the planet, all countries on Earth, all religions, all political parties, all languages spoken...shit, everything and everyone participated in the Eco War directly or, as hard as it is to imagine, indirectly. The earth was almost ruined due to greed and carelessness over many years.

I do harbor some resentment for those things from so long ago, though I know it is somewhat illogical. Maybe it's mostly my sorrow at what had to be endured by everyone, or almost everyone, on Earth to halt the damage and correct the environmental destabilizations. OK, I'll spit it out: It seems so monumentally stupid.

The full understanding of the damage done to the planet must have caused great anguish and distress, softening my harsh opinion. The losses: forests of trees lush with endless varieties, stunning oceans and seas, beautiful beaches, verdant plant life, surface-dwelling animals of a huge variety, and critically, the unseen life of precious fungi. All were caught up in the cascading events that threatened the comfortable existence of humans, and that of their descendants.

In my research, I came across a statement attributed to the leader of the United Kingdom—a country and party to both world wars—Sir Winston Churchill. He was a man mentioned in the book written by my relative, which has been handed down from generation to generation. My relative was an American, also a country and party to those big wars. Churchill is quoted as saying, "Americans can always be counted on to do the right thing...after they have exhausted all other possibilities." It was a statement of diplomacy to encourage the Americans to assist in World War Two. It could easily be applied to the Eco War by replacing "Americans" with "humanity."

Or so it appears to me.

It took decades of doing the right things to halt the environmental damage to Earth that had accrued over two centuries. It seems rather quick to me, but "decades" to those enduring the necessary and significant changes to their lives seemed much longer. And humans don't like change when it involves their lifestyle, religion, or traditions.

I pay homage to you, my distant relative Duane Eastman, although I know that is a pseudonym. You were so fortunate to have lived in an era when Mother Nature still had the upper hand. There were less than half the number of humans shouldered by the earth then as during the Eco War. Travel was real, not a viz. And the suffering for the damage done to Earth was largely in the future.

I give thanks and stand here in gratitude for the sacrifices made by your generation and the tough years of the next generation. The Earth has existed long before humans arrived, and it wouldn't miss our presence here much at all, if any. But we add spice to life; humans are an interesting study for the other highly intelligent sentient life that we have encountered and learned to accept without prejudice.

And so far, we've not found another planet so perfectly suited to the human being.

I personally doubt we ever will.

Repose

In my mind, there's no question that Dots exist and influence the course of human life. Perhaps their influence is even more far-reaching than that. As stated before, the recognition of a Dot in the moment of connection isn't always a factor in the effect or ramifications—then or in the future. But on an individual basis, understanding that Dots are a thing, embracing their existence, and recognizing them at the moment can be the vehicle to a life-changing path. Would that be an expression of free will?

Several predominant scientific theories interpret quantum mechanics to explain existence and what humans perceive as reality. Those include two derivatives of string theory: the multiverse and many worlds, and the Copenhagen interpretation.

At least one of these theories posits humans and all that we perceive are part of a computer simulation.[56] The simulation would have to be sufficiently finely detailed to be indistinguishable from the "real thing." That would be an astonishing accomplishment.

The best I can determine, all mentioned theories recognize and incorporate the laws of physics. In physics, the overwhelming constituent of the universe, at the estimate of 95 percent, is dark matter. For our purposes, we've renamed it karma based on the premise they named it "dark" for lack of understanding what the structure and content are. I'm taking the further liberty to use the adjective form of karmic as *karmic matter*.

If karmic matter is the home of Dots, I posit that Dots should exist, regardless of the scientific theory one wants to embrace as support for their reality.

It follows that Dots would also exist and have the same features, functions, and implications as in the other interpretations of quantum mechanics. An unexpected but welcome life-changing Dot would be no less exciting to me in a simulation as it has been in this version of my life.

So, what's the story about Dots' attraction to a specific person, at a specific time, in a specific place? Or is that individual attracted to the Dot? Does the story include a component of quantum mechanics? Does karmic background influence matter in a way that resembles the forces that attract particles to one another at the subatomic level?

Another possible connection is what I've previously posited: That a Dot might be compared to a particle in a waveform. When recognized, the Dot materializes. That seems too limiting in my experience. Before this book, there were few Dots that I gave a second thought to at the time. Nonetheless, even unrecognized, they proliferated into a meaningful and even important event.

Many would argue that a positive attitude is good for your health and fosters a climate of goodwill in one's life. By extension, a positive attitude creates an environment for attracting the goodness of life. Traditionally, it's believed that good karma results from living one's life along those lines. Does that attitude extend to other human qualities, like enthusiasm, passion, and healthy curiosity? It's hard to argue against that positive attitude belief when there's proof to be had—just look at all the wonderful examples on Instagram. It's all true, right? No BS there!

The Theory of Dots has karma as the medium, replacing dark matter or at least co-inhabiting with it in the void of space. Under that premise, it's an easy jump to connect a positive attitude to Dots, along with the close allies of passion, enthusiasm, and curiosity. And to close the loop, travel is, or at least was, a deep well of experiences that generates a positive attitude and healthy curiosity. That leads me to the logical conclusion that travel facilitates contact with Dots.

Back to string theory[57] in quantum mechanics. Like many theories before it and currently still supported, it has not been fully validated. It also has not been disproved. In the simplest of terms, it posits that the fundamental smallest particle is a vibrating loop. The strength and frequency of the vibration determines its behavior, and all sub-atomic constituents are derived from that string.

There are many uses of the word "vibration" and the concept of it. Good vibes, bad vibes, "picking up vibes from him/her/it," "good vibes from the audience," and so on. More examples exist of under-current human emotions that are skipped past, ignored, or dismissed. We've identified other examples previously, the common identifier being along the lines of "I had a feeling that <fill in the blank>."

I can easily connect string theory to music because it is an elegant connection and a beautiful idea. And my lack of any scientific credentials is well established, which further allows me to careen off the walls of science and land in that opinion.

The concept of the symmetry of a vibrating loop as the basis of everything, extended to music, which is vibrations arranged in beautiful collections, is intuitive in nature. Furthermore, music also generates the emotions of enthusiasm, passion, and curiosity. Many living organisms respond to music. I'm one of them. You probably are, too.

I enthusiastically nominate music to the Dot Hall of Fame. The import and prevalence of music in the history of humans can't be accidental. There's a very good reason beyond entertainment, because music is as important to humanity as strings are to superstring theory.

Dots, questions, travel, and music are the touchstones of this story. Music and travel are undoubtedly Dots and, with a little wiggle room, so are questions. Traveling with music is the way to go. Dots are welcome passengers.

Afterword

Including A Request and A Promise

ZZ Top: *La Grange > Lyrics*

The booty was buried deep in several locations. Over fifty years, I kept it safe during countless moves, aware that one day I would need to excavate it and reveal the treasure inside. Approximately 10,000 unique moments frozen in time awaited me: Photographs!!

A copious and frequent collection of slides, negatives, and prints, all saved with little forethought about how valuable they would become to me in later years.

I'm blessed with a wonderful recall for photos I've taken. I remember the moment I snapped the photo, its location, and the approximate time, with few exceptions.

In the fall of 2021, I found myself in one of my storage places and in front of me was a cardboard moving box labeled "Save." Glad I had saved it, as it contained eight Kodak Carousel boxes of full slide trays. I knew the time had come. No more excuses! I was going to digitize all my photos. Well, at least get started on the project.

The work I took on was a little overwhelming and expanded beyond my original plan. I've reached the age to accept that I probably won't live forever. I don't have children, and the thought had crossed my mind from time to time regarding my life as witnessed in my photos. Opening that first box of slides brought it quickly to the fore: "Who's gonna accurately pass on to future generations what Uncle Duane was like, and what's the story with all those photos?" Assuming anyone would be interested. Good question. Answer: Me! Who else could choose and create the narrative better than me?

But it also meant a monumental task that needed to be done meticulously. The box of slides that galvanized me into action was marked "Kabul & Afghanistan." So there it was…the process began there. Some photos were slow to move past. Forgotten memories triggered emotions of joy or sorrow or angst, or even a chuckle. Once in a while, incredulity. In six months, I digitized roughly 500 photos from the original boxes and over a thousand slides and negatives from the second dive into the storage area. A few photos are in this book. I created a website https://ctdbook.com, to share more from that era.

The project escalated from scribbling notes that matched some of the travel photos into a memoir with overtures of a self written legacy and then morphed into Destiny Rides Shotgun. I had no idea of how much time and energy were required to write a book! The self publishing was another level of learning and doing.

An observation from my wife, Arielle gave me pause: "All of the research, rewriting, and editing you're doing is more work than I did for my masters degree thesis."

When all was said and done, I held a paperback proof of Destiny Rides Shotgun in my hands. I'm satisfied it's a fair representation of that part of my life for my future relatives to digest and find in me a scapegoat from the past to explain their current genetic woes and shortcomings.

But wait, they say. "Aren't you going to pass on some bit of wisdom that we can't live without?" Glad you asked. Here's a few:

- Travel is a doorway. Once chosen and traversed, it presents a myriad of opportunities to improve oneself while making room for differing opinions.

- Travel is the antitheses of boredom.

- And since we're discussing relatives... Ignorance is a blood relative of intolerance, and the best friend of a tyrant.

- You're welcome. Now, live your lives in happiness and may Dots find you, or vice versa. And ask a lot of questions!

• • • • • • • • • • •

My Request and Promise to Readers

A glutton for punishment, I've started my second book. This is an opportune time for me to hear from you what you think of this book, so I can learn from your comments. Please do me the honor of writing an Amazon review for Destiny Rides Shotgun. ***I promise you I will read it carefully!***

Link to the Amazon review page: https://amzn.to/3R9dVnJ

Thank you. Your purchase of the book is huge. A review is a special gift that will help me improve my writing.

Acknowledgements

Authors seek help to write a book and some authors require more help than others. Take me, for example—I needed all the help I could muster. Fortunately, the cavalry arrived just in time.

I gratefully acknowledge those who gave their time and support, with or without a bugle call from me. Those not included below know who you are. Thank you, thank you very much!

My gratitude in memory of my grandparents: Grannyo and Hank, and Grandpa and Grandma. The contribution of RD and Mimi, my parents, was huge—they gifted me my brother and sisters. They also provided a stable and supportive home. And that generosity extended to our friends who made it their backup home as well. That is until my father drew the line at my friend Rod's toothbrush in the bathroom.

In spite of their oldest sibling—me—being a jerk and mostly ignoring them growing up, they still like me. Maybe even love me. I certainly love Deré, Melissa, Jeb, Leigh, and Maureen. The money they sent to me in Germany helped me at a critical time when I was as close to broke as a fish to water. I'm forever grateful for that, and for the warped sense of humor we share!

My dear wife, Arielle Thomas Newman, endured my annoying habit of talking to myself. Her sharp eye caught many an error and she frequently pulled me back from the wordy philosophical brink. You were correct, my love…at least most of the time. You're the one!

Professor Emeritus Joyce Generali is a special friend and my first editor. She has published several books and hundreds of articles. Joyce produced several instructive manuscript edits that set me on a path to recognizing my subpar writing habits. The self-described "coma queen" also gifted me *On Writing* by Stephen King and *The Elements of Style* by William Strunk Jr. Mil gracias, Joyce.

John Norton Simonson, a published author and a best friend, directly—and without mincing words—informed me that I had not written a book. He was referring to my manuscript disguised as an advanced reader copy book. Norton knows what he is talking about. His three historical novels and many published articles have appeared in newspapers, magazines, websites, museum exhibits, and jazz recordings. He detailed his opinion, and I paid close attention. I was smart enough to follow his advice. Muchas gracias, Norton!

Rick Watkins, dear friend, running buddy, entrepreneur extraordinaire, and environmental crusader for decades—you be da man! Gracias for soldiering on to read my manuscript in it's very early stages. You gave pointed opinions, valid criticism, and actionable advice. Gracias, amigo!

I salute Susan Uttendorfsky of Adirondack Editing, my copyediting and proofreading editor. Wow, if she were in a real cavalry, she'd be the sergeant major! I would be a raw recruit doing hundreds of pushups for grammatical errors. And that was only the beginning of my infractions. Her observations and instructions were always fair, concise, and appropriate. I needed each and every one. Gracias, Sarge, you're the best. I'll be reenlisting. Sergeant Uttendorfsky: "At ease, soldier."

A huge round of applause for my Beta readers: Anke Mous, Bailey Beatt, Bruce Scott, Caleb Newman, Dere Newman, Hawk, Maureen

Newman, and Mike & Janet Kaplan. You gave me a boost in morale by making me believe that I did have something interesting to share with readers. Along with comments, praise, and kind criticism, you delivered feedback at a critical time. And Mike, a.k.a. Lt. Harrisson, your support and generosity in all things automotive allowed me to focus on writing!

A special acknowledgement to Hawk and his daughter Anke, who supported me in deed and thought in Amsterdam. Some of Hawk's photos are in the book, as are parts of his colorful life. Anke provided essential backstory insights, and some photos and videos from her father's archives. Muchas gracias!

Scott Brewster and Dave Smith: my two partners in adventure. Without you two, "no trippy, no story." Gracias for the good times and the good memories, particularly those that I can recall.

Three wise men remain in my thoughts and psyche: Frank Hruska, Buford Guittar, and Jim Bernard. They were pillars of integrity, delightful wit, and honest humility. I miss them dearly.

About the Author

He was born in the Midwest of the United States in the middle of the last century. He was fortunate to have highly intelligent and enterprising parents, whom he promptly dismissed as impediments to having fun. Several decades passed before it dawned on him that perhaps he was a bit quick to judgment and in fact had loving and supporting parents who gifted him five incredible siblings. That notwithstanding, it took another decade or so to fully get it.

Along the way he traveled, learned and forgot lessons, had a helluva lot of fun, and heaven forbid, gained some wisdom. One of the most important insights he gained was humans are all different in the way they look, think, and behave—and no particular way is the best. And those differences make the world a very interesting place to live. He currently resides in Playa del Carmen, Mexico.

Photo Credits

Book Cover Photos ©Don Newman

Book Cover Design by 100covers

Page 3 ©Don Newman

Page 6 ©Don Newman Illustration

Page 17 Mimi Newman

Page 27 Map data ©2024 Google

Page 28 Map data ©2024 Google

Page 34 ©Don Newman

Page 50 ©Scott Brewster

Page 69 ©Hawk

Page 70 ©Hawk

Page 85 Map data ©2024 Google

Page 92 ©Scott Brewster ©Don Newman

Page 100 ©Scott Brewster ©Don Newman

Page 112 ©Don Newman

Page 113 ©Scott Brewster

Page 123 Map data ©2024 Google

Page 126 ©Don Newman

Page 134 ©Don Newman

Page 154 ©Don Newman

Page 155 ©Don Newman ©Scott Brewster

Page 174 Map data ©2024 Google

Page 175 ©Don Newman

Page 176 ©Don Newman

Page 177 ©Don Newman

Page 199 Map data ©2024 Google

Page 200 ©Don Newman

Page 204 Map data ©2024 Google

Page 205 ©Scott Brewster ©Don Newman

Page 206 ©Scott Brewster ©Don Newman

Page 222 Map data ©2024 Google

Page 224 ©Don Newman

Page 225 ©Don Newman

Page 226 ©Don Newman

Page 227 ©Don Newman ©Scott Brewster

Page 246 ©Don Newman ©Scott Brewster

Page 249 Illustration adapted from http://www.chinasilkcarpet.com/silk.htm and https://jacobsenrugs.com/blog/knots-used-in-weaving-oriental-rugs/

Page 276 ©Don Newman

Page 277 ©Scott Brewster ©Don Newman

Page 298 ©Don Newman

Page 302 ©Don Newman

Page 303 ©Don Newman ©Scott Brewster

Page 321 Mimi Newman

Endnotes

Print book pages are referenced. Electronic book version will differ.

[1] p. 31 Transition period: the "early out" program for Vietnam Vets who had completed their tour of combat duty.

[2] p. 52 Rafferty, John P. *Britannica*, Homo Sapiens, https://bit.ly/3 wOcZxR.

[3] p. 52 Tobias, Phillip Vallentine et al. *Britannica*, Homo erectus https://bit.ly/438KAyF

[4] p. 53 Gigerenzer, Gerd. *Gut Feelings: The Intelligence of the Unconscious*.

[5] p. 57 Sisters and Brother: Deré, Melissa, Leigh, and Maureen. Brother Jeb. Each is an individual with high standards and integrity. Generous and honest. The best siblings I could ever hope for.

[6] p. 62 Chillum: from the Hindi word *cilam*, which means "pipe." Use of chillums span thousands of years, documented as being used by Hindu monks called *sadhus* in rituals relating to Shiva. More recently, chillums were regarded as something of a status symbol among travelers.

[7] p. 73 Wikipedia, Einstein, Spooky action, https://bit.ly/3VOy5Xz

[8] p. 73 Wikipedia, Special relativity, https://bit.ly/3PRaXUj

[9] p. 76 Brown, Lachlan. *Karma Definition: Most People Are Wrong,* https://bit.ly/4a4prYx

[10] p. 80 *Tot Ziens*: Dutch slang for "Goodbye."

[11] p. 86 Yugoslavia: like many Communist era countries, it had artificially been created after World War Two with no regards for the diverse cultures and ethnicities that had been there for centuries. After the Berlin wall came down in 1989, it dissolved into Bosnia and Herzegovina, Croatia, Macedonia, Slovenia, Serbia and Montenegro.

[12] p. 86 Communist country: in this sense, Eastern European countries dominated by the USSR, largely resulting from the post-World War Two settlements. Controlled by dictatorships, there seemed to be rules against anything that was fun, rebellious or sexy. No place for a young Westerner!

[13] p. 89 *Dag*: Dutch slang for "Hello."

[14] p. 92 Buzkashi: an Afghan tribal game played on horseback. Not many rules; horses can bite humans, kick or generally cause mayhem. People the same. The goal is to throw a goat skin stuffed and sewed up into a round stone enclosure. Click for Video

[15] p. 103 *National Institute of Health,* Sixth sense: proprioception,, https://bit.ly/3TygiSY

[16] p. 103 Wikipedia, Intuition and Decision Making, https://bit.ly/3PMeoeR

[17] p. 117 *Open Skies*, Rise and Fall of the Hippie Trail, https://bit.ly/3VGryxN

[18] p. 117 Hopkirk, Peter. *The Great Game.*

[19] p. 129 Ethan B. Russo et al., National Institute of Health, https://bit.ly/3Ts3Wvs

[20] p. 130 Escohotado, Antonio. *The General History of Drugs, Volume One*

[21] p. 131 Kushka, *Wernard Bruining Interview*, https://bit.ly/3Ts3Rb8

[22] p. 135 Sheldrake, Merlin, *Entangled Life* p. 4.

[23] p. 135 *National Park Service*, Slime Molds, https://bit.ly/3VNYtk7

[24] p. 137 Sheldrake, *Entangled Life* p. 17.

[25] p. 138 Jabr, Ferris. *Nature*, How brainless slime molds redefine intelligence, https://bit.ly/3vCZdxT

[26] p. 138 Andreoli, Claire et al, *NASA, Slime Mold Simulations*, https://bit.ly/48OVZEX

[27] p. 139 Andreoli et al, *NASA*, https://bit.ly/48OVZEX

[28] p. 139 Andreoli et al, *NASA*, https://bit.ly/48OVZEX

[29] p. 139 Stamets, Paul. *Fantastic Fungi, The Source of Life*, Suzanne Simard p. 21.

[30] p. 140 Sheldrake, *Entangled Life*

[31] p. 151 Churchill, Winston, S. *My Early Days*

[32] p. 183 Brown, *Karma Definition*, https://bit.ly/4a4prYx

[33] p. 196 Wikipedia, *Desert of Death*, https://bit.ly/3POgKKi

[34] p. 198 BBC, *Partition: Why was British India divided 75 years ago?*, https://bit.ly/4agXXzw

[35] p. 210 Encyclopedia of Philosophy, *Quantum Mechanics* https://iep.utm.edu/int-qm/

[36] p. 229 Lawson, Denise. *Karma*, https://bit.ly/3xwj7uR

[37] p. 230 Chalmers, David J., *The Matrix as Metaphysics*, https://bit.ly/43dKndA

[38] p. 231 Wikipedia, *Quantum Entanglement*, https://bit.ly/3VaQuNE

[39] p. 248 Wikipedia, *String Theory*, https://bit.ly/3TTGpCO

[40] p. 249 CCCB Lab, "*Any sufficiently advanced technology is indistinguishable from magic.*", https://bit.ly/43KF4m6

[41] p. 250 Stanford Encyclopedia of Philosophy, *Intentionality*, https ://bit.ly/3PeDWBl

[42] p. 251 Dcode similar to a cellular phone number it's envisioned as a 9-to-12-digit personal identifier for access to the Dot Net or other messaging or communication system. The basic dcode provides un-encrypted information similar to a business card with contact info and geographical data. The dcode can also be used for general purposes much like an email address or WhatsApp address. Dcode format for a human born on Earth: Star, orbiting platform, habitat, longitude, latitude.

[43] p. 251 Crypcode encrypted data that provides specific personal info such as precise date, time, and location of birth for a human or emergence for a nonhuman. It is appended to the 9 to 12 digits of the dcode to create a full access passcode. The crypcode is private and highly personal. Both dcode and crypcode must be used in conjunction to allow access to the most sensitive of information. The dcode plus the crypcode would be needed for the Dot Net algorithms to search for Dots and connect two or more Dots. It would also be an individuals ID for other purposes.

Crypcode: format for a human born on Earth: precise longitude (to the second), latitude (to the second), elevation, and EST time of birth.

Dcode Terms as of Early Twenty-First Century

- Star—0 for Sol then sequential numbers for the order in which inhabited star systems are added

- Orbiting platform—planet, moon, asteroid or manufactured structure

- Habitat—geographical location, artificial environment supporting life (dome or otherwise)

- Longitude—degree North (1) or South (2)

- Latitude—degree East (1) or West (2)

- Earth Standard Time—formerly UTC (Universal Time Co-ordinated) before that, GMT

- Emergence—local time that a nonhuman entity is allowed access to human defined space

- Elevation—in meters above or below Earth's designated sea level

Examples:

<u>dcode</u> example for human born on Earth: 013152141 (0 = Sol, 1= Earth, 31 = Netherlands, 52 = degrees, 1 = North, 4 = degrees, 1 = East)

<u>crypcode</u> example for human born on Earth: 521212734151537293195013243601 (Born in Sol star system, Earth, Netherlands (from Dot Code), Amsterdam, at Driehoek Straat on October 20, 1950 at 1324 hrs, 36 seconds, at sea level.) This code would be encrypted and accessible only by password.

[44] p. 281 BioSignal conceived as a novel medical intervention instrument capable of revolutionizing treatment of serious medical conditions. Structured much like a software update for an operating system or app to address a security threat. It would function as a treatment potentially replacing a prescribed medicine or surgery. Delivered via the Dot Net to the individual and administered at the microscopic level. A BioWare specialist software writer would write it.

[45] p. 281 Deveau, Aurélie et al. *Bacterail Fungal Interactions,* http s://bit.ly/4ckMcJY

[46] p. 281 Angheleanu, Roberta. *The Mystery of Microbes,* https://bit.ly/4aaJDIB

[47] p. 282 Marshall, Michael. *Why the human genome was never completed,* https://bit.ly/3V7kr1e

[48] p. 282 Irum, Natasha et al. *The Role of Gut Microbiota,* https://bit.ly/4c5Urcx

[49] p. 283 Silberner, Joanne. *Studying the link between the gut and mental health is personal,* https://bit.ly/49IcVyc

[50] p. 283 Windsor, W. Jon. *How Quorum Sensing Works,* https://bit.ly/4a1LfnI

[51] p. 285 Sagan, Carl. *Pale Blue Dot,* https://bit.ly/3V9vhUo

[52] p. 286 National Geographic, *Anthropocene Epoch,* https://bit.ly/3Te3Eqy

[53] p. 287 Merriam-Webster, *Arrogance,* https://bit.ly/49S7I7

[54] p. 290 Water Science School, *The Distribution of Water on, in, and above the Earth,* https://bit.ly/48NwbJm

[55] p. 290 NASA, *Ocean Warming | Vital Signs – Climate Change: Vital Signs of the Planet,* https://bit.ly/4cbyHMi

[56] p. 309 Bostrom, Nick. *Living In a Computer Simulation?* https://bit.ly/43dXBXH

[57] p. 311 BBC Reel, *String theory - a simple way to understand the universe,* https://bit.ly/43aLRFm

Bibliography

Andreoli, Claire. 2022. *Slime Mold Simulations...* https://bit.ly/48OV ZEX

Bergreen, Laurence. 2007. *Marco Polo*. Vintage.

Bostrom, Nick. 2022. *Are You Living in a Simulation?* Philosophical Quarterly (2003) Vol. 53, No. 211, pp. 243-255, https://bit.ly/43dXB XH

Chatfield, Tom. 2022. *The Man Rethinking the Definition of Reality* BBC Future. https://bit.ly/3v5SDj4

Cline, Ernest. 2011. *Ready Player One*. Ballantine Books.

Cline. 2021. *Ready Player Two*. Ballantine Books.

Crouch, Blake. 2022. *Upgrade*. Ballantine Books.

Gigerenzer, Gerd. 2008. *Gut Feelings*. Penguin.

Gladwell, Malcolm. 2006. *Blink*. Penguin UK.

Greene, Brian. 2000. *The Elegant Universe*. First Vintage Books Edition. Vintage Books.

Greene. 2005. *The Fabric of the Cosmos*. First Vintage Books Edition. Vintage Books.

Greene. 2011. *The Hidden Reality*. First Edition. Alfred A. Knopf.

Greene. 2020. *Until the End of Time*. Vintage.

Hawken, Paul. 2021. *Regeneration*. Penguin.

Hawking, Stephen. 2001. *The Universe in a Nutshell*. Bantam.

Hawking. 2018. *Brief Answers to the Big Questions*. Bantam.

Hawking, Stephen, and Leonard Mlodinow. 2010. *The Grand Design*. Bantam.

Heinlein, Robert Anson. 1982. *Stranger in a Strange Land*. Berkley.

Hopkirk, Peter. 1994. *The Great Game*. Kodansha Globe.

Kaku, Michio. 2006. *Parallel Worlds*. Anchor.

Keay, John. 1979. *The Gilgit Game*. Oxford University Press: John Murray.

Kerouac, Jack. 2002. *On the Road*. Penguin.

King, Stephen. 2002. *On Writing*. Simon and Schuster.

Library of Congress. 2022. *The Great Game & Afghanistan*. https://bit.ly/3wOhUPr

Richards, Keith. 2010. *Life*. Little, Brown.

Robinson, Kim Stanley. 2020. *The Ministry for the Future*. Orbit Books.

Sagan, Carl. 1997. *Billions & Billions*. V3.1_r1. Ballantine Books: The Random House Publishing Group.

Sagan, Carl, and Ann Druyan. 2011. *Pale Blue Dot*. Ballantine Books.

Sexton, Paul. 2022. *Charlie's Good Tonight: The Authorized Biography of Charlie Watts*. Harper Collins UK.

Sheldrake, Merlin. 2021. *Entangled Life*. Random House Trade Paperbacks.

Simard, Suzanne. 2021. *Finding the Mother Tree*. Penguin.

Smith, Elaine. *Humongous Fungus*. University of Toronto News. https://bit.ly/3TwRevA

Stamets, Paul. 2019. *Fantastic Fungi*. Earth Aware Editions.

Strunk Jr., William. 2010. *The Elements of Style*. Original edition. Singer.

Szondy, David. 2022. *Large Hadron Collider Restarts After Three Year Refit.* https://bit.ly/48NPy5g

Thompson, Hunter S. 2010. *Fear and Loathing in Las Vegas.* Vintage.

Wikipedia. 2002. *Mohammed Zahir Shah.* https://bit.ly/4a8afda

Wikipedia. 2002. *Silk Road.* https://bit.ly/49JgGnh

Wikipedia. 2002. *The Great Game. https://bit.ly/4c2gKjk*

Wikipedia. 2003. *Hippie Trail.* https://bit.ly/4c3S8XD

Wikipedia. 2005. *Cannabis Indica.* https://bit.ly/4a7MvFT

Wikipedia. 2005. *Oriental Rug.* https://bit.ly/49mRO3r

Wohlleben, Peter. 2016. *The Hidden Life of Trees.* Greystone Books.

Wolfe, Tom. 1999. *The Electric Kool-Aid Acid Test.* Bantam.